The Boy
I Love

The Boy
I Love

MARION HUSBAND

Published by Accent Press Ltd – 2012

First Published 2005
Reprinted 2008

ISBN 9781908262721

Printed and bound by CPI Group (UK) Ltd, Croydon, CR0 4YY

Cover design by Sarah Davies

Chapter One

November 1919

HIDING IN ADAM'S PANTRY, Paul remembered how he was once forced to eat marmalade at school, a whole pot of marmalade, Jenkins twisting his arms up his back as Nichols held his nose and clattered the spoon past his teeth. He stared at the jar on Adam's shelf. Its contents were all but finished; only a dark orange residue speckled with toast crumbs and marbled with butter remained. He unscrewed the lid, wondering if marmalade could taste as bad as he remembered. The scent of bitter oranges assaulted him as outside the pantry door his father's voice rose a little, as close to anger as he ever came.

'He's not well enough to be out on his own.'

'Doctor Harris, I swear I didn't even know he was home.'

'He writes to you.'

'He wrote occasionally.'

Paul placed the marmalade back on the shelf, listening more carefully. That pinch of truth would help the lie down – that "occasionally" held the right note of disappointment. His father might almost believe his letters to Adam were infrequent.

George sighed. 'If you do see him ...'

'I'll bring him straight home.'

Paul listened as Adam showed George out, waiting until he felt sure his father had gone before pushing the pantry door open. In a stage whisper he asked, 'All clear?'

Adam sat down at the kitchen table. Taking off his glasses he ground the heels of his hands into his eyes.

'Jesus, Paul. He knew you were in the pantry. He bloody knew.' He looked up. 'He didn't speak to me. He spoke to the bloody pantry door.'

Sitting opposite him Paul reached across the table and took his hand. 'At least you didn't give us away.'

Adam drew his hand back. 'He could smell your cigarette smoke.'

'Maybe he thought you'd taken up smoking. Maybe you should.' Paul shoved his cigarette case towards him. 'Calm your nerves.'

'You know I hate it.'

Lighting up, Paul blew smoke down his nose. 'Hate what? Lying, smoking or having a one-eyed lunatic hiding in your cupboards?'

'Smoking.' Adam sighed. 'No point hating the rest of it, is there?'

Adam polished his glasses on the corner of his shirt. Hooking the wire frames over his ears he smiled at Paul. 'Cup of tea?'

'I should go. He's had enough worry, lately.'

'Haven't we all.'

'I'd better go.'

'Yes. Of course. Better go.'

Neither moved. Paul's bare toes curled against the cold lino. The kitchen of Adam's terrace house was always cold, always smelt of yesterday's frying, always made him want to take boiling, soapy water and a scrubbing brush to the sink and stove and floor. He thought of the stale-biscuit smell in the pantry, the damp in the corners, the nagging suggestion of mice. He shuddered and wiped imaginary marmalade stickiness from his fingers.

That morning he had turned up on Adam's doorstep, leaving his father to his breakfast, using up another lie about needing fresh air. He had seen Adam only yesterday, his first day home, and all he could think about was seeing him again, of lying down in his bed and breathing in the fug of sweat and come and cigarettes as he slept. Adam would work downstairs, marking his piles of ink-smudged essays. Later he would slip under the covers beside him, warming himself against his body. As the room darkened they would make love whilst in the street children called to one another and dogs barked and church bells closed the day. There would be none of yesterday's fast, furious fucking, the sex that came from relief and awkwardness and lust. Adam would make love to him and he would be loose-limbed and lazy. Afterwards he would sleep again. He would sleep all night in Adam's bed, Adam's legs entwined with his, Adam's breath warm on his face. He had wanted this day and night for years.

Adam, however, had wanted to feed him – eggs and bacon and thick slices of bread, cups of sweet tea, a rice pudding he'd made especially for him. He was an invalid to be fattened; he was too thin by far, a bag of neglected bones. Quick with embarrassment Adam had fussed between sink and stove and table. Later they had fucked routinely and Paul had left his eye patch on although he had planned to take it off. Taking off the patch would have been a kind of unveiling. Such theatrics had seemed inappropriate after the ordinariness of rice pudding.

Paul stubbed his cigarette out, crushing it into a saucer so that it all but disintegrated and Adam ducked his head to smile into his face.

'Paul? You've gone silent again.'

'I'm fine.' He smiled back. Like George, Adam needed constant reassurance. 'I've left my shoes and socks upstairs.'

Adam laughed. 'You know, I half expected to see you in uniform. I almost didn't recognise you, standing there in civilian clothes.'

'Disappointed?'

'No, of course not.'

'You said once I suited the uniform.'

'Did I? You suited the cap, I think.'

'I'll keep it. Wear it in bed.'

'I'm glad you're back.' Adam laughed again. 'Glad. Christ, what kind of word is that, eh? Glad. Bloody glad.'

'I'm glad to be back.' Paul stood up. 'I'll go and get my shoes.'

As he went past Adam caught his hand. 'I love you.'

'I know. I love you too.'

Paul took a shortcut home through the park that separated

Thorp's long rows of back-to-back terraces, its steel works and factories from the small, middle-class ghetto of Victorian gothic villas where his father lived. He sat down on the graveyard wall opposite his house and lit a cigarette, imagining his father in the kitchen toasting cheese, his usual supper. Cheese on toast then cake made by a grateful patient, then tea, strong, just a little milk, no sugar. George was a man of habit. Paul looked at his watch; it was later than he'd thought – the tea would be drunk, the cup and saucer and plate washed and dried and put away. His father would be reading the *Telegraph* in front of the kitchen fire. In France, and later during his months in St Steven's, he had remembered his father's rituals and almost wept with homesickness. Now, as the cold from the wall seeped into his bones, he wanted to walk away from the smallness of them, back to one of the pubs he had passed along the back streets. At the Stag's Head or the Crown & Anchor he would order beer and share a joke with the hard men of Thorp. Paul smiled to himself. He would get his head beaten in along a dark alley, called a fucking little queer as boots smashed his ribs. He had only to look at one of them in the wrong way. Best if the fucking little queer went home and faced his father's disappointment. Tossing the half-smoked cigarette down he crossed the road towards the unlit windows and locked door of his father's house.

Margot said, 'He's home.'

'Who, dear?' Her mother looked up from her knitting, rows of grey stitches that were beginning to take the shape of a mitten. Mitten production hadn't stopped just because the war had. There were orphans' hands to keep warm now. Absently she repeated, 'Who's home?'

'Robbie's brother. Paul.'

'Oh?' Iris Whittaker laid the knitting down on her lap. 'That poor boy. He was so handsome, wasn't he? I remember how handsome he looked at your birthday party. Such a beautiful face. It must be quite dreadful for him.'

'It would be dreadful for anyone. Even an ugly man.'

'Yes, of course, but worse, somehow, for such a good-looking boy. Such a courteous boy, too. So charming. Poor George. I thank God every night you were born a girl. If we'd had boys like poor Doctor Harris …'

They would be dead, Margot thought, and considered saying it aloud. Dead as dodos. Dead as doornails. Stone, cold, dead. No one said the word dead in this house, although whichever of the vicarage windows you looked from you could see the weeping angels and floral tributes that marked out dead territory. Dead was such a stark word when death was so close, so her father, when he'd told her of Robbie's death, had cleared his throat and said, 'That boy's been taken from us.'

She knew, of course, exactly who and what he meant. That boy: Robbie. Dead.

Her mother picked up her knitting. 'He'll have a glass eye, of course. It might look real, from a distance.'

'Look but not see,' Margot said quietly.

'Pardon, dear?'

'Didn't you think he was horribly vain?'

'Vain?' The wool was held taught and crossed over the needles. 'All men are vain, dear. At least he had the right to be.'

Margot closed her eyes. Robbie had said, 'It's amazing that Paul and I have leave together.' He'd grinned. 'I can show you off to him – introduce you as my fiancée.'

'I thought we weren't going to tell anyone.'

'We can tell Paul. He's so self-centred he'll have forgotten by tomorrow.'

Margot remembered how Robbie had pulled her into his arms, holding her tightly so that her cheek felt the scratchiness of his uniform. Khaki smelt of dry hessian, of sweat and metal polish that she imagined was the stink of gunpowder. Beneath the khaki his body felt hard and spare. She tried to remember how she had responded, if she had drawn away a little or pressed herself closer. She remembered he groaned. Perhaps she had encouraged him.

'I think I'll go to bed.' Margot closed the book she'd been pretending to read and stood up.

Iris glanced at her. 'Say goodnight to your father.' The knitting needles picked up speed. 'Tell him if that sermon isn't finished by now it's too long.'

In her father's study a picture of Jesus surrounded by children hung above the fireplace. Christ was white and pale gold, the children dark and dressed in bright colours. A lamb knelt at Jesus's side, a garland of flowers around its neck. The picture was titled *Suffer the Little Children*. Robbie had frowned at it. 'I was in Palestine before the war. The children wore rags.' She tried to remember the tone of his voice. Not quite so pompous, maybe, just matter-of-fact.

Her father looked up from his desk. 'Margot. Off to bed?'

She sat down opposite him on one of the chairs arranged for those about to inform him of marriages, births and the passing-on of loved ones. Placing his pen down the Reverend Daniel Whittaker smiled at her.

'Sermon on the Mount. For the memorial service tomorrow.'

'Oh.'

'Blessed are the peace-makers.'

'Yes.'

'It's so important to strike the right note. So difficult.' He sighed. 'I've asked Mr Baker to read the lesson.'

Mr Baker: three lost sons. Margot nodded. 'That's good.'

'I hope it won't be too much for him.'

'Daddy …?' she began. More quietly she went on, 'I'm going to have a baby.'

'Sorry, dear?' Looking up from the sermon he frowned. 'You do look peaky, my dearest heart.' He sighed again. 'You should go to bed. Up the wooden hill.' He smiled. 'Remember how I used to say that when you were small?'

'Yes.'

'Yes.' After a moment he said, 'Go to bed, Margot. Try not to worry.'

As she was about to close the door behind her he called out, 'Say your prayers, Margot. God always listens.'

On the stairs she looked back towards the study door. She had deliberately left it ajar so she might spy on him from the wooden hill. He was lighting his pipe, packing the tobacco down with his thumb as he sucked on the stem to draw the flame. She knew he knew. For now it was their secret, stored

6

against her mother.

Her mother had no idea how wicked she was. Although Robbie had said I love you only once, she hadn't stopped him when he slipped his hand under her camisole. She had lost her voice; the shock of his cool, hard palm against her breast seemed to cleave her tongue to the roof of her mouth. He had drawn away, smiling at her hands clenched into fists at her sides. 'You're not going to box my ears, are you?'

'No!' She remembered blushing.

Robbie laughed a little, his eyes avoiding hers. 'I wish you were older, sometimes.'

Her blush deepened and she dug her fingernails into her palms, a counterpoint to the pain of humiliation. 'I'm old enough!'

'Then try and behave as though you are!' Vehemently he said, 'Don't look at me as though you want to eat me alive, then turn stiff as a corpse the minute I touch you.'

Later he was penitent, his head bowed as he held her hands. She'd been afraid that he might cry. A little later still and he was pushing her down into the long grass beside the Makepeace tomb, covering her face with frantic kisses as his hand scrambled beneath her petticoats. When he had pressed his hand between her legs she hadn't protested. 'Let me,' he whispered, and she'd nodded, not knowing how to refuse him: the war had made him strange, an infectious strangeness, she realised now.

She splayed her fingers over her belly. She would show soon and even her mother would notice. Then there would be tears. All the listening Gods in the world wouldn't help her then. She thought of nunneries; a nunnery would be her mother's solution. Nuns with hard hands and stern voices would take charge and smooth it over and send her home a sinner still, but a sinner whose sin was taken away, a Mad Hatter's riddle. She wouldn't think about it any more. Turning away she climbed the stairs to bed.

Paul had vomited twice that morning. Once just after his father told him they were going to church and again as they were about to leave, when he told him that it was to be a special service of remembrance and they were expected for lunch at the vicarage afterwards. That second time had exasperated George.

Placing his hand firmly on his son's forehead he barked, 'Any stomach pain?'

Paul twisted away. 'No.'

'Bowels moving normally?'

'Dad! For Christ's sake.'

George ushered him out. Locking the front door behind him he said, 'You smoke too much. It's enough to make anyone sick.'

Across the road St Anne's Church loomed from the leafless trees. Sunday-best parishioners snailed their way towards the church doors. Paul began to worry that he would be expected to talk to these people, that they would tell him about lost sons and husbands and brothers as though they expected some kind of comfort from him because he survived. He felt the bile rise in his throat again and he closed his eye.

'Paul.' George's voice was sharp. 'Pull yourself together. Remember what your doctors said.'

'They said, "Lieutenant Harris, we've dug out your left eye with a rusty spoon. Any questions?"'

'Don't be idiotic. And I wish you wouldn't hide your glass eye behind that patch. You look like a pantomime pirate.'

They crossed the road. George took his elbow and steered him like a very old man along the graveyard path, past the angel weeping over his mother's grave, past the urns and obelisks of those who had died comfortable deaths. Frosted leaves crunched beneath his thin-soled shoes and the cold kept his hands deep inside his trench coat pockets, making him a sloppy civilian from capless head to ill-shod foot. In some hospital or another he'd lost the leather gloves Rob had given him. He thought about the gloves, concentrated on remembering their beautiful stitching, the way they kept the shape of his hands when he took them off, the expensive, masculine smell of them. He thought about the gloves as George led him up the aisle and gently pushed him down on to a pew. Only when his father pressed a handkerchief into his hand did he realise he'd been weeping over their loss. From the pew in front a child turned to stare at him and was slapped on the legs for her rudeness.

'Have you met Reverend Whittaker, Paul?' Standing in front of the vicarage fireplace George was forcing himself to smile.

Paul nodded. 'We met during my last leave, at Margot's party.' He held out his hand. 'How are you, sir?'

Daniel Whittaker shook his hand briefly. 'Would you like a drink before lunch? Whisky or sherry?'

'Oh, whisky, I think.' George seemed to relax a little. 'Lunch smells good.'

Whittaker turned towards an elaborately carved sideboard crouching against the dining room wall. 'My wife's cooking beef.'

Handed his own short measure of Scotch Paul said, 'Do you mind if I smoke, sir?'

'I presume you smoke cigarettes?'

'Yes, sir.'

'Then would you mind if I asked you to smoke them in the garden?'

George said, 'It's a disgusting habit, dirty and disgusting.'

'I smoke a pipe myself.'

To hide his smile Paul bowed slightly. 'Would you excuse me?'

'Don't be long, Paul. I don't want you catching cold.'

To avoid catching cold Paul walked back to the hallway where Whittaker had hung his coat. He put it on, turning up the collar and buttoning it, trying not to think of those wretched gloves that once lived in the pockets.

As he fastened the belt a voice behind him asked, 'Are you leaving?'

Paul turned round, his fingers going to check that the eye-patch hid all it was supposed to.

The vicar's daughter smiled at him, her own hand going to the blush that was spreading over her throat.

'Hello, Margot.'

She was standing on the stairs, so much higher than him he had to tilt his head back to look at her. Touching her left eye she said hesitantly, 'The patch … it makes you look dashing.'

He laughed.

'No. Really. It suits you …' Her blush deepened. 'Sorry, I didn't mean that, exactly. It must have been horrible.' She came down. 'Are you leaving?'

'Leaving? Oh, no. No, not leaving. I wanted a cigarette.'

'Daddy wouldn't let you smoke in the house?'

'No.'

'I smoke.'

'Really? Well, if you'd like one of mine …'

'Yes, thank you.'

She had thought he was Robbie, returned from the grave, wearing the same coat she imagined they buried him in, the same coat he had spread on the grass behind the Makepeace tomb. He had lost his captain's cap, and those strips of cloth like khaki bandages he wrapped around his shins, but it was Robbie, not dead, only lost. She'd stood on the stairs watching him, holding her breath to be as silent as possible until slowly she realised that this was only Paul, the boy who had looked so close to weeping as her father spoke of the importance of remembering, everyone had seemed embarrassed for him. Afterwards, when he was in the queue to shake her father's hand, most people had kept their distance, as though madness was contagious.

In the garden Margot watched as he fumbled with a cigarette case and matches. His hands shook and he smiled apologetically as first one match and then another broke.

'Let me,' she said, and took the matches from him.

He stepped closer, accepting the light she held out. Just like Robbie, he blew smoke down his nose and smiled at her. 'When did girls start smoking?'

'Same time as boys.'

'1914?'

She felt her face flush. 'Probably.'

They stood side by side, smoking in silence. From the corner of her eye she noticed his fingers go again and again to the eye-patch as though checking its straightness. Tossing her finished cigarette down she pulverised it into the crazy-paved path.

'I have to help my mother serve lunch.'

'Margot ...' He caught her arm as she turned away, immediately releasing her as she faced him. 'I'm sorry about Rob.'

'I should say that to you, shouldn't I?'

'I know how close you and he were.'

'What do you know? What did he say about me?'

'That you were going to be married.'

'Yes! We were!' She laughed harshly. 'He promised me. We would have been married by now.' She began to cry and he took a handkerchief from his pocket and handed it to her. 'I'm sorry.' Dabbing at her eyes she said, 'I don't know what came over me.'

'Misery? That's what comes over me, anyway.'

She gave back the handkerchief. 'Thank you for the cigarette.'

As she walked away she had a feeling he was watching her. When she looked back she saw that he had turned away and was staring out towards the graves.

Chapter Two

IN PARKWOOD'S KITCHEN PAUL slumped into the armchair by the fire. He took off the eye-patch and threw it at the hearth where it caught on the coal scuttle handle.

Hanging up his coat George asked, 'How are you feeling?'

'Tired.'

'Why don't you go and lie down for an hour?'

'I'd rather stay here, if you don't mind.'

'I don't mind. Glad of the company.' He sat down in the armchair opposite him. 'You can smoke, if you like.' As Paul lit a cigarette George said, 'Margot's a pretty girl, isn't she? She sent me such a nice letter after Robbie was killed … reading between the lines she seemed quite fond of him.'

Paul remembered Robbie's own description of Margot's feelings. Shyly he had told him, 'She loves me. In fact …' He had glanced away. 'She allowed me to, well, you know.'

Allowed. Paul shuddered.

'Are you cold?' George got up and put more coal on the fire, delicately placing aside the eye-patch. Sitting down again he pressed on. 'Margot's such a sensible girl, a nice, sensible girl.'

'I'm not interested, Dad.'

'Why not?'

'She's a fat little girl.'

George was silenced, gazing into the fire as the room's clutter was tidied away by the dusk. Nothing had changed in this room since Paul's childhood. Even the bookcase was still full of his grandfather's books, their spines cracked with age, their titles fading. Paul wondered how long it was since anyone had unlocked the glass doors and taken a book down. Not since his last leave, probably, when he had taken *A Tale of Two Cities* on the journey back to the front. He frowned, trying to remember what had become of it, and saw Jenkins hunched against the cold, a candle dripping wax on the thin pages.

Jenkins snorted. *'A far, far better thing* my arse. Bloody fool that's what I say.'

Jenkins. It was dangerous how the most innocent thoughts could remind him – he should have learnt that by now. All the same, each reminder was a jolt, as though he'd been suddenly woken from sleep walking. Unable to sit still, Paul got up. 'I think I will have that lie down.'

Jenkins sang *The Boy I love. 'There he is, can't you see, smiling from the bal-con-neee...'* He made the words up as he went along. Some of the words were filthy.

Lying on his bed in his room, Paul blew a smoke ring, squinting as it disappeared into the gloom. The wind roared in the chimney and threw the bare branches of the trees against the window. He lifted his hand and its enormous shadow played in the candlelight as Jenkins's catchy tune played inside his head. Jenkins, in balaclava and muffler, grinned at him.

'*The boy I love is up on the balconee. The boy I love is …*'

'For Christ's sake, Jenkins.'

'You're a miserable bastard, Harris. But then having to read the men's pitiful letters would make anyone a miserable bastard.'

'I'm censoring, not reading.'

Jenkins laughed. 'Of course! One's mind becomes numb to the blather, eventually.' He put on a Tyneside accent. '*Me darling lass. I hope this letter finds you as it leaves me: utterly, utterly buggered.'*

Paul closed his eyes, smelt the burnt patties and boiled potatoes they'd eaten that evening. He could taste them still, greasy as mutton, salty as sea water. He thought of ice cream sundaes, eaten with long spoons from tall glasses in Robinson's café, of the cold lemonade that always accompanied them. He groaned softly. Next to him on the table made from planks and barrels, the yellow flame of a candle drowned in its pool of wax.

Jenkins came to sit next to him. He rested his hand on Paul's thigh. Paul's skin crawled beneath his fingers and he fought to keep from shuddering. He should have shoved him away but something held him back, some idea about protesting too much, of being the obvious queer pretending to be appalled by queerness. He waited for Jenkins to tire of this game and felt his leg tense with the effort of not moving. Jenkins looked at him, digging his fingers into his flesh before lifting his hand away.

Staring at his bedroom ceiling Paul flicked ash into the saucer balanced on his chest. He remembered the day Jenkins joined his platoon, his shiny boots yet to be broken in and creaking with each step, his trench coat and uniform stinking of newness. He remembered his own stink: damp khaki and sweat overlaid with lousy sweetness. As Captain Hawkins introduced them, he could have sworn Jenkins's nose wrinkled as he held out his hand. Jenkins hadn't recognised him for a moment. Plenty of men called Harris, after all, and he supposed he'd changed a little, grown up. Paul shook his hand, all the time his heart hammering as he grinned like an idiot to hide his shock. Not used to seeing him smile, Hawkins had eyed him suspiciously. 'Are you all right, Harris? You look like you've seen a ghost.'

'I have that effect on people, sir.' Jenkins at last let go of his hand, his eyes questioning. Finally recognising him, he laughed, a short, startling burst of noise that made Paul want to vomit with fright. 'Harris! Jesus – *Paul* Harris?' Jenkins looked at Hawkins. 'We were at school together, sir!' He turned back to Paul. 'Good God! Harris! I'd have thought they'd let you sit this one out!'

Paul exhaled sharply. His room was becoming colder and he thought of getting up and drawing the curtains against the chilly moonlight, of climbing fully dressed beneath the slippery eiderdown and blankets George had piled on his bed. Too much effort. He thought about having a wank and his hand plucked faintly at his fly buttons, but all the familiar filthy images evaded him. He thought about Jenkins in school, twisting his arms up his back, forcing his face down into the nest of dead, newly hatched sparrows he'd hidden in his bed. His nose had brushed the fragile flesh and he'd closed his eyes tight, trying not to breathe the green-meat smell. Later, he'd carried the nest to the bins outside the school's kitchens, feeling responsible for the little corpses that looked so dismayed by their pointless deaths. Around that time, Jenkins's bullying had become more inventive, and he remembered the sense of dread of what might come next. Constantly afraid, he'd felt as disgusting and powerless as the birds.

To stop himself thinking about Jenkins he made himself think about the vicar's daughter, the way she'd smoked her cigarette like Jenkins at his most needy. Robbie would have shown her how to smoke like that, reluctantly at first, then amused by her efforts, then taking it for granted that she should smoke as he did, the whole process taking place over the weeks of his sick leave, during that last summer of the war.

'Don't you think she's marvellous?' Robbie had grinned at him from the foot of the bed. His sleeves were rolled up and his forearms were deeply tanned. His smell of outdoors invaded the comforting stuffiness of his room, making Paul pull the bedcovers over his head.

'Go away, Rob.'

Rob had tugged the covers away. 'I've been up for hours. I've mowed the lawn. What are you going to do? Waste your leave sleeping?' Sitting on the end of the bed he said, 'Margot *is* marvellous, isn't she? We're going to be married.'

'Congratulations.'

'What do you think of her?'

What had he said? Something that had made Rob sulk. That she was too young, or too plump, that when he'd danced with her at her birthday party she'd smelt of steamed roses.

Paul frowned as this memory came back. Dancing with her he had wanted to bury his nose in her hair, to hold her closer and breathe her in, so distracted by her scent she must have thought he was touched.

He covered his face with his hands. Imagine, linking her arm through his as they strolled around the graves. Imagine, taking off his coat and spreading it out beside the Makepeace tomb, laying her down on its black silk lining. Imagine, whispering endearments and lies, promises and reassurance as the Makepeace dead listened impotently beneath the hard earth. He imagined the words Robbie said when he finished: 'I'm sorry.' Knowing Robbie he would have apologised. The rest he knew for definite, Robbie had told him.

'She cried,' Robbie said.

'I should think all girls cry, the first time.'

He had been sitting opposite him on St Stephen's lawn and Robbie had looked away, fumbling in his tunic pocket for his cigarettes. Fiercely he said, 'Bloody hell.'

'You haven't asked me to be your best man.' Paul leaned forward in his invalid's bath chair to light his brother's cigarette. 'Should I be polishing my best eye, or not?'

'Of course I want you there … when you're better, of course.' He shifted uneasily, glancing at some of the other patients wandering the grounds in their pyjamas and plaid dressing gowns. Stiff and correct in his captain's uniform, his fingers went to the knot of his tie, adjusting it minutely. At last he said, 'We won't be married for a while. Plenty of time for that when I'm discharged.'

The war had been over for ten months. For the first few weeks of peace Paul had been blind on his back in an army hospital bed, under orders not to move in case what remained of his sight should be dislodged for good. It would be his own, careless fault if he lost the use of his right eye as well. He'd kept silent, refusing to acknowledge responsibility, wanting to be deaf, too: deaf, dumb, blind, the ultimate retreat.

Halfway recovered that day in September, he'd smiled at his brother. 'You don't have to hang around, Rob. Thanks for coming to see me.'

Robbie frowned at him. 'You're better now, aren't you? Properly, I mean. In the head.'

'Maybe.'

'They should let you go! It's idiotic keeping you here! Good God, Paul. You're so bloody *thin*!'

He remembered laughing – being thin seemed the very least of it – and Rob had frowned again, further discomfited. He stood up. 'I'd best be off. Take care of yourself, Paul. Tell them they should send you home, where you belong.'

Paul watched him as he walked away, remembered how his brother adjusted the fit of his cap with both hands before brushing a speck of lunatics' dust from his tunic. He had pulled on a pair of gloves, preparation for his ride home on the borrowed motorbike. Later Paul was told that the bike had skidded on spilled oil. He imagined its wheels slowly spinning as it lay on its side, sun glinting in its spokes as his brother bled into the earth from the gash in his skull. The farmer who found his body had thought at first that he was only sleeping, peaceful on his back in a verge of grass and poppies.

There had been unspoken irony in the condolences. Rob had joined the army in 1913 – was one of the first to fight. It seemed wrong that he should die on an English road, that there should be some natural law against it. Told he was too frail to attend the funeral, Paul had spent the day completing a jigsaw of Buckingham Palace with another lieutenant who believed the war was still raging and in an hour or two they'd be out on patrol. The fantasy was oddly comforting; he'd gone along with it until the last piece of the jigsaw was fumbled into place, imagining a close crawl across no-man's-land instead of his brother's burial.

His room was completely dark now. George called him for his supper and he got up, fumbling like a truly blind man towards the door. Downstairs, he realised that he'd tricked himself into forgetting about Jenkins for almost half an hour.

Every Wednesday and Saturday Thorp held a market along its High Street, a choppy sea of white canvas stalls from the Georgian cube of its town hall to the medieval stone cross outside the Shambles. Catholic martyrs had once burned at that cross, Margot had been told, but although she had examined the pitted stone she didn't believe it. Thorp had always seemed too sensible a place for such carrying on, a commercial, agnostic place halfway between the cities of Durham and York, with no tradition of mining to ally it with its neighbours.

The Wednesday streets were littered with cabbage stalks and bruised apples, the stalls strung with lanterns to light the late afternoon. Margot walked quickly past the butcher's stall. Lately, all smells had intensified and she covered her mouth and nose with her hand so that she smelled only her own woolly mitten smell instead of the cold-blood stink of freshly slaughtered chickens. The creatures hanging from their scaly feet stared at her with dull slits of eyes in the yellow light. She looked away and bumped into Paul.

'Oh, I'm sorry ...'

'Hello, Margot.'

She hadn't realised who it was until he spoke. The voice was unmistakably Robbie's. She jerked her head up in shocked recognition, her heart pounding fiercely. Paul Harris frowned at her.

'Are you all right?'

Disappointment tasted like metal against her teeth. She nodded breathlessly.

Paul took her arm. 'Perhaps you should sit down.'

Where the make-believe martyrs had once burned stood a pair of wooden benches. Paul sat her down then crouched in front of her. 'You look terribly faint.'

She sat up straight, breathing deeply to try to subdue the nausea she felt. When she was almost certain she wasn't about to be sick, she said, 'I'm fine.'

Sitting next to her he took out his cigarette case. Opening it, he held it out to her but she shook her head.

'Not in public, eh? We have to care what people think. People will think we're a courting couple. They'll think isn't it marvellous how she's standing by the poor soul, some girls wouldn't look at him again in that state.'

Margot looked around, exaggerating an interest in passing shoppers. 'Aren't they thinking about what to buy for supper?' She turned to him. 'You're not a poor soul.'

'No, I know. I'm a very lucky boy.' He held her gaze. 'May I buy you a cup of tea?'

She hesitated. Paul got up and waited expectantly in front of her. It seemed rude to refuse him. Getting to her feet she said, 'All right. A cup of tea would be nice.'

* * *

In Robinson's Department Store café they were shown to a window table. As Paul passed other tables Margot noticed how heads turned to watch him go by, their conversations pausing only to resume in more hushed tones. She felt like a chief mourner at a funeral, ostracised from normal society. For a moment the urge to reach out and take his hand was so strong she curled her own hands into fists inside her mittens.

They sat down and he glanced at a menu. 'Toasted teacake? How about muffins? They used to do marvellous cream cakes here. Éclairs, meringues, that kind of thing.'

'Nothing for me, thank you.'

He closed the menu and placed it down beside him. 'Just tea, then.'

'You have something.'

A waitress hovered, pencil poised. Paul's fingers went to the eye-patch. 'Tea for two, please.'

Margot took off her hat and gloves and placed them on the chair beside her. Self-conscious suddenly, she glanced out of the window to the street. Three floors below them, the lamps on the market stalls twinkled. A hurdy-gurdy man turned the corner into view. She could just make out the red of his monkey's fez as the man stopped his machine and began to wind its handle. She heard Paul strike a match and turned to look at him.

He was beautiful, as beautiful as she remembered Robbie to be, although his dark hair was cut brutally short, his skin pale against the black of the eye-patch. If she were honest she would say he was more beautiful than his brother. He made her feel large and solid. She looked down at the starched white tablecloth.

Paul said, 'There's a monkey dancing in the street.' He was looking out of the window, his face reflected in the dark glass. 'I think its owner only has one arm. Poor devil.' He turned to her. 'I've been wondering what I should do for work. Perhaps I should ask him where I might buy a monkey.'

The waitress came back with the tea and Paul turned to stare out of the window again as she set out the cups and saucers. Margot waited until she had gone before asking, 'What if there are no monkeys to be had?'

He turned to face her. 'Trays of matches? Or newspapers. I could sell the *Gazette* outside the station.'

'That spot's already taken.'

'Then I don't know.'

'What do you want to do?'

'Nothing.'

'What did you want to do before the war?'

He frowned as though trying to remember. At last he said, 'I should go and give that man some money. He'll be freezing, he should get some hot food.'

Margot looked out of the window. The hurdy-gurdy monkey had climbed on to the man's shoulder; the music had stopped and they were walking away. An excited band of children ran after them and Margot found herself remembering the picture of Christ and the children in her father's study. She closed her eyes, the hot metal smell of the teapot making her feel suddenly sick.

Gently Paul said, 'Are you really all right, Margot?'

'I'm pregnant.'

She half expected him to change the subject, to pretend not to hear just as her father had. Instead he said flatly, 'Oh.'

'Oh?' She almost laughed. 'You said oh!'

'Did Rob know?'

She looked away, unable to face his concern, wishing she hadn't told him but at the same time wanting to talk about Robbie's baby. She forced herself to look at him.

'You won't tell anyone, will you?'

'What will you do?'

'Sit in a hot bath and drink gin? I tried, it doesn't work.'

The gin had tasted of perfume and had cost most of her savings. She hadn't allowed herself bath salts. The water was so hot she had cried out, half-drunk, self-pitying mews of pain as her feet were scalded. She'd grasped the side of the bath, arms quivering with the strain of supporting her bottom just out of the water. When she finally sat down she expected to see blood cloud between her legs. That evening, red-faced and giddy, she'd almost told her mother.

Hesitantly Paul said, 'Margot … have you seen a doctor?'

'Your father?' She heard her voice rise incredulously.

'There are other doctors.'

'I don't know any.'

'Margot …'

'Stop saying my name like that!'

'What will your parents say?'

'That God always listens? Do you think he does?'

'No.' The sharpness in his voice made her look at him. He was paler than before. His hand went to the eye-patch, all five fingers checking its position. Just as sharply he said, 'They'll send you off somewhere, won't they? The baby will be taken away?'

She thought of nuns, of the black crucifix on the white wall and the high, barred windows of a room she had imagined so often it had become real. A tear rolled down her face. She wiped it away quickly but he had already taken a handkerchief from his pocket and handed it across the table.

'I'm sorry, I didn't mean to make you cry.'

She laughed, snivelling into his handkerchief. 'I cry all the time. Haven't you noticed?'

'Do you want to give the baby up?'

His handkerchief smelt of Robbie. She wanted to cover her face with it and weep great abandoned sobs that would have the fox-furred old ladies on the next table tut-tutting in disapproval. Instead she stifled her tears, making her sinuses ache.

Softly he repeated, 'Margot, do you want to give the baby up?'

She looked down, watching her fingers crumple the handkerchief. 'What else can I do? What? There's nothing else I can do!' Her voice rose and he seemed to cringe. Taking a breath she said, 'I shouldn't have told you. I'd better go.'

As she made to get up he caught her hand. 'Don't go.'

He sounded too much like Robbie, just like Robbie when he said, 'Did I hurt you?' She remembered how he'd rolled on to his back, his fingers scrambling to button his flies. The uneven ground bruised her back through his coat; a smell like flour and water paste leaked from between her legs.

She pulled her hand away from Paul's, desperate now to get away. 'I have to go.'

'Then let me walk you home.'

She nodded, too concerned with the nausea watering her mouth to protest.

He'd decided almost as soon as she'd told him about the baby that he would ask her to marry him. All the way down the stairs from the café he wondered how she would react, although it seemed an obvious solution to him; he even felt a sense of relief. He thought about the ordinariness of being married, remembering the fellow officers who'd shown him their carefully staged photographs of their wives and babies. He remembered that occasionally he had envied them, imagining an easy, undemanding state of domesticity, safe and shameless. Their wives probably respected them, looked to them for support; at the very least there had been a settled air about such men, they'd seemed calmer and more self-assured, although some of them were younger than he was. Most of them spoke to him of their wives with smiling pride. He had written to one such wife, her photograph, salvaged from her husband's corpse, propped beside him. Struggling with inadequate sentiments, he had finally turned the photo face down, feeling as though he was trespassing in a world he knew nothing about. His letter was brief and no doubt of little comfort. By then, words had already begun to fail him; even his letters to Adam were becoming shorter.

He thought of Adam, his reaction. Perhaps he would see such a marriage as a smoke screen for their relationship, a trick to play on the gullible. He glanced at Margot and at once felt an overwhelming pity for her. He had an idea what kind of husband he would make.

The market traders were dismantling their stalls as they walked along the darkening High Street. Behind them someone dropped part of a stall's metal skeleton, the iron pole clattering to the pavement with a din like broken church bells. Paul felt his heart leap. Fighting the urge to throw himself to the ground, he stopped and lit a cigarette, shielding the match with cupped, shaky hands. Margot stopped too, glancing away in embarrassment when he caught her eye.

He smiled awkwardly. 'Still not good with loud noises.'

'Robbie told me about how poorly you were.'

Poorly. That was a nice, Robbie, word. 'Well, I'm better now. Officially.'

Looking along the street again she said hurriedly, 'You really don't have to walk me home.' Quicker still she added, 'Don't tell anyone, about what I told you.'

On impulse he took her hand. The words came on a rush of breath. 'I could marry you.'

She stared at him. 'You?'

'Yes.'

'It's ridiculous!'

'Why?'

'*Why?* We hardly know each other. Why would you want to do such a thing?'

'Why did you tell me?'

'What do you mean? I don't know why!' She seemed lost for words. At last she said, 'It wasn't so you'd propose! It wasn't that! I'd never have thought of such a thing.'

'I would have, if I were you.' He glanced away, awkward now, his small store of bravado exhausted. He watched the market traders load their trucks, the clangs of metal poles punctuating the noise of her breathing. Eventually he forced himself to look at her. 'I'm sorry if I've upset you. It seemed the best solution.'

'You'd really marry me?'

'Yes, if it meant we could keep Robbie's baby.'

Her face was white in the darkness, her relief obvious, and she stifled a cry with her hand. Putting his arm around her shoulders he held her as she wept.

Chapter Three

'DEAR LIEUTENANT HARRIS,' PATRICK wrote. 'Congratulations on your forthcoming marriage.' He paused, tapping the pen against his lower lip. Should he congratulate him? He read the words again; they were too formal, too distant. And how should he address him now he had lost his army rank? *Dear Paul.* Patrick smiled to himself. *Dear Paul, remember me?*

'Mr Morgan!' From the front of the shop Hetty shouted, 'Mr Morgan, we need more sausages.'

The shop was packed. A queue snaked past the window. Dull, patient faces stared in at the trays of pork pies and the grinning, winking plaster of Paris pig that was Morgan's High Class Butcher's mascot. Putting the pen down, Patrick walked through from the back with the sausages and the queue shuffled forward. A few of the women smiled at him. He smiled back obligingly.

Pointedly Hetty said, 'Thank you, Mr Morgan.'

Patrick looked to the next customer. 'Mrs Taylor. How can I help?'

From beneath the rim of her black straw hat Mrs Taylor eyed him suspiciously. 'Not like you to be so cheerful, Patrick Morgan.'

He thought of Paul, suddenly brought back to life by that short marriage announcement in the *Gazette,* and he smiled. 'Mrs Taylor, today I've reason to be.'

At six o'clock Hetty turned the sign to 'closed' and leaned back on the bolted door. 'Oh my aching feet.'

Patrick laughed. Counting the takings, he glanced at her over his shoulder. 'Go home. Give them a good soak.'

'I'll stay, if you like. Help you clear up.' Standing beside him she said shyly, 'It's been a good day.'

He handed her a ten-shilling note.

'What's this for?' She frowned at him.

'Christmas bonus.'

'It's too much.'

'As you said, we've had a good day. Besides, you deserve it. I couldn't do without you.'

The note was folded into her skirt pocket. Without meeting his eye she said, 'Thanks.'

He sensed her hesitation. Quickly, before she could say anything more, Patrick said, 'See you bright and early in the morning?' He turned back to the till. After a moment he heard the door close and knew that she had gone.

Slamming the till drawer he thrust the money into a cloth bag, folding it so that it would fit neatly in the inside pocket of his coat. He wouldn't go home, not straight away. He'd go to the Castle & Anchor and drink two pints, one after the other, and then a whisky to warm him. He would think about the letter he'd started. The excitement he'd been trying to disguise all day burst out of him and his laughter echoed off the white-tiled walls.

It had been Sergeant Thompson who first pointed out Lieutenant Paul Harris. Walking to the pub Patrick remembered how, on the day he joined Paul's platoon, Thompson had leaned close, lighting their cigarettes behind a cupped hand.

'See that officer?' Thompson had nodded in Paul's direction. 'Fucking little Nancy.'

A Very light lit the indigo sky, showing up Thompson's filthy smile. Patrick stared into the exploding darkness, excitement stirring inside him. Mirroring Thompson's leer he said, 'Bent over for you, has he?'

Thompson threw back his head and laughed, 'I'd split him in two, man.'

Smiling now, Patrick pushed open the door of the Castle & Anchor and was bombarded with light and noise. He remembered Thompson naked in the de-lousing queue. He'd scratched his balls with all the casualness of someone who knows he's watched. Patrick had gone on watching, knowing he was above suspicion.

'Patrick. What can I get you?' Maria held a polished glass up to the smoky light, squinting at streaks. 'Pint?'

Patrick nodded. In the mirror behind the bar he saw that he was still smiling – an unfamiliar expression was suspended maniacally between the *S* and *T* inscribed in the glass. Placing the beer in front of him, Maria jerked her head towards a group of men in the corner of the bar.

'Mick's holding court again.'

His smile disappeared. 'Who brought him this time?'

'Jack Watts, but he says he hasn't the strength to push him back home.' She laughed. 'Mick organized a draw to see who'd get that honour.'

'There's no need for that now.'

'Oh, let someone else do some work for a change!' She turned to the bottles ranged in front of the mirror and poured a small measure of Scotch into a glass. 'Here. On the house.' She glanced towards the group of men, wincing against their burst of loud, dirty laughter. 'Go home, Patrick. Get a bit of peace before they wheel him back.'

He downed the Scotch in one. Picking up his pint he turned towards the still laughing men. 'Wish us luck, Maria.'

She smiled grimly. 'Good luck, pet.'

In confession he'd told Father Greene he hated his twin brother. Behind the intricately carved screen the priest had remained silent for a while before sighing, 'You must pray for patience, Patrick. Remember Mick's difficulties.' There had been no penance. He had wanted a penance. Greene's leniency had seemed like an insult.

I don't hate him, Patrick thought as he sat beside his brother's wheelchair. Not hate, exactly. Mick grinned drunkenly at him, lifting his glass and clinking it against Patrick's.

'I'm pissed.'

'I'd never have guessed.'

Leaning towards him Mick said in a loud, mock whisper, 'I

also *need* a piss.'

Men on either side of them shifted uncomfortably. Patrick finished his pint and stood up, manoeuvring the chair around the table, careless of feet that weren't quick enough to get out of harm's way. As he wheeled him towards the pub doors, Mick turned back to his drinking partners. Putting on a high-pitched, frightened voice he called, 'Help! The bastard's kidnapping me!'

Awkward laughter followed them into the street, where Patrick stopped and walked around the chair to button Mick's coat against the cold.

Sullenly Mick said, 'I said I wanted a piss. I didn't say I wanted to go home.'

Patrick looked up at him. 'Don't call me a bastard in front of other people.'

'Can I call you a bastard at home?' He groped in his pocket and took out cigarettes. Without offering them to Patrick he lit one and blew smoke into his face. 'Can I call you a bastard now?'

Patrick began pushing the chair towards home. 'Did Hetty's mother come?'

'That useless bitch, she knows I hate liver and onions. I threw the disgusting mess at the wall.'

Patrick sighed and wondered if he really had, and if Annie had stayed long enough to clean it up. Carefully he asked, 'Did she stay?'

Reading his mind Mick said, 'Don't worry, Jack's dog ate it. Cleaned up better than that old hag would.'

'What will we do if she refuses to come back?'

Mick hunched further into the chair. After a while he said, 'I can look after myself.'

Patrick stopped at number six, Ellen Avenue, unlatching the gate and wheeling the chair up the black and white tiled path of their Edwardian villa. Stooping for the key hidden beneath the smiling Chinese lion that guarded the front door, he turned to Mick.

'Hungry?'

Mick nodded.

'Scrambled egg and bacon, how's that sound?' He tipped the chair back, lifting its front wheels over the step, and pushed his brother into the dark house.

Preparing supper, Patrick added up the months since he'd last seen Paul. It had been thirteen months in all, over a year of missing him.

He'd been one of the lucky ones, discharged only five months after the end of the war. He'd returned to Thorp, to his childhood home, empty since his parents' deaths in a road accident a year earlier. Walking through the house he'd thrown the windows open, imagining he could still smell his father's brassy scent, that odd mix of fresh blood and copper coins. In the garden he'd made a bonfire of their clothes, even the brushes and combs on the dressing table that were still matted with his mother's hair. As he'd carried bundles of their belongings to the fire, he'd fantasised that he was preparing the house for Paul's return, that they could live together quietly and that no one would think it unnatural or improper that he should take care of him.

As it was, he brought Mick back from hospital, to a house cleared of their parents' effects. Even the ashes of the bonfire had been raked over.

He'd begun on the shop next, scrubbing away the stink of its neglect with bleach and boiling water. A pile of sacks squirmed with maggots, the rotting hessian disintegrating under his brush. Maggots and all were swilled down the yard drain, along with the sweetly rotten residue from a butcher's shop that hadn't been properly cleaned since he'd joined the army in 1915. He saw a rat escaping beneath the yard wall and, sure there'd be more, laid down poison, his lip curling in disgust as he remembered the rats in France.

When the first batch of pigs was delivered the flurry of activity attracted old business associates of his father, the pretence of paying their respects a thin cloak for their curiosity. The animals' squeals drowned out their rheumy-eyed reminiscences and he'd allowed them to drone on about how sorry they were about his parents. Some even bothered to be sorry about Mick, too. As he poleaxed pigs, as he disembowelled and dismembered, he wanted to tell them to save their breath, he wouldn't do business with any of them: they were all too tainted by association with his father.

With Hetty newly employed behind the shop counter, Patrick went to bed and slept for fifteen hours. He'd dreamt of Paul, bloodied and disfigured in Thompson's arms.

Patrick arranged bacon and scrambled egg on to plates. About to call Mick, he hesitated, thinking of Paul's marriage announcement in the paper. The wedding was to take place on Christmas Eve, a week away. There was nothing to stop him going to the church. He would see him, even if only from a distance. Wondering why he hadn't thought of it before, he smiled to himself. His appetite killed by excitement, he spooned more of the eggs on to Mick's plate and called his brother to the table.

'I dreamt my legs grew back last night.' Mick looked up from mopping bacon fat from his plate with a slice of bread. 'I dreamt Mam was still alive and when I saw her I just got up and walked.' As though he had just thought of it he said, 'Let's visit the grave tomorrow. Take some flowers.'

'If you want.'

Patrick began to stack the plates as Mick lit a cigarette and deftly manoeuvred his chair away from the table and over to the fire. Reaching up to the mantelpiece he took down a book and began to read. He became absorbed almost at once, his expression becoming softer and losing the anger that so often animated his face. About to carry the plates through to the kitchen Patrick asked, 'Can I get you anything?'

Mick barely glanced at him. 'Nothing, thank you.'

'Call me when you want to go to bed.'

In the kitchen Patrick held a plate under the running tap, remembering Paul sleeping beneath a lilac tree. He remembered squatting beside him, watching as his chest rose and fell, fighting the urge to kiss his mouth, to run his hands beneath his shirt. He breathed the scent of white lilac blossom, heavy as gas on the warm air. Grass grew high, brushing pollen against his puttees and his cock's aching hardness. He groaned.

Paul woke, squinting against the sun. Drowsily he said, 'Sergeant Morgan?' His hand went to shade his eyes as he sat up. He frowned. 'Morgan?'

'Captain Hawkins wants you, sir.'

He knew he sounded sullen. His Thorp accent made even ordinary words sound like a threat. Paul had fallen back on to the grass, pushing his hand over his face as if to rub the sleep away. 'I'll be along in a moment, Sergeant.'

Patrick hesitated, still squatting at his side. Paul had frowned up at him. 'Was there something else?'

Patrick loosened his grip on the still running tap. It had left a star shaped imprint on his palm and he pressed it hard against his erection. Thinking about Paul he could bring himself to climax in no time, come right here at the kitchen sink and swill the evidence straight down the drain. Remembering Mick in the next room he turned off the tap and began on the day's dirty dishes.

Hetty said, 'What do you want for Christmas, Mam?'

'Peace and quiet.'

'What would you like really? I've seen a lovely scarf in Robinson's.'

Her mother grunted, 'You keep your money.'

Hetty fingered the ten-shilling note in her pocket. The scarf was thick and soft, a rich navy blue; it would go with her mother's wardrobe of black; it wouldn't upset her invented rules of mourning. All the same she knew her mother wouldn't wear it. Taking the note out, she placed it on the kitchen table.

'He gave me this as a bonus.'

As her mother held the money up to the light Hetty laughed. 'He's a butcher, Mam, not a master forger.'

She placed the note down on the table again where it looked dull and insignificant against the bright greens and reds of the new oilcloth. 'It's got something nasty stuck to it.'

Hetty hadn't noticed the small clump of sausage meat

sticking to one corner. She picked it off. 'It'll still spend.'

'Then spend it on yourself.' She turned back to the stove where her husband's supper of mince and onions was boiling noisily.

'What about Dad. What would he like?'

Her mother laughed harshly. 'A crate of beer?' Looking at the clock on the dresser she said, 'He promised he'd be home by now. He'll be sat in that pub, laughing and joking. How can he laugh and joke, eh? How can he behave like … like …'

'It's his way of coping, Mam.'

Her mother stared at her scornfully. '*Coping*! How do I cope, eh? How do I cope with it?'

Badly, Hetty thought. Next to the clock her brother Albert's photograph was draped in a square of black crepe. In the parlour a candle was kept burning in front of another, larger photo of Albert in uniform, a crucifix propped against the ornate frame. Bertie's shrine, her father called it once, and never mentioned it again.

Her mother sat down at the table and picked up the ten-shilling note. Holding it out to Hetty she said, 'He must think a lot of you.'

Hetty took the note and crumpled it into her pocket. 'He says I work hard, that's all.'

'It's a pity you have to work at all for riff-raff like him. I remember when his father ran that shop, so filthy you wouldn't have set foot in it.' She got up again. Going to the back door she opened it and peered out into the yard. 'Where's your father got to? His tea's ruined.'

'Shall I go and fetch him?'

'I don't like you going in pubs.'

'I don't mind.'

'Are you sure?' She twisted her apron in her hands, looking from Hetty to the door and back again. 'Maybe just walk up the street and see if you can see him.'

Hetty put her coat on and stepped past her mother into the yard. 'I won't be long.'

At the corner of Tanner Street Hetty saw her father walking

towards her.

Joe Roberts sighed. 'She sent you out to look for me?'

'She was worried. Besides, it was my idea.'

'Was it?' He smiled at her. Linking her arm through his he patted her hand. 'How's my girl? That big bruiser of a butcher asked you to marry him yet?'

'I'm working on him.'

'Good. Plenty of money, the Morgans. No harm marrying money.'

'Mam says he's riff-raff.'

Joe laughed. 'Patrick Morgan might be but she thinks the sun shines out of that brother of his. Him being a major has gone to your mother's head. Anyone would think he'd won the war single-handed, if they listened to her. What's she cooking for tea?'

'Mince.'

'God love us. Can't you smuggle a nice bit of sausage home, pet?'

They had reached the back yard gate and Hetty drew her arm away from her father's. Joe pulled at the hem of his jacket and straightened his tie. He grinned at her. 'Once more into the breach?'

She grinned back. 'Once more.'

As she was about to go in Joe caught her arm. 'I was joking just now. Money's nowt – you marry for love. Life's hard enough with it.' He sighed. 'Come on. Let's not keep your Mam worrying.'

When she told Elsie and the others she was leaving the sugar factory to work in a butcher's, Elsie had summed up the general feeling.

'You must be bloody mad.'

'It's better money.'

'You'll stink of meat.'

'Well, I'm sick of stinking of sugar.'

Elsie smirked. 'He comes as a set, you know. Him and that crippled brother.'

'I'm going to work for him, that's all.'

'Of course you are.'

Lying on her side in bed, Hetty pretended that Patrick was beside her, his body fitting together with hers, close as two spoons in a drawer, and her hand moved to rest between her thighs. She lay still, waiting.

Through the wall came her parents' furious whispering, the usual row fuelled by her mother's anxiety and her father's exasperation. She listened, not wanting to, wishing they had found Bertie's body. They should've told them he was dead rather than only presuming. The shrine was just a pretend acceptance.

She heard their bed creak and held her breath to listen to the sudden silence. After a while all she could hear were her father's snores.

Chapter Four

HER MOTHER SAID, 'YOU'VE made your bed, you lie on it.'

Her father said, 'Margot, please think carefully about this. There are three lives involved.'

The doctor said, 'My dear, you are a fit, well young woman and I don't envisage any problems.' He had pushed her knickers down so that they gathered beneath the hard bump and pressed his hands over her in a blind search for problems he had decided wouldn't exist. He gave her iron tablets and told her to eat liver. She craved oranges. To Paul, who waited outside, he said, 'Congratulations, young man. Please give your father my best regards.'

'You look tired,' Paul said, and handed her a cigarette as they waited for the tram home.

When they arrived at the vicarage Margot led Paul through the house to her father's study. For the first time in her life, she tapped on the door. Turning to Paul she smiled nervously as her father called, 'Come in.'

The study was filled with the smell of pipe tobacco and Margot breathed it in greedily. The pipe itself lay extinguished in the ashtray. He never smoked in front of his parishioners. He glanced at her briefly. 'Sit down, both of you. Now.' He looked down at his open Bible. 'I thought we'd have the reading about Christ turning the water into wine. Have you chosen some hymns?'

Before Margot could tell him they hadn't, Paul said quickly, '*All Things Bright and Beautiful*, sir.'

'And the others?'

'*Praise My Soul the King of Heaven*,' Paul said. 'And because it will be Christmas Eve we thought *O Little Town of*

Bethlehem. If you think that's appropriate.'

'No, I don't. Think of another one.' Writing the accepted titles down he said, 'Now, I shall give you away, Margot, of course, and the Reverend Collins will conduct the service. We don't want any fuss, so your mother and I have decided to hold just a small reception here at the vicarage.' To Paul he said, 'Mrs Whittaker would like a guest list from you.'

Paul took a folded piece of paper from his pocket and handed it across.

He frowned at it. 'Only one guest apart from your father?' For the first time he looked at Paul directly. 'Adam Mason? Is he your best man?'

Paul looked down at his hands clasped together on his lap. Margot guessed he wanted a cigarette as much as she did. Her father repeated his question and Paul stood up abruptly. 'Would you excuse me, I need some fresh air.'

As he left the room Daniel sighed. He sat back in his chair, pinching the bridge of his nose between his fingers. 'Are you absolutely sure about this?'

Sullenly she said, 'What else can I do?'

'You could do as your mother said.'

She had been wrong about the nuns. Her mother's solution had been worse. She would go to Aunt May's in Carlisle and stay there until the baby could be given up for adoption. Margot remembered the aunt from childhood visits, a spinster who smelt of camphor and attended spiritualist meetings. There were cats, she remembered, and shuddered.

'Do you honestly think that boy is fit enough to marry you?'

'He's fine. You make him nervous, I think.'

'He makes me nervous. At least he's given up wearing that eye-patch. He looks almost normal, at least.'

The patch had been abandoned the day they'd told her parents. She remembered how startled she was, for a moment imagining he'd been miraculously healed. The dead glass, a paler green than his eye, was horrible, and so she ignored it.

'Has he found a job yet? You can't live with his father for ever.' Bitterly Daniel added, 'Even in a great big mausoleum like that.'

35

Hesitantly Margot said, 'He's found a house to rent. In Tanner Street.'

'Tanner Street's a slum!' He shook his head. 'I'll talk to him. I'm not having you and the baby living there.'

The baby. It was the first time he'd referred to it directly. She felt herself blush. Looking down to hide it she heard her father sigh. 'Oh, Margot. How did this happen? I thought it was Robbie you were sweet on, but then this, this *other* one comes along and ...' He closed his eyes and his face became pinched with anger. At last he said, 'How could he? He hardly knew you ...'

The door opened and Paul came in and sat beside her. He took her hand. 'Is there anything else you want to talk to us about, sir?'

The Reverend dropped the pretence of civility. 'Do you have a job yet? How do you intend to pay for a decent home for my daughter, because she won't be moving into Tanner Street, I'm telling you that now.'

'If you saw the house yourself, sir, I think you'd find it's not as bad as you imagine.'

'For heaven's sake stop calling me sir, boy! You're not in the army any more!' He glared at Paul. 'And I have been inside those houses. Members of my congregation live in those streets.'

'Then you'll know decent people live there.' Releasing her hand he stood up. 'Is that all, Reverend Whittaker?'

'Yes. So what do I say now? Dismissed, lieutenant?'

He was never sarcastic. For a moment he looked ashamed of himself and Margot blushed for him.

Paul took her hand again. 'Goodnight, Reverend.'

He waited. When there was no reply he turned and led her out of the room.

She saw him outside.

'I'm so sorry,' she said. 'He's upset.'

Paul took out his cigarettes and lit two at once. Handing her one he said, 'He'll get over it, they all will, eventually.'

'I think Mummy likes you.'

He looked at her. 'Did she like Robbie?' Her silence made

him laugh. 'Mothers usually did like me best.'

Margot leaned back against the vicarage wall, tilting her head to rest on the cold bricks, wanting to press her hot face against them. A bright moon shone its ghostly light and the air was sharp with frost. She shivered.

Paul said, 'Dad's out at a patient's.' He hesitated. 'We could go to Parkwood ...'

She glanced back. 'I should go and tell Mummy where I'm going.'

'Do you have to? She knows you're safe with me.' Taking off his coat he put it over her shoulders. 'Come on. I've set the fire in the kitchen – it only needs a match. We might even stretch to a cup of cocoa.'

Paul wondered if she'd been in the house before but she looked around her with such curiosity he guessed she hadn't. Picking up a pile of newspapers from one of the kitchen armchairs he tidied them on to the floor.

'Please, sit down. Would you like some cocoa?'

She nodded absently and went to stand in front of the bookcase, tilting her head to read the spines of those books too large to stand upright. Opening the case she took a book out.

'*Health During Pregnancy*. Do you think your father would let me borrow it?'

He took it from her only to hand it back immediately, hating the shrivelling feel of its dust-dry cover. 'Keep it. Dad never looks at books.'

She sat down on the edge of the chair he had cleared, holding the book on her knee and watching him as he whisked cocoa powder into the warming milk. At last she said, 'You chose hymns.'

'I remembered them from school. You can change them if you want.'

'No, they're fine.' She laughed awkwardly. 'I remember them from school, too.' She blushed. She blushed often and he wondered if this was as much a symptom of pregnancy as the sickness she suffered from. He didn't know. *Health During Pregnancy* was the only book in the house he hadn't read.

He handed her the cocoa and sat down. After a moment she got up suddenly and took a framed photograph down from the mantelpiece. She smiled at it and then at him.

'When was this taken?'

'1915.' He remembered how George had wanted a studio picture of them both in uniform. To please him they had gone to Evans, Society Photographer, and posed in front of a turquoise backdrop that developed as a grey, Flanders sky. Evans posed them standing back-to-back, heads tilted towards each other, arms folded across their chests. Paul had tried hard to keep a straight face, concentrating on the sharpness of Rob's shoulder blades through the thickness of their tunics. Neither smiled, and because their caps shaded their eyes they didn't look ironic as they had intended, only fierce. Noble, Evans said, his two noble warriors. Paul had wondered if Evans was queer or just patriotic.

Margot replaced the picture and sat down. 'He talked a lot about you.' Her blush deepened. 'He told me he never thought he'd see you in uniform.'

Paul sipped his cocoa, aware that she was watching him. Sitting on the edge of the chair she held her cup in both hands, her face still hectic with colour. Her mouth opened, only to close again. He saw her bite down hard on her lip.

He said, 'He called me a fool when I volunteered.'

'But he was so proud of you ...'

He laughed. 'I'd just started medical school. Robbie said they needed doctors more than they needed foolhardy boys. Well, he was right. I just couldn't wait, though. Couldn't wait. The day that photograph was taken was the happiest of my life. I didn't care that Rob was angry. He took me for a drink anyway.'

'Where did you go for a drink?'

He glanced at her from lighting a cigarette and she smiled slightly. 'I like to picture him in different places. Make more memories of him, I suppose.' Staring down into her cocoa she said, 'Sorry. It must be painful for you to talk about him.'

'We went to the King's Head. Afterwards he went into Morgan's butchers and bought two pork pies and a pound of

38

sausages. We ate the pies on the way home. He had the sausages for breakfast, before he went back to France.' Looking over his shoulder he said, 'He stood there, at the stove, pricking the sausages with a fork. His sleeves were rolled up and his braces hung at his sides. Afterwards I walked with him to the station and I didn't see him again until your party.'

'He was so pleased you had leave, he even told Daddy.' She laughed, 'I think Daddy was expecting Alexander the Great, the way Robbie built you up.'

'He was disappointed, then.'

Avoiding his gaze she said, 'I didn't know you wanted to be a doctor.' Quickly she said, 'I'm ruining your life, aren't I?'

'No. Don't think that.'

'I can't help thinking it. You don't have to marry me if you don't want to. Mummy can arrange for me to go away.'

'I want to marry you, Margot.'

'Why? I mean, apart from the baby …'

'Isn't that a good enough reason?'

Tears ran down her face. 'It just seems so unfair on you.'

Taking her cup he put it down and crouched in front of her. 'Have you thought it might be unfair on you? After Robbie, having to marry a one-eyed, nervous wreck isn't every girl's dream, is it?' He took her hands. 'It's pointless talking about fair and unfair. It just *is*. Besides, believe it or not I'm happy. I feel settled for the first time in my life.' Squeezing her fingers he laughed a little. 'Maybe I should ask if I'm ruining your life?'

'No, of course not! Please let me tell them it's Robbie's baby. Daddy won't be angry with you then.'

'He won't be angry for long.'

She wiped her eyes, avoiding his gaze, and he ducked his head to look up at her. 'Margot, I don't want this baby to grow up and find out from someone else I'm not its father.'

She began to cry more desperately and he helped her to her feet. He caught her scent, that smell of rose petals seeped in a hot bath, and he thought of Rob, wondering if he had been astonished by it too, or if all women smelt like her. Wanting to catch her scent again he pulled her into his arms and held her tightly. Desire stirred inside him, sweet and surprising.

Later, after he'd walked her home, he wondered how long they had stood there. Eventually she'd stopped crying and her arms had moved cautiously around his waist. As she rested her head on his shoulder he could see the way her hair had been combed and held into place. There was something affecting about it and he touched her head lightly so that she wouldn't feel it but would go on standing still and quiet in his arms. He had closed his eyes and allowed himself not to remember anything.

The memories came back when he woke in the night.

He was blind; both eyes were covered in gauze and bandages that smelt of his father's surgery. They might save one eye, if he could lie very still. That was very important. He had to lie very still on his back and not move. The sheets became creased and uncomfortable, a pungent heat seeped from the rubber mattress and from time to time a nurse would slide a bedpan beneath him or wash him with brisk thoroughness. Whatever they did they warned him in advance, breaking from their private conversations to explain what they were about to do. Only when they changed the dressings on his eyes did they give him their complete attention. Then their voices were quiet, their commentary frighteningly precise as what seemed like yards of bandages were unwound.

The last person he'd seen was Sergeant Thompson, an ex-miner with coal dust tattoos etched beneath his skin. The sergeant smiled into his memory, showing off the gold tooth that looked too soft to break skin and made his breath smell of gun barrels. Thompson had held him in his arms screaming, 'Get the bastard stretcher bearers!' And then, remarkably tenderly, he'd heard him whisper, 'It's all right, sir. Take your hands away from your face and let me see.'

Paul closed his fingers into fists, crumpling the sheets. Across the landing his father coughed. He too was wakeful and soon Paul would hear him get up and pad to the bathroom in his felt slippers, not flushing the lavatory, not closing the bathroom

40

door in case these sounds might wake him. The noise of his father pissing was proof of his love.

He'd asked only, 'It's Robbie's baby, isn't it?'

'No.'

'I don't believe you.'

He listened as George made his way back to his room. He imagined leaving his own bed and climbing into his like he had as a child. Those excursions had been rare; his father suffered them only so long before carrying him back, kissing his forehead with quick finality as he tucked him tight between cooling sheets. And if he did climb in beside his father, if he buried himself in the stuffy sleepiness of his double bed and said, 'I'm scared, Dad,' what could George do? He was scared, so what? Being scared was normal. Scared had its own peculiar comfort.

Lying on his bed, Paul curled on to his side. Closing his eye he forced himself to concentrate on sleep, trying to ignore Jenkins's quiet humming of *The Boy I Love*.

Chapter Five

'ARE THEY STARING AT me?'

Standing beside Paul at the front of the church, Adam turned very deliberately and looked at the bride's side of the congregation. 'No,' he said. 'They're just whispering amongst themselves.'

'About what a bastard I am.'

'A handsome bastard, though.' He touched Paul's hand discreetly. 'Listen – if you look round they'll all smile at you. They think this is terribly romantic.'

'I look idiotic, don't I? Should I have worn the eye-patch?'

'No.'

'I'm so sorry, Adam.'

'Hush. Don't say that now. Try and calm down.' He frowned at him. 'You're not going to faint are you?'

'I don't know. Maybe. I need some air, I think.'

'I'll come out with you.'

'No.' He smiled, hoping to reassure him that he wasn't going to run away. 'I need to be on my own for a while.'

He'd told Adam he was going to marry Margot the day after he'd proposed to her. They had been in bed, feathers from Adam's pillows and eiderdown curled into the dusty corners of the room and drifting in the draught beneath the door. There were so many feathers it was as though he and Adam had been pillow fighting. Beside the bed a pillow slumped like a weary, defeated body, its insides poking through its worn ticking. He had picked it up and hugged it to his chest. Very quickly he'd said, 'I've asked a girl to marry me.'

'What?' Adam had laughed, a harsh burst of noise that had

made him cringe. Adam had sat up and reached for the spectacles he always removed before sex. Hooking their metal arms over his ears he'd repeated, 'You've *what*?'

Paul had actually quaked, and that had been the worst part of it, feeling so afraid that the ordinary contempt Adam felt for him would finally erupt into something vicious. Adam had stared at him, his face suspended above his so that he could smell his own scent on his breath, and at last he'd said coldly, 'Did this girl say yes?'

To his shame he had began to cry because he cried too easily, even now when he was supposed to be cured of crying. Adam hesitated a moment too long before pulling him into his arms. He held him awkwardly as though sex had made him unclean. 'It's all right,' he said unconvincingly. 'Just tell me how it's happened.'

Adam had believed he was being told the truth. He believed the story that he'd laid down with Margot in the long grass of a meadow beyond the asylum's grounds. He believed that she'd allowed him – a lunatic – to push her skirts up and shove her legs apart. He believed they had both been overcome by a passion that stemmed from their shared grief over Robbie and it was this last shameful invention that stopped Adam short of hating him. He'd said he could understand, he knew all about grief and passion. He said that it could even work out for the best if one of them was married – who could suspect them if he had a wife and child? He'd held him tighter and it seemed he was almost excited at the prospect of fucking a married man. 'I'll talk to the headmaster about getting you a job at the school,' he'd said. 'Don't cry any more. Everything will be all right.' Suddenly Adam had planned a life for him: he was a family man and schoolteacher and undercover queer. He had an urge to tell Adam the truth just to see him look ashamed.

The fact that Adam believed him, that Margot's parents believed him and hadn't simply laughed at such patently obvious lies, seemed bizarre. He wondered what their belief said about him and about Margot, who surely deserved better. He'd considered telling the truth only to realise that if he did no one would allow them to marry. They would say it was too

43

much of a sacrifice on his part, meaning that he wasn't fit to be a husband, let alone bring up another man's child.

Margot and her father appeared at the entrance to the churchyard. They paused, the Reverend glancing at his watch, angry and impatient as ever, as Margot nervously adjusted her veil. The plain, old-fashioned white dress she wore made her look pale and frightened and the shiny material strained across the small bump of her belly, guaranteeing that all eyes would be drawn to it. He could hear the tongue-clicking already. Moved by the sight of her, he swallowed back the ridiculous tears and went back quickly inside the church before she saw him.

In the vicarage dining room, Paul looked down at the glass of sweet sherry he'd been nursing since Margot's mother had ushered him into the house. The feeling he was being stared at persisted, along with the idea that everyone knew where he'd been for the past year. They would be speculating on the nature of his madness, whether he was a potential danger or mere nuisance. Lunatics were usually one or the other, aside from embarrassing, of course. He sipped the sherry, relieved that Whittaker had decided to do away with the formality of speech making. Beside him Adam said quietly, 'Don't look now.'

'Ah, Paul!' His new father-in-law smiled with forced heartiness. 'Won't you introduce me to your best man?'

Whittaker shook Adam's hand. 'Now, Adam, let me introduce you to a few of the other guests. Paul, shouldn't you be with Margot?'

To be with Margot he would have to edge his way through a group of women. Margot stood quietly amongst them, holding the small bouquet in front of her like a shield. The women's voices rang around her, rising in pitch before their sudden laughter made her look down at the carpet. Side-stepping through the women, Paul took her hand.

She smiled at him shyly and from the corner of his eye Paul saw the women exchange knowing looks. One of them reached out and touched his arm flirtatiously. 'We were just saying what a very handsome pair the two of you make.'

He turned away, leading Margot through the crowded room.

When they were alone in the garden he lit her cigarette. 'Are you all right?'

'I think so.' She glanced away from him, blowing smoke towards the graves. 'Better when it's over, I think.'

She had put her hair up, making her look older. Fine tendrils escaped, curling at the nape of her neck and around her ears. Her veil had been discarded as soon as the ceremony was over, leaving the top of her hair flat where it had been gripped in place. She shivered. 'Handsome pair, eh? Silly woman.' She drew deeply on her cigarette. 'When shall we leave?'

'Now?'

'I have to get changed.'

'Hello, you two.' Stepping forward Adam said, 'Sorry, I wasn't eavesdropping. I just came out to say your mother's looking for you, Margot.'

She threw her cigarette into the bare brown soil of the rose bed. 'I'd better go and see what she wants.'

Adam watched her walk towards the house. 'Childbearing hips.' He glanced at Paul. 'Funny, I imagined she'd be ever so fragile-looking. A frail, delicate doll with an obscene little bump. But she has tits *and* an arse. I'm surprised at you, Paul.'

'Are you?'

Taking off his glasses Adam took a handkerchief from his pocket and polished the lenses vigorously. 'Sorry. I suppose I'm just a bitter bastard.' He sighed. 'She seems sweet, really. And she smokes! You've one thing in common, at least.' Quickly he said, 'I've left you both a bite of supper in the pantry – just cheese and bread, that kind of thing. Milk and tea of course – I presume you're not going away anywhere?'

'No.'

'Probably best, this time of year. Not much fun.'

'Thanks for standing by me today.'

'We coped, didn't we?'

'Yes. We coped.'

Adam stepped forward and hugged him, the stiff, awkward embrace of an ordinary best man. Stepping away hastily he said, 'Shall we go in? I think you have to cut the cake.'

From the house George called, 'Paul, for heaven's sake boy,

come in out of the cold!'

Adam laughed emptily. 'He's always wanted you in out of the cold, hasn't he? Well, at least someone's happy.'

They turned to walk back to the house. Startled, the graveyard rooks hurled themselves into the sky.

In the house on Tanner Street, Margot stood in the bedroom doorway and looked around the little room. Paul had brought furniture from his father's house, a chest of drawers and a bedside table made from some dark expensive wood, recently polished and smelling of beeswax. On top of the drawers stood a jug and basin, decorated with the cheerful faces of blue and yellow pansies. Tucked discreetly under the bed was a chamber pot in the same pattern. Beside the jug was a vase full of holly, heavy with berries.

Placing her suitcase beneath the sash window Paul said, 'Sorry about the smell of paint.'

'That's all right.'

'I kept the windows open for a while but I didn't want the place getting too cold.'

'Really, I can barely smell anything.'

'Right, well, I'll go and light the fire downstairs. Would you like a cup of tea?'

'Tea?'

'Unless you want something stronger?'

'No! I mean I just thought …' Lamely she said, 'Tea would be nice.'

He went downstairs. Margot took off her new, going-away hat and tossed it at the chair in the corner of the room. Suddenly exhausted, she lay down on the bed. The stink of fresh paint hung heavily in the air and she tried to breathe only through her mouth, turning to bury her nose in the eiderdown. Smelling lavender she tugged the quilt back to reveal freshly laundered sheets. He had taken care with their wedding bed. She shivered.

That morning, as she'd twisted and tugged her hair into place, her mother said, 'Your father's not a good judge of character, for all that he's supposed to be.' She'd met her eye in the mirror. 'I like Paul. You should consider yourself lucky to catch him.'

'I didn't *catch* him.'

Her mother had laughed grimly, pinning a lump of hair with a quick stab. 'Perhaps you should put a little lipstick on. You look far too pale.'

Paul returned with a cup of tea and placed it on the bedside table. He sat down at the foot of the bed. 'I've made up my bed in the other room.'

'Oh.' She felt herself blush and busied herself reaching for the cup of tea, only to spill some of it on the eiderdown. The stain spread darkly. 'Sorry.' She looked up at him. 'I'm so clumsy.'

'It's nothing, don't worry.'

To the tea cup she said, 'You don't have to sleep in the other room, if you don't want to.'

A silence grew between them, going on and on until she hardly dared look at him. At last he took her hand, holding it between both his own. After a while he said, 'You're tired, I'll sleep in the other room tonight.' He smiled shyly. 'I'm making some sandwiches. Come down when you're ready, if you're hungry.'

When he'd gone she got up, going to the mirror above the chest of drawers. She pushed her fingers through her hair. In the vicarage bathroom she'd rubbed away the last of the sticky lipstick and she looked pale, more like a mourner than a bride. Catching sight of the holly from the corner of her eye she touched the prickly leaves, imagining their sharpness might pierce her skin, that the pain might shock her out of her numbness. Instead the leaves gave against her touch, soft and glossy as funeral lilies.

Chapter Six

PATRICK WATCHED THE BRIDAL party from his hiding place behind a yew tree, close to the church porch. He watched as Paul smiled for the camera and turned to kiss his bride at the photographer's insistence. A reluctant kiss, Patrick thought. The girl on his arm didn't even close her eyes. All kisses should be received blindly, but this girl stared wide-eyed at some point beyond Paul's shoulder. Behind the newlyweds, the doctor, the vicar and his wife forced smiles. Patrick had witnessed few weddings in his life, but those he had attended he remembered as exceptionally joyful compared to this sad little gathering. He smiled to himself, grimly satisfied.

Earlier he had watched Paul and another man walk up the path to the porch and wait outside the church while Paul smoked a cigarette. The other man was weedy and bespectacled, nervously checking his watch and smiling fleetingly at guests who hurried past them into the church. Paul ignored everyone. Later, Paul came out on his own and the sudden conviction that he had changed his mind and wouldn't be going through with it had made Patrick's heart race with the idea that he might step from his hiding place and take him home. Eventually, however, he went back inside the church and Patrick had noticed how his hand went to his face as though checking on a non-existent eye-patch.

'He's blinded.' He remembered the pity in Thompson's voice as they watched the stretcher-bearers take Paul away. He'd been about to run after them, all sense and discretion lost to grief and shock, when Thompson had caught his arm to hold him back. 'Leave him be. Someone else can look out for the poor little bastard now.'

Walking back to the shop Patrick remembered how until then he'd always thought he'd been so careful, that no one would ever guess except Paul himself. He day-dreamed that Paul would one day notice and then, during some routine business, would catch his eye, would smile that all too rare smile of his and lead him to some quiet, private place where a sergeant could fuck an officer senseless.

In the shop, Hetty glared at him. 'Where have you been?'

He ignored her but she caught hold of his sleeve. 'It's Christmas Eve, our busiest day!'

'Be quiet!' He glared back at her, keeping his voice quiet and immediately turning to the customers. 'Right. Who's next?'

She didn't speak to him for the rest of the afternoon until, as she was about to leave, she said grudgingly, 'Have a nice Christmas, Mr Morgan.'

'Hetty …' She glanced at him from buttoning her coat. 'I hope you and your family have a nice Christmas, too.' From beneath the counter he brought out the chicken he'd put aside. 'I kept this back for you.'

'What is it?'

'A pound of apples – what do you think?' He bundled the cold, heavy parcel into her arms.

Looking at it suspiciously she said, 'I thought I'd had my bonus.'

He sighed. 'Leave it, if you don't want it.'

'I didn't say that.' She readjusted the parcel in her arms. 'It's heavy.'

'Would you like me to carry it home for you?'

She hesitated only briefly. 'Would you mind? I don't want to take you out of your way.'

He took the chicken from her. 'You live on Tanner Street, don't you?' She nodded. 'It's on my way home.'

Her mother had made no preparations for Christmas, just as last year. The year before that Albert had been home on leave from the training camp, still yet to go to France, and they had decorated the house with paper chains and Chinese lanterns and lined his favourite pink sugar mice along the mantelpiece. Now the only thing on the mantelpiece was Albert's shrine. Its candle leapt in panic as Hetty showed Patrick into the parlour.

'Take a seat. I'll make you a cup of tea.'

'Really, Hetty, I should be getting along.'

'Stay. Mam'll want to thank you for the bird.'

'It's nothing.'

'It was very generous. Now,' she pulled out a chair. 'Sit down. Shan't be long.'

In the kitchen Hetty took the best willow pattern cups and saucers from the dresser and set them out on a tray. She worked quickly, afraid that if she took too long he would come and find her, making his excuses to leave. As the kettle boiled she cut a slice of the plain, yellow rice cake her mother made for her father's bait, and then, as an afterthought, cut another slice. They would eat cake together. Hetty smiled to herself, her anger at his disappearing act that afternoon already forgotten in the novelty of having him in the house. Remembering the chicken, still wrapped in its newspaper, she patted it gratefully.

With everything laid neatly on the best doily, she carried the tray through, kicking the parlour door open with her foot. Patrick stood up at once, crossing the room quickly to hold the door open for her.

The little room seemed even smaller with him in it. Tall, broad men looked out of place in these little houses, Hetty thought; they were made clumsy by the mean proportions. Expecting him to knock over one of her mother's china dogs she said, 'Sit down, I can manage.'

As she poured the tea he said, 'Is that your brother's picture?'

Hetty glanced at the mantelpiece. 'Yes.'

'Were you and he close?'

'Not really.' She hesitated before saying quickly, 'Not close like you and your brother.'

He laughed. 'You think we're close, Mick and I?'

'Aren't you?'

'Sometimes.'

'I always wanted a twin.' She pushed the plate of cake a

little closer to him. 'I thought a twin sister would always be a friend, no matter what.'

'Sometimes twins don't get on.'

'But blood's thicker than water, isn't it? And a twin, well …'

'Their blood is thicker than most?'

'Yes, I suppose so.'

He took a piece of cake that looked like a doll's portion in his huge hand, and ate it in two bites. Finishing his tea he placed his cup back in its saucer. 'I have to go, my *twin* will wonder where I've got to.' He stood up. 'Thank you for the tea.'

'Stay till Mam gets back, at least.'

He was already buttoning his coat. He smiled at her. 'Happy Christmas, Hetty.'

She saw him to the door, standing on the front step and watching until he turned the corner out of sight. He'd been in the house all of fifteen minutes. No ground had been won. In the parlour she cleared away the cups, and noticed that he'd left his gloves behind. She lifted them to her nose, breathing in his familiar scent, before hiding them away.

Patrick and Mick spent Christmas day alone together, eating turkey and fried potatoes from their mother's best china and drinking beer from her crystal glasses. Crackers were pulled in a series of loud bangs that had them both screwing their eyes up tight in a parody of fear. Mick wore a pink paper hat rakishly over one eye and read cracker mottoes in an exact impersonation of Father Greene. The room became hot from the many candles that dripped wax on to the mahogany sideboard and table and illuminated the sepia faces of the unsmiling dead: mother, father, two little sisters, a grandmother stuffed into black bombazine; all stared disapprovingly from their gilt frames.

In his own voice Mick said, 'Here's to us.' Pouring the last of the port, he clinked his glass against Patrick's. 'God bless us, everyone.'

'To the future,' Patrick said.

'Forget the past.'

'Seconded.'

'Although it had its moments.'

Thinking of Paul asleep beneath the lilac tree, Patrick nodded. 'It did.'

Mick frowned at him, his dark eyes smiling questions. 'It did, did it? Tell me more.'

'You first.'

'Nothing to tell.' Mick looked down at his glass, swilling its contents and splashing a ruby stain on the white tablecloth. 'Major Michael Morgan has never been kissed.' He glanced up at him. 'There. Tell the truth and shame the devil.'

'I don't believe you.'

'No?' He laughed. 'Well, it *is* hard to believe, me being so handsome an' all.'

'Never?'

'For Christ's sake.' Reaching across the table Mick pinched his cheek. 'Don't look so appalled, Patty. It's not so terrible, is it? I just never got around to it. Too busy being promoted.'

Mick drained his glass then wheeled his chair away from the table and over to the fire. Taking off the paper hat he screwed it into a ball and tossed it into the flames. The fire flared, sending flimsy charred scraps up the chimney. On the mantelpiece their parents scowled from their wedding portrait. Reaching behind it, Mick produced two cigars. 'So,' he smiled. 'Tell me who made your war bearable.'

Patrick drew out the ritual of trimming his cigar and lighting it, sitting back in his chair and stretching his legs out in front of him. He blew smoke rings at the ceiling. Mick watched him, smiling indulgently until he said at last, 'Did I know her?'

'*Her*!'

'Him, then.'

Patrick studied the tip of the cigar, a good, Havana cigar, the best that could be bought in Thorp. It was sweet and delicious. He poured himself some of the brandy used to fire the pudding, offering the bottle to Mick who shook his head. Taking a large sip Patrick said, 'I think Hetty's sweet on me.'

Mick laughed. 'Poor thing. Well, when she gets tired of

barking up the wrong tree, send her home to me.'

Patrick thought of Paul outside the church with his new wife. 'Perhaps I should get married.'

'And perhaps I'll grow new legs, but it wouldn't be what you'd call natural, would it?'

Patrick drained his glass and poured himself another. Knowing Mick was watching him he snapped, 'I can get drunk, can't I?'

'As long as you can stand to put me to bed later.' Mick held his gaze and Patrick laughed drunkenly.

'Have I ever let you down? Ever? Remind me.'

Mick drew on his cigar. 'You've never let me down. Never. Not yet.'

The room had become even warmer. If Patrick squinted the candle flames danced and the frozen faces of his family blurred into one. He had meant to burn the photos, along with the rest of his mother's favoured possessions, but in the end he couldn't bring himself to do it, his own superstitions surprising him. Getting up, he took his parents' wedding photograph down, slamming it on the table in front of Mick.

'When I heard they were dead I told the officer who broke the news, "I'm an orphan." I laughed – we both laughed. It was bloody ironic.'

Mick picked up the photograph and frowned at it. He looked at him. 'You laughed, eh?'

'Didn't you?' He felt drunk, more drunk than he'd ever been in his life. He thought of Paul walking towards the church with that unknown runt of a man and jealousy swept over him. Because he was drunk he said thickly, 'Paul Harris got married yesterday.'

'So?'

'So nothing, I'm just telling you.'

'I knew his brother, Rob.' Mick gazed at him. After a while he said, 'Paul was the *very* pretty one, wasn't he? I mean, Rob was handsome, but Paul ... it's a wonder he got past the recruitment sergeant. Crying out to be gang raped, that one.' He smiled slowly. 'You wear your heart on your sleeve, Patty. So, I'm listening, tell me about Paul. How you met, his first words

53

to you, everything.'

'Fuck off.'

Mick held his hands out to the fire. 'It's cold in here, isn't it? I'm always freezing cold.'

'Have a brandy, that'll warm you.'

'I've had enough. How did you know he got married?'

'It was in the paper.' Patrick hesitated. Sullenly he added, 'I went to the church. I watched him as he went in and waited until he came out again.'

'Did he see you?'

'No. I don't think so.'

Mick turned back to the fire. 'Be careful.'

'I'm so fucking careful he's forgotten I exist.'

'Are you going to remind him?'

Patrick stared down at his drink. He thought about the letter he'd written and hadn't sent, a stiff, formal letter as though he was still playing sergeant to his officer. It wouldn't do at all. He had to be bolder. Remembering Paul asleep beneath the lilac tree he said, 'Yes, I'm going to remind him.'

Not wanting to disturb the pain expanding inside his head Patrick lay stiff and still in bed. He could hear Mick snoring and he opened his eyes only to close them again against the winter sunlight. He was still dressed, stinking of yesterday's cooking and cigar smoke. Reaching out, his hand covered Mick's. He had put him to bed only to fall asleep beside him.

Mick stirred, crying out soft, unintelligible commands and flinging out his arm so it rested on Patrick's chest. Patrick lifted it aside and sat on the edge of the bed, holding his hangover carefully in both hands. Slowly, more and more of last night's conversation came back to him and he groaned. Mick always had to know everything – everything had to be told, discussed, resolved; there'd never been a single thing he could keep to himself.

For a while he watched his brother sleeping, making sure dreams no longer disturbed him. At last he stood up gingerly, going to close the curtains so that he'd sleep on.

Chapter Seven

THE HEADMASTER HIMSELF SHOWED Paul around the school.

'Of course you realise you'll be teaching only the most junior boys.'

'Of course, sir.'

The school smelt as his own school had, of sweaty plimsolls and damp gabardine and Paul wished he could smoke as he struggled to keep up with the headmaster's impatient quickness. A cigarette would at least be a distraction, something to keep the memories at bay. He remembered Jenkins lying in wait at the end of long school corridors and the bowel-loosening fear of what he might have in store for him. The memory made him feel ashamed but he willed himself forward, even as he imagined himself running back the way they had come, the startled headmaster staring after him.

Adam had arranged this interview with the headmaster. The man had opened the school especially for him, taking a day from what he called "the wasteland" between Boxing Day and New Year to interview him. He raced a few steps ahead of Paul, his shoes squeaking on the parquet floor of the corridors and from time to time he flung open an empty classroom door, briskly shouting out its form number. To Paul each room appeared identical to the last: rows of desks facing a huge blackboard, the teacher's desk raised on a low platform. He tried to picture himself behind such a desk, controlling thirty or so boys. Half of them would be on his blind side. Perhaps he could rig up a mirror.

In the headmaster's study Paul watched him shuffle through his references before tossing them down on his desk. The reference Adam had written was on top and he tapped it with his index finger, smiling at Paul.

'Our Mr Mason thinks very highly of you. He seems to think you'll make a very good teacher.' He sat back in his chair, putting on a show of studying him. At last he said, 'In the army for how many years?'

'Three, sir.'

'And you're quite well, apart from …' He waved his hand vaguely around his own left eye.

'I'm fine.'

'Well, that's good. A lot of my staff are past retirement age – certainly not as fit as they used to be. But with so many of you youngsters away … to be blunt, we need fresh blood pretty desperately. I've got classrooms full of boys with no one to teach them.' He got up and went to the window that looked out across the playing field. 'You were in university for a short time, before the war?'

'I was taking a medical degree.'

'Yes, quite. Well, you're certainly educated. In normal times, of course, I would expect more, but these aren't normal times …' He sighed as though the seriousness of the decision he was about to make weighed heavily. At last he said, 'I'm sure we can work something out, come to some arrangement … term begins again on January sixth.' He looked at Paul over his shoulder. 'Shall we see if we suit each other?'

They had been married five days. Every night Margot lay stiffly in bed, waiting and listening. Every night Paul sat downstairs, reading and endlessly smoking until midnight or later when she would hear him climb the stairs. As he reached the landing her heart would pound so hard she imagined he could hear it. She wondered if he would stop and tap on her shut-tight door and she would tense, listening intently as she slowly counted to ten. It usually took around ten seconds before she heard his bedroom door close behind him. It seemed sometimes that he listened, too, standing outside her door as shy and awkward as she was, so that idiotically she had begun to imagine ways to seduce him, knowing she was too clumsy and gauche to make a success of such absurd plans. She remembered how tightly he had held her that evening in his father's house; she should have kissed him then and got it over with.

He had gone out that morning in his wedding suit, washed and shaved and shoes polished. As he'd combed his hair in the mirror above the sitting room mantelpiece he'd caught her watching him and smiled at her reflection.

'How do I look?'

She had blushed, caught out in her act of spying, wondering if he realised how beautiful she thought he was and whether he would be offended by her use of such an unmanly word to describe him.

The house still smelt of paint. She wandered from sitting room to kitchen and back again, half-heartedly dusting the furniture Paul had brought from Parkwood: a table that dominated the little room, a sideboard intricately carved with bowls of fruit and flowers, empty apart from a cheap, wedding-present tea-set. The furniture was even more depressing than the dark, poky house and she trailed upstairs, only to pause outside the closed door of Paul's bedroom.

Telling herself she didn't want to intrude on his privacy, she hadn't been in his room, shy of his underwear, his pyjamas, his shaving things, everything that made him real and ordinary and disappointed. Now boredom mixed with curiosity and she opened the door, hesitating only a moment before going in.

The room was freezing, the curtains drawn back and the window open. He had made the bed, turning back the sheets and blankets as she imagined he had been taught to in the army, so neat and precise it looked as though a ruler had been taken to the edges. Beside the bed a book lay open, face down on the floor, a stack of books beside it, bookmarks inserted between the pages. On top of the books was an ashtray containing a single cigarette stub and a spent match. His clothes, his shoes, everything was put away. The only things to be shy of were books and cigarettes.

Sitting down on the edge of his bed, she remembered watching Paul at her birthday party. Standing next to her, watching too, her friend Edith – older and more worldly than she – had said, 'He's so handsome, isn't he?'

'I suppose so.'

Still looking at Paul, Edith smiled. 'He's probably having a passionate, unhappy affair with a Parisian actress. She's very neurotic and threatens to kill herself if he ever leaves her.'

Margot laughed, but was ready to believe that some beautiful, willowy French woman would throw herself at his polished boots. When Robbie came back with their glasses of punch he frowned.

'That's Paul over there. What's he doing on his own?'

'Smoking.' Edith grinned and Robbie turned his frown on them.

'He looks lost. Has he been introduced to anyone?'

'He's only just arrived.'

It was the first time she had seen Rob angry. Coldly he said, 'I'll go and fetch him.'

Her father had brought the gramophone out of the house and Edith and her other friends were gathered around it. Across the lawn she watched as Robbie embraced his brother, only to hold him at arms' length as through inspecting the correctness of his uniform. She heard them both laugh and as one they turned to her. She looked down, her face burning, knowing she had been the subject of their laughter. In a moment they both stood in front of her.

Robbie was smiling now. 'Darling, this is Paul, my brother.'

'Pleased to meet you, Margot.' Paul glanced towards the makeshift dance floor laid out on the lawn. The gramophone had begun to play a waltz and he smiled at her. 'Would you like to dance?'

She was still blushing, aware of everyone watching them as he led her on to the floor. With his back to the on-lookers he bowed slightly. Only she could see his grin. Holding her in his arms he said quietly, 'Are they watching?'

'Yes.'

'Good. Happy birthday, by the way.'

She had tried to keep a little distance between them, keeping her body stiffly away from his so that she danced badly. All the same, she remembered that he had a pimple on his chin, that there were dark rings under his eyes, that his wrists protruded stick-thin from the sleeves of his tunic. He had smelt of coal tar soap and cigarettes and seemed too frail to wear a uniform. She had thought him vain and arrogant and was glad when the dance was over.

Duster in hand, Margot stared out of Paul's bedroom window. Girls turned a skipping rope in the street, their chanting carrying on the still air as the rope lashed the cobbles. She thought of Paul dancing with Edith, remembering how Robbie had squeezed her hand too tightly.

'I'll start to get jealous if you don't stop staring at my brother.'

'I wasn't!'

He laughed, his own eyes on Paul. 'It's all right. He has the same effect on everyone.'

'And what effect is that?'

'You were the one staring at him, Margot. You tell me.'

Bristling she said, 'I was only thinking how arrogant he seems – can't even be bothered to hide his boredom.'

Robbie lit a cigarette, shaking the match out slowly as he watched Paul dance. After a while he said, 'He only got home yesterday. He goes back the day after tomorrow. I expect he's exhausted.' He looked at her. 'I would expect so, wouldn't you?' After a moment he laughed. 'Don't look so sulky. I want you to like Paul. I know you and he will get on fine.'

A week later Robbie was back in France. Just before the armistice he wrote to tell her Paul had been wounded. *Would you write to him? He gets so few letters. Dad tells me the nurses read our letters to him and it's the only diversion he has. I can only imagine how truly bored he must be ...*

She had tried to compose a witty, entertaining letter fit for an unknown nurse to read to a bored, blind man. The task had been too difficult. The half-page she wrote had lain abandoned on her desk. Eventually she threw it on the fire.

From the kitchen Paul called her name and she ran downstairs too quickly, making herself breathless.

Standing in the passage he frowned. 'Are you all right, Margot?'

'I'm fine.'

'Are you sure? You look pale.'

'Never mind me. Tell me how you got on.'

'I start next week. Scary, isn't it?'

'It's wonderful. Congratulations.' She stepped towards him, only to stop, unsure of herself.

With sudden decisiveness he said, 'I think we should go and celebrate.'

'Where?'

'I don't know. We'll take the train somewhere. The seaside.'

'It's winter.'

'So? Come on, I'll buy you lunch in the Sea View Hotel.'

The sea was out, the beach a wide expanse of dull yellow sand they shared with only a few seagulls. She walked ahead of him, from time to time stooping to pick up a shell. Her dark wool skirt brushed the sand and a strand of hair escaped from her navy blue tam-o'-shanter. She tucked it impatiently behind her ear, turning to smile at him before looking out at the still, grey sea.

'I feel like we're playing truant,' she said. 'No one knows we're here and they'd disapprove if they did.'

'I've felt like that all my life.' He lit two cigarettes and handed her one. 'In the army, even at boarding school, I was always expecting someone to tap me on the shoulder and say, "Harris, you idiot, what are you doing here? You should be somewhere else"'

'I would've hated boarding school.'

He thought of Robbie holding on to the sleeve of his brand new blazer in the school hall. George had told him to hold his hand but that wasn't done. With each word Rob spoke he jerked his sleeve until he thought he would pull it from its seams. *Don't cry. The others will think you're a baby if you cry.* He was seven. Despite Jenkins's best efforts over the next fourteen years he hadn't cried once.

They began to walk again, keeping to the firm, wet sand at the edge of the water and following a trail of spiky seagull footprints. When the headmaster had offered him the position he'd almost told the man he'd changed his mind, that the very thought of setting foot in a classroom again made him want to throw up. Instead he'd heard himself accept, meek as ever. He sometimes wondered if he'd agree to anything. Such a sense of duty he had! From the corner of his eye he glanced at Margot. He knew she'd be pleased that he'd got himself a nice, middle-class profession. He smiled to himself bitterly, hoping she was the type who could manage on the slave-wage he'd agreed to.

Above them on the front was the Sea View Hotel, its grand Edwardian façade shuttered for the winter.

Paul said, 'Sorry about lunch.'

She glanced up at the hotel. 'I was wearing the wrong hat for it, anyway.'

'I imagined it would be decked up for Christmas, all lights and flunkies.'

'Perhaps next year.'

'The Grand Hotel is holding a New Year Dance. Shall we go?'

She looked down at her bump. Hesitantly she said, 'Would it be seemly?'

'Are you supposed to hide away?'

'No, but …'

'I think I'd like to go dancing.'

'All right.' Avoiding his gaze she nodded. 'I'd like that, too.'

'Good.' He slipped her arm through his. 'Now, let's find a nice warm café and have a cup of tea.'

All the cafés were closed, their windows opaque with condensation, their doors locked. They walked up and down the promenade and along side streets lined with little shops advertising candy rock and ices, their windows decorated with miniature Union Jacks for the victors' sandcastles. All were closed. The whole town seemed deserted, all life stored away for the winter beneath a dustsheet of grey sky.

'There's a pub along there.' Margot smiled. 'You could buy me a port and lemon.'

'Are you sure? It looked a bit rough.'

She laughed. 'That's all right. I've got you to protect me.'

*　　*　　*

The King George was as hostile as he'd suspected, the landlord eyeing them suspiciously as he settled Margot at a table furthest away from the men leaning against the bar. Taking off her hat and mittens and unwinding her scarf, she looked around curiously. Her face was pink from the cold sea air. She looked too young to be in such a place.

He bought a port and lemon and a pint. As he went back to the table, Margot lit a cigarette, shaking the match out and tossing it into the ashtray like a practised smoker. Picking up her drink she laughed. 'Down the hatch.'

'Down the hatch.' He clinked his glass against hers.

'I've never been in a public house before.'

He lit a cigarette. 'They're usually a bit nicer than this.'

She looked around her again, at the dark brown walls, the spluttering gaslights that made the absence of comfort or warmth even more obvious. Too lightly she said, 'I suppose you've been in lots of places like this.'

'A few.'

'In France?'

'They're different over there.'

'How?'

'Just different.'

'You don't want to talk about it. That's all right.'

He laughed. 'Over there they call them cafés. They put tables on the pavements outside and serve wine and food.' He looked at the barman slowly twisting a dirty cloth into a pint glass. Turning back to Margot he said, 'You can order a cup of coffee and a glass of cognac and sit and watch the world go by.'

'And French women go by?'

He took a long drink. Wiping away a beer froth moustache he caught Margot's eye and smiled. 'Thirsty.'

'You've almost finished it!'

Draining what was left in the glass he stood up. 'I'll have another while you finish that.'

As he returned with a second pint Margot asked, 'Have you ever been to Paris?'

'No. I haven't been anywhere, really.' He laughed shortly,

lighting another cigarette. 'Nowhere exciting, anyway.'

'I've never even been to London.'

'Then one day we'll go. Perhaps if you're with me I won't get so lost.'

'You got lost?'

'Hopelessly.' He smiled at her. 'Didn't you go on holiday when you were a little girl?'

'Once. We went to Scarborough for a week.' Quickly she said, 'What did you do in London? Were you on your own?'

'Yes, on my own. I was on leave, early in the war, ages ago. I didn't have enough time to get home and back so I got lost in London.'

'All on your own.'

He laughed. 'Yes, completely. Very sad.'

'But on your other leaves, what did you do?'

'I didn't have many. There was that one, in London, one other when I came home and slept for two solid days, and that last one, when I met you.'

'But the army sometimes held receptions for officers, dances, that kind of thing …'

He frowned at her. 'Who told you that?'

She blushed. 'Robbie.'

'I think that was before the war.' He gazed at her, her sweet embarrassment making him smile. 'Margot, I left school and like an idiot joined the army almost at once. Unlike Rob, who was his regiment's pride and joy, I was never invited to balls or the general's parties.' Gently he said, 'You were the first girl I danced with in my life.'

She looked down, running her finger around the rim of her glass. 'But you're such a good dancer.'

'We were made to dance together, at school. I was usually the girl.'

She smiled at her drink. 'May I have another of these?'

As he took Paul's money the landlord jerked his head in Margot's direction. 'On honeymoon, are you?'

'Visiting.'

The man laughed. 'Visiting, eh? We don't get many *visitors* this time of year.' Handing him an overflowing pint he said

63

matter-of-factly, 'We've a room here. I do a nice cooked breakfast if she's up for it.'

Paul sat down and Margot said, 'What were you talking about with that man?'

'The weather.'

She smiled, closing her eyes as she took a long sip of her drink. 'I feel quite light-headed.'

'We should get you something to eat. You shouldn't drink on an empty stomach.'

She smoothed her skirt over the small bump. After a moment she said, 'That man was talking about me, wasn't he? Saying what a hussy I must be for drinking and smoking and …'

'And?' Paul smiled.

'And going out with soldiers.'

'Soldiers?' He looked around the darkening, shadow-filled pub. 'I don't see any soldiers.'

'You.' She sighed. 'You know what I mean … anyone can see you were a soldier … especially when you wear that coat.'

Finishing his drink he hauled her to her feet. 'I think we'd better go and find you something to eat.'

Along with everywhere else, the fish and chip shop was closed and they walked towards the station, both sobered by the cold evening air. Margot looked at him sheepishly. 'He wasn't talking about the weather, was he?'

'He thought we were on honeymoon.'

'Honeymoon? Here?' She looked at him, astonished. 'Who would come here on honeymoon?'

Carefully Paul asked, 'Would you have liked a honeymoon?'

'I don't know.' She blushed. 'I suppose I thought it wasn't appropriate somehow.' Brightening, she smiled at him. 'I'd like to go dancing at New Year, though. I think that would be nice.' She laughed slightly. 'Remember when we danced together at my party?'

He remembered the feel of her in his arms, her body so stiff, as though he repelled her. Although he'd bathed in almost scalding water he'd imagined he stank, that itchy, lousy smell, sweet as decay. She had smelt of steamed roses. He smiled to himself, remembering how much he had wanted to lead her away to some quiet place just so he could breathe her calming scent in private.

Margot was laughing. 'When we danced you looked so pained and bored, I told Robbie I thought you were very rude.'

Recollecting himself he said, 'And Rob agreed.'

'No. No, he didn't.'

'He told me I should buck up.'

'It was a terrible party, anyway. You had every right to look bored.'

'I wasn't bored.'

'No. I realise that now. You're just shy, like me.'

She stopped walking and turned to face him, holding his gaze for so long he imagined he could see himself in her eyes, a slight, shy boy trying to live his brother's life. At last she reached up and touched his cheek. 'You look so sad, sometimes. I'm so sorry, Paul, for all this.'

Her hand was cold and he pressed his face against it, turning to kiss her palm. She groaned softly, a low needy sound and he pulled her into his arms. He kissed her, tasting the sweetness of port wine as she held him tightly. She must have felt his erection through their clothes because she made that same raw noise again.

Holding her face so that she'd meet his gaze he said, 'Let's go back there …' He searched her eyes, smiling because they were so bright and large. Kissing her again he said, 'Let's have a honeymoon.'

'Shall we?' She seemed shy suddenly, glancing away towards the dark sea and the distant lights of ships. Managing to look at him she said awkwardly, 'I think you're terribly handsome, you know.'

Taking her hand he led her back along the street towards the lighted windows of the King George public house.

The bed was hardly wider than a single bed, its sheets smelling of rainy back streets. There were thin, satin-trimmed pink blankets gathering in deep furrows at their feet and trailing on to the floor. The room was too warm for blankets; it seemed to have sucked up the heat from the room below, drawing it through the cracks in the floorboards just as it drew the laughter and chatter from the bar. Naked, with only a sheet covering her, Margot lay still, listening. Laughter rose and fell; greetings and insults were exchanged. Paul slept on, mumbling anxiously at a sudden burst of noise.

The landlord had been deadpan when they arrived back at his pub. Taking a key from a hook behind the bar he had led them up a steep flight of stairs and along a short corridor, its carpet as sticky as his pub tables. His swinging lantern cast his huge shadow on the wall ahead of them, a hunched, scary monster, intensifying her nervousness. Unlocking the room he'd stood back, smiling broadly at Paul only to resume his poker face as he handed him the key.

Paul turned to her as soon as the man had left. 'You don't have to go through with this.' Taking out his cigarette case he sat down on the bed and lit two cigarettes at once. He handed her one and she noticed his hands were shaking. 'We can still go home, if you want to.'

There was a chest of drawers beside the bed, the only other piece of furniture in the room. Balancing the cigarette on its wooden edge she took off her hat and began to unbutton her coat. Without another word Paul got up, keeping his back to her as he began to undress. Naked, he climbed into the bed, lying on his back and staring at the ceiling until she climbed in beside him. The sheets were cold and she shivered.

He turned on his side, drawing her close to him. His erection nudged her belly and she was shocked into stillness, afraid as she remembered the hot, tearing pain of that first time with Robbie. From the pub came a shout of laughter and he held her even tighter.

He smelt of musk, nothing like his usual scent. The smell made her want to bury her face in his chest and the pits of his arms. He was hairier than she had expected, his chest covered in coarse, springy hair, jet-black against the paleness of his skin. She curled her fingers into it and he pressed her hand flat against his chest. His heart beat steadily beneath her palm and he kissed her.

'You taste sweet, of port and lemonade. It's delicious.'

'You taste of cigarettes.'

'Sorry. Such a filthy habit.'

'You were smoking the first time I saw you. Just standing in our garden, staring out into space, smoking. You looked so sophisticated.'

'And you thought "What an arrogant boy".' For a while he was silent and she shifted in his arms until her head rested on his chest. He stroked her hair steadily. At last he said, 'I feel clumsy, a bag of sharp bones.' He hesitated, then, 'Should I just hold you? Would you prefer it if I just held you?'

Her disappointment surprised her. Carefully she said, 'We're married, now.'

'I've never done this before.'

He shuddered and she sat up a little, causing the sheet to fall away from her. Daring herself to be bold she took his hand and pressed it against her breast. Her nipple hardened against his palm and he closed his eyes, before pulling her down on top of him.

Going home on the train Margot fell asleep, her head resting on his shoulder. Paul avoided eye contact with the other passengers. Dishevelled and unshaven, he imagined he stank of sex, that everyone must surely be able to smell it on him. He closed his eyes, Margot's body a weight against his. She smelt only as she always did, of fat, blowsy roses.

As the train trundled towards Thorp, he thought of Adam, feeling the same guilt he always felt on the very few occasions he'd been unfaithful to him. He opened his eyes, staring out of the window, remembering.

He'd been sleeping in a chair beside his hospital bed, and had woken, startled at the sound of Adam's voice.

'I'm sorry,' Adam said, 'I didn't mean to make you jump.' He'd stood over him, smiling with all the awkwardness of any visitor to an asylum, although he'd visited often. 'Here.' He held out a package. 'I bought you some sweets.' Pulling up another chair Adam sat down, watching uncomfortably as, one after the other, Paul ate all the toffees he'd brought.

'You'll be sick.'

'Would you like one?'

'No, I bought them for you. I just didn't expect you to eat them all at once.'

As though he thought he wouldn't be heard above the rustle of wrappers, Adam waited until the last sweet was finished. 'I heard about Rob. I'm so sorry, Paul. I don't know what to say.'

The toffees had made his tongue raw. All the same he craved another. He looked down at the empty wrappers on his lap, feeling through them for one he might have missed.

'Paul? Did you hear me?'

'Yes.' He looked up at him. 'Robbie's dead. There's nothing to say.'

After a long silence Adam said, 'How are you?'

He lit a cigarette, wanting a contrast to the burning sweetness. Pinching a stray strand of tobacco from the tip of his tongue he said, 'You know how I am. They cut my eye out. Other than that, I'm fine.'

Adam sighed. 'I'm still missing you, counting the days until you're home.'

'Do you really miss me?'

'What kind of a question is that? Of course I do! I love you, you know that.'

He thought of Jenkins, his body slumped against his own. At last, remembering Adam's presence, he said, 'You wouldn't love me, if you knew what I'd done.'

'What? Paul, I can't hear you if you mumble.' Frustrated, he said. 'Paul, won't you *try* to pull yourself together?'

The train began to slow. Fellow passengers folded their newspapers and collected coats and briefcases. Margot smiled at him, sleepily. 'Are we home, already?'

He nodded. Getting up he busied himself with buttoning his coat so that he wouldn't see the fragile happiness on her face.

Chapter Eight

HER MOTHER FOUND THE gloves Patrick had forgotten on Christmas Eve. She laid them on the kitchen table in front of Hetty, silently waiting for an explanation. Unable to keep the exasperation from her voice, Hetty said, 'If you must know he carried the chicken home for us on Christmas Eve.'

'Who did?'

'You know who. You know they're Patrick's gloves.'

'Oh, it's Patrick, is it? Not Mr Morgan any more? I suppose you're all free and easy with him now you've asked him into our home? Well, next time, Madam, you ask me if you can bring men into this house. You don't do it behind my back.'

'It would have been rude not to ask him in. Especially after he'd given us the chicken.'

'I didn't ask for his charity. Tough as old boots, anyway. I've told you before I don't want meat from that shop.'

Hetty picked up the gloves, turning them over in her hands, wanting to press them to her face to see if they still smelt of him. He hadn't missed them, as far as she knew. Planning to return them to his house each evening, each evening her courage failed and the gloves remained in their hiding place.

She said, 'You shouldn't go looking through my things.'

'Looking through your things?' Her mother laughed scornfully. 'Tidying up after you, don't you mean? Putting *things* away. If you want to keep secrets you should keep them more carefully.'

Hetty put her coat on, thrusting the gloves into the pocket.

'Where're you going?'

'I'm taking them back to him.'

*   *   *

She would say, 'You left your gloves at our house on Christmas Eve. I'd forgotten all about them until this evening, and as I was passing your house anyway …'

Hetty sighed, nervously fingering the gloves in her pocket. With luck he'd be home. If she missed all the cracks in the pavement he would smile and ask her in and his brother would be safely tucked up in bed.

Outside his house she stood at the gate, surprised to hear music coming from the lighted room that looked out over the small front garden. A man spoke above the music that came to a sudden end with the sound of a gramophone needle being scratched across a record. Another voice, unmistakably Patrick's, decided her. Walking up the path she pulled the front door bell.

'There's someone at the door, Patty. Go and see.'

'I'm not expecting anyone.' Patrick slipped the gramophone record into its sleeve and put it away. 'They'll go away if we ignore it. It's time for your bath, anyway.'

The bell rang again and Mick wheeled himself over to the window. Lifting aside the lace curtain he peered into the darkness.

'It's that little shop girl of yours.'

'Are you sure?' Patrick caught sight of Hetty over Mick's shoulder. He groaned. 'I'll get rid of her. Wait there.'

Hetty said, 'Oh, Mr Morgan … you're home, then.' She looked surprised to find herself there. Her usually pale face was even paler against the dark scarf wrapped around her throat. Awkwardly she said, 'I hope I'm not bothering you.'

Behind him Mick said, 'Hello, Hetty. Please, come in. You must excuse my brother keeping you on the doorstep. He's not used to visitors.'

Patrick ignored him. Still standing in the doorway he said, 'There's nothing wrong, is there?'

'Oh, no. No!' Hetty laughed as though the idea was outrageous. 'I was passing and …'

'For God's sake, let the girl in. You can see she's freezing.'

'It's all right. I'll go if it's inconvenient.'

Patrick stood aside. 'You'd better come in.'

Mick poured her a glass of sherry; he even cut her a slice of the last of the Christmas cake. He talked too much, as he always did when he felt others were embarrassed. Eventually, as Hetty calmly sipped her drink, Patrick realised that it wasn't Hetty who was embarrassed, but Mick himself. His stream of words had dried up and he smiled desperately at Patrick, willing him to end the silence.

Patrick cleared his throat. 'That's a pretty scarf, Hetty.'

'Thanks. It's Mam's. I bought it for Christmas but she lets me borrow it.'

Mick said, 'Did you have a nice Christmas?'

'Quiet.'

'Ours was quiet, too. Wasn't it, Patrick?'

'Very.'

Mick laughed, a short, embarrassing burst of noise. 'We should all have a rowdy New Year to make up for it. We should go dancing …'

'That would be lovely.' Hetty grinned. 'Somewhere posh with a nice band.' She looked at Patrick, adding, 'Somewhere they let balloons down from the ceiling at the stroke of midnight.'

'The Grand used to do that kind of thing, didn't it, Pat?'

'I don't know.' Turning to Hetty he said, 'I was just about to help my brother to bed, Hetty.'

She fumbled in her coat pocket. 'Oh! Nearly forgot.' Handing him a pair of gloves she said, 'You left these at our house the other day. I was passing and I thought …'

'It was kind of you.' He stood up. 'Well, if that was all.'

'Yes. Right.' Placing her glass on the table she smiled shyly at Mick. 'Thank you for the drink, Mr Morgan. And the cake.'

'My pleasure, Hetty, and call me Mick, please.'

Patrick held the door open. 'I'll see you out.'

As Patrick came back into the room Mick glared at him. 'You shitty, bloody bastard.'

Gripping the arms of the wheelchair Patrick brought his face

71

up close to his brother's. 'I told you I'd get rid of her, didn't I? But no, you had to ask her in *and* show me up as well! Thanks, Mick. Was that little charade worth it?'

Mick took his cigarettes from his pocket. His hands shook as he struck a match. 'You were rude.'

'Rude!' Patrick laughed. 'That's bloody priceless coming from you.'

'She's a nice girl.'

Patrick stood up straight. 'I don't want to encourage her. She's an employee, not a friend.'

'Of course! God forbid we might have any friends!'

Patrick gazed at him, his anger slowly ebbing away. 'You're tired. She could see how tired you are. She wasn't going to stay long, anyway.'

'All the same you had to remind her how bloody helpless I am.'

'I'm sorry.'

'No, you're not. You like everyone to know you do everything for me. Well, what a great big bloody selfless bastard you are! I wish you'd left me in the hospital. At least there …'

'Go on. At least there what?'

'I had people to talk to.' Sullenly he said, 'I wasn't alone all day, every day.'

'Shall I take you back there? You can take up basket weaving again. So, seeing as you miss it so much, first thing in the morning off we go.'

'All I'm saying is she could have stayed a little longer.' He bowed his head. 'She could have stayed. We were getting along.'

Patrick sighed. 'She came to see *me,* Mick. You know what she's after.'

'So? Marry her. Once she finds out you can't get it up for her maybe she'll find her way into my bed.'

'Don't be so disgusting.'

'You're disgusting. A lovely girl like that showing an interest and all you can think about is buggering some whey-faced, lisping boy.'

'He doesn't lisp.'

Mick laughed. 'Doesn't he? I could have sworn …'

'What do you know?'

'Oh, we've met, *Paul* and I.'

'When? When did you meet?'

'Oh, sometime. Can't remember.'

'Liar! Fucking liar!' Patrick seized Mick's arms, digging his fingers into the flesh. 'You're just lying now.'

'Let go.'

'And what can you do about it if I don't?'

Drawing his head back Mick spat in his face.

'You filthy bastard.' Patrick wiped the spittle away, glaring at his brother as he stepped back. 'I think I will take you back to that hospital. I really think I will.'

'And close the shop for a day? I don't think so.'

'No? Well, wait and see.'

Mick tossed his cigarette stub into the fire. He smiled slowly. 'I suppose you could always dump me there on a Sunday when the shop's closed. Bit of a bugger getting there on a Sunday, though. And on Sundays there'll be no one at the hospital to do the paperwork. They're very strict about their paperwork.'

'Well, they can just leave you sitting in the drive until Monday, then, can't they?'

'Oh dear.' Mick lit another cigarette. 'You *are* cross. Poor me.'

'You're pathetic.'

'You and me both.' He looked up at Patrick through a haze of cigarette smoke. 'I bet Hetty's got gorgeous tits. Not too big. Just nice. You didn't have to be so off-hand with her.'

'Yes, I did. Now, do you want that bath or not?'

They were identical twins, a novelty act dressed up in matching outfits: sailor suits with beribboned caps, blue velvet breeches with white knee socks. Their mother spent too much time brushing their hair, smoothing it into exactly matching neatness. She wanted others not to be able to tell them apart, a trick she played on the world until even their own father couldn't be bothered to tell which was which.

Patrick stooped over the bath, dipping his hand in the water to test its temperature.

Mick smiled at him. 'Just the right degree of boiling?'

'Just. Ready?'

Mick nodded, putting his arm around Patrick's shoulder as he was lifted from the chair. He closed his eyes, sighing as the water covered him.

'Hot enough?'

Mick nodded.

'Call me when you've finished.'

'Pat … don't go for a minute. I've been thinking …' He laughed, frowning down at the water. 'What have you put in this bath? It smells like one of Mother's handkerchiefs.'

'Lavender. It's supposed to help people sleep.'

'People? How about bad-tempered cripples?'

'It might help. You never know.' Patrick sat on the edge of the bath. 'So, what were you thinking?'

Drawing a deep breath Mick said quickly, 'I was thinking maybe we could go dancing, Hetty and I. Oh, you could come too.'

'Could I? Thanks. Where shall we go? Paris?'

'The Grand Hotel.'

Patrick laughed. 'The Grand Hotel? The Grand Hotel with all the steps leading to the doors?'

'We could manage a few steps.'

'You mean I could.'

'All right. You could.'

'You're joking, aren't you?'

'They're holding a New Year Dance. I saw it advertised in the paper. And Hetty said she'd like to go.'

Patrick stared at his brother. The lavender-scented steam seemed to blur his features, making him look younger and less like himself. His eyes were wide with hope.

Shaking his head Patrick said. 'She's made quite an impression on you, hasn't she?'

'I can't stop thinking about her tits.'

'Mick …'

'Oh, don't *Mick* me. I don't want your sympathy. I just want to take a girl out.'

'To a dance? You know how people stare at the best of times.'

'I stare back.'

'Hetty will want to dance.'

'You can dance with her.'

'Which will give her the wrong idea entirely.'

'Not if you behave as you did tonight.' After a moment he said, 'We still look alike, don't we? Even now. If she likes you ...'

'No, Mick.'

Mick sank lower into the water. 'Fuck off, then. Fuck off so I can have a wank in peace. After all, it's the only relief I'm ever likely to get. I knew you wouldn't agree to it. So fucking scared of a few stares! Just keep me hidden away till I rot.'

'You go out sometimes.'

'And you wheel me back again.'

'Because you get drunk and spew your guts all over me.'

'Once.'

'I get scared for you, when I'm not there.'

Mick looked at him. The cold tap dripped like the measured tick of a clock, timing the silence. At last he said, 'Please, Pat.'

'I don't know ...' Patrick sighed, unable to think of a good enough reason why they shouldn't go. Knowing he would regret it he said, 'All right. I'll ask her.'

Mick exhaled a long breath. 'Thanks.' He closed his eyes and Patrick recognised this as his cue to go.

Cleaning the bath, hanging towels over the clothes-horse to air, Patrick tried to imagine asking Hetty to the hotel's dance. He saw her face brighten only to fall when he said, *'Mick's coming as well.'* He hoped she would turn him down, certain she wouldn't.

He ran cold water into the bath, sluicing away the last of the lavender suds. As children they had bathed together, their mother sitting where he had, on the edge of the bath, watching them with rapt indulgence.

No girl would ever have been good enough for her boys, but she would have hated Hetty more than most. So common, so coarse, with her rough hands and scrawny features. Such women didn't even wash properly. Involuntarily Patrick curled his lip in disgust. Hetty would smell of milk and blood and bone. All women did.

He remembered the whore's room, papered with a pattern of abstract flowers and Chinese dragons, hump-backed, serpent-like creatures with manic, goggle-eyed smiles. He had stared at them, counted their repeat around the walls and tried to imagine such creatures breathing fire as the girl worked on him. Her hands were small and brown with half-moons of dirt beneath her fingernails, her fingers surprisingly strong around his cock. She frowned over her task, tipping her head to one side so that he imagined her as a bird, poised over a half-buried worm. He'd closed his eyes. Reaching out he'd grasped her wrist and lifted her hand away. 'I can't.'

'Don't worry, pet, it happens.' Her voice was singsong Geordie. Into his silence she laughed. Lowering her voice she said gruffly, 'Not to me it doesn't.'

'What?' He opened his eyes to look at her.

'You all say it. I say *it happens* and you say *not to me it doesn't.*'

She had been kneeling at his side on the bed and she got up, the flimsy robe she wore falling open. A trickle of blood ran down her thigh and she drew the robe tighter around her. All the same he caught her scent, his mother's scent, ripe and fecund and suffocating. He gagged, stumbling to the basin in the corner of the room, vomiting Dutch courage under the grinning eye of dragons.

Chapter Nine

HER FATHER HAD A new curate: a stocky, cheerful redhead who shook Paul's hand too vigorously, studying his face as though trying to decide which eye was real. As the curate, Martin Peters, asked Paul if he had accepted Jesus into his life, her father smiled at Margot as though some need for revenge had been partly satisfied.

Taking her to one side her father said, 'Your mother tells me he's found a job. Will he cope with a class full of boys, do you think?'

'Of course he will.'

'Well, I hope so, Margot. I hope he can take care of you.'

'He can.' She looked at Paul. Without thinking she said, 'Isn't he like Robbie? He even laughs like him.'

He frowned. 'I don't see Robbie in him at all. Robbie was a fine boy. And perhaps you've forfeited the right to mention his name.'

Humiliated, she looked away so he wouldn't see her eyes fill with tears. Her father sighed heavily.

'Have you a handkerchief? Then use it. We have a guest, please don't embarrass him.'

Margot walked out through the French doors into the garden, ready to cry as much as she liked. Once outside though she only felt childish, shivering in the cold without even a cigarette to occupy her. She glanced back into the brightly lit dining room. Her father stood with the curate and Paul, his expression still pained and angry. After a moment he touched the curate's arm, excusing himself.

Standing beside her in the garden he said, 'I'm sorry. Of course you can talk about Robbie if you wish.'

Unable to speak she smiled tearfully, taking his hand.

'Oh, you're cold!' He rubbed her fingers. 'Let's go in.'

'Not yet.'

'Don't cry, Margot. I'm sorry.' Exasperated he said, 'I'm just so angry still.' He looked back at Paul. 'What he did to you makes me angry. But I'm trying. I'm trying to get over it.'

'He's not as bad as you think – I really like him ...' She thought of the night in the seaside pub and blushed.

'Like! You should be head over heels in love with him. Instead you're crying alone in the garden.'

Quickly she said, 'He's taking me to the New Year Dance at the Grand tomorrow.'

'And so he should! Now, dry your eyes and let's go in. Your mother's serving the tea.'

The curate reminded Paul of a sailor he had once fucked in the lavatories on Darlington Station. The sailor had a short, stubby cock nesting in the most vividly coloured pubic hair he'd ever seen. His skin smelt of hot, dry canvas and a mermaid tattoo swished her tail over his coccyx. He thought often about that mermaid. He was thinking about it now as the curate said, 'I'm afraid I spent the war in Blighty. Spent a lot of time pushing paper around in the War Office.'

The sailor hadn't been wearing underpants. He still wondered why this had seemed shocking. The mermaid had long, golden hair, of course, her tail undulating as he fucked him. Suddenly ashamed, he closed his good eye, leaving only the glass eye to look at the curate.

'Paul?' Margot slipped her hand into his, squeezing his fingers hard. She laughed awkwardly. To the curate she said, 'His eye gets tired.'

'Yes, of course. I understand.' They both blushed.

Placing a trifle in the centre of the table her mother called, 'Now, everybody, come and sit down. Help yourselves to tea.'

'Have some more trifle, Paul.'

Paul smiled at his mother-in-law. 'No, thank you, Iris.'

He hadn't used her name before and she smiled back at him,

pleased. Her plump, pink hands reached for the curate's bowl and spooned in another wobbling helping of raspberry sponge and yellow custard. Still smiling at Paul she said, 'You won't say no, will you, Martin?'

'No indeed, Mrs Whittaker.'

'Paul's about to become a teacher, Martin, we're very pleased.'

'A teacher?' He raised his eyebrows at Paul. 'That's important work.'

'Isn't it?' Iris beamed. 'I do think you'll make an awfully good teacher, Paul.'

'Do you, dear?' Reverend Whittaker frowned as though surprised. 'What makes you think so?'

'Daddy …'

Whittaker ignored Margot's anxious look. 'I think teaching is going to be quite a challenge for him.' He turned to Paul. 'Perhaps you should think about a less demanding career.'

'What would you advise, sir?'

'Clerical work? I don't know. What has the army equipped you for?'

'Oh, Daddy. Please …'

'No, Margot, let Paul answer. He's always so quiet, listening, watching.' He laughed shortly. 'We hardly know anything about you, boy, nothing at all, in fact.'

'What would you like to know, sir?'

'Don't call me *sir*. Are you deliberately trying to anger me?'

Coldly Iris said, 'What should Paul call you? Father? Reverend? Or Daniel, even?'

Whittaker stood up, tossing his napkin down on the table where it knocked over a jug of cream.

Paul set the jug upright again and used the napkin to mop up the spill. No one else at the table moved as Whittaker turned and walked out, slamming the door.

The curate laughed nervously. 'Oh dear. I'll go after him.'

'Yes,' Iris snapped. 'Go after him. I'm sure none of us can be bothered to.' She turned to Paul. 'He liked your brother, I'm afraid. He liked him very much.'

Paul said, 'We should take this cloth off the table before the cream stains.'

Quickly Margot said, 'Don't worry about that, Paul.'

Iris stood up. 'No, Margot, Paul's right. Help me clear the table.' She touched his hand. 'Why don't you go and have a cigarette? We can manage here.'

In a ruined church in a village close to Arras, Jenkins had sat down beside him. 'If you could eat anything, Harris, anything in the world, right now, what would it be?'

Walking along the path leading from the vicarage to his mother's grave, Paul remembered how Jenkins had reminded him of the hunger he'd been trying to ignore all day. Knowing Jenkins wouldn't leave him alone until he replied, he'd said, 'I don't know. Anything.'

'God – you've no imagination have you, Harris? You're no fun at all! Think about it, man! I know what I'd have – my mother's mince and dumplings. Custard for dessert. Just very thick custard, skin an' all. Mother's brilliant at custard.' After a moment he said, 'Your mother's dead, isn't she?'

Above their heads starlings darkened the sky, ready to roost amongst the charred rafters. Jenkins looked at him questioningly. 'That's right isn't it? I seem to remember you had a dead mother. What was that like, having your mother die on you?'

Brusquely Paul said, 'I don't know.'

'You don't know? Really? Your mother dies and you haven't a thing to say about it?' He moved closer to him, his forehead creased in mock puzzlement. 'And I would have thought you were quite the Mummy's boy, Harris. Yet you don't seem to care about her at all. You really are the limit, aren't you?'

He had wanted to keep silent to prove to himself that he didn't always have to rise to Jenkins's bait. Instead, hating the pompousness in his voice he said, 'She died when I was born.'

'Oh.' Jenkins turned away. Huddling further into his trench coat he stared straight ahead at the overturned altar. 'You killed her, then.' He laughed suddenly, making Paul jump. 'You know, Smith's custard tastes of onions. Christ knows what he does to it.'

They'd been marching to the forward trenches. Hawkins had seen the church and allowed them to stop for ten minutes. The men sprawled out on what was left of the pews, some sleeping, others staring into the spaces the shells had made, their faces grey with exhaustion, their uniforms caked in drying mud. From time to time one of the men coughed harshly, breaking the unnatural quiet as the crucified Christ looked down on them, his face and body taken up with his own agony. Paul stared at the cigarette smouldering between his fingers. The food Jenkins had conjured made his stomach growl with hunger and Jenkins glanced at him, and patted his knee before getting up. Paul kept his head bowed feeling every inch a coward as Jenkins stood over him. He heard him snort and flinched as Jenkins nudged his foot with the toe of his boot. 'Come on. Best foot forward, eh? Before you burst into tears.'

Crouching now at his mother's grave, Paul rested his hand on the angel's hip as he took the dead chrysanthemums from the urn at her feet. He turned away from the stink of their water, holding the slimy, dripping stems at arm's length as he carried them to the bin. Walking back to the grave, he pulled up a dandelion that had braved the cold, raking back the disturbed chips of white stone with his fingers. The angel wept into her hand, and he remembered his grandfather standing here next to her, weeping for his daughter. As a small child he'd imagined that the old man and the angel were trying to out-grieve each other.

'Paul?'

He turned around and Margot smiled at him shyly. She stepped towards him. 'I was looking for you.'

'The flowers had died. I didn't want to leave them for Dad.'

She stepped closer. 'Are you all right?' She stood across the grave from him seeming to read and re-read the names and dates inscribed on the stone. At last she said cautiously, 'Let me tell them about the baby.'

'No.'

'I want him to like you.'

'He wouldn't have liked me anyway.'

'That's not true! He liked Robbie.'

He looked at the angel, imagining the bodies of his mother, brother and grandfather buried beneath her feet, only to remember other bodies at the side of a French road, a neat row covered in blankets. Care had been taken for those particular dead; nothing for the camera to see but small differences in the lengths and sizes of the corpses. His men stood behind their shovels, posing solemnly, and the photographer, fussing over his equipment, caught his eye and smiled at him, queer to queer. Paul had only stared back, angered at the man's lack of respect for the dead, hating that he should capture their images inside the camera's black box. Even now he worried whether faces had been sufficiently well hidden.

He grasped the angel's wrist, wanting to pull her hand away from her face. The stone was worn, as though other fingers had worried it. He thought again of Jenkins. He remembered sitting in that ruined church, glancing at him surreptitiously from the corner of his eye, trying to work out if his growing paranoia was justified. Whether it was or not, he'd decided then that the only defence against him was to be silent, to give nothing of himself away.

The familiar paralysing guilt returned. He closed his eyes, appalled all over again at his own wickedness.

'Paul? I think we should go home.'

He had forgotten Margot and looked up in surprise. She smiled anxiously and took his hand. Curling it up in her mittened fist she led him towards the cemetery gates.

Chapter Ten

HETTY'S FATHER SAID, 'Do you think they should be taking that crippled lad out on a night like this?'

Her mother sniffed. 'He'll catch his death. I just hope he wraps him up warm.'

Smoothing down her freshly washed, misbehaving hair, Hetty said, 'Do I look all right?'

'You'll do.'

Behind her mother's back her father winked at her. 'She'll do, will she, Mother?'

'If she has to go at all.'

'Dancing at The Grand!' Joe shook his head in mock amazement. 'My little Henrietta.'

There was a knock on the front door and Hetty jumped. Wearing a dress in the new, shorter style and new, heeled shoes instead of her usual button boots, she felt less like herself than she had ever done in her life, her chilly ankles indecently exposed. Even her underwear was new and too scratchy; the new-fangled, flesh-toned silk stockings she'd squandered her savings on seemed to rustle with each move she made. Too late to change into something else, she wished she'd worn at least one thing that was soft and quiet and reassuringly hers.

Hetty felt the cold air as her father opened the door on to the street. Her heart beat faster as she heard him invite them in. Nervously she went to the door herself, finding the three of them on the pavement, a gang of neighbours' children gathered around Mick's chair.

Mick smiled at her. 'Hetty. You look lovely. All set?'

The wheelchair made Joe awkward and he grinned too broadly. 'Doesn't Major Morgan look smart, Hetty?'

'I'm not a major any more, Mr Roberts. Please, call me Mick.'

Tersely Patrick said, 'Are you ready, Hetty?'

'Yes.' She smiled as brightly as her father had.

'Have a nice time, pet.' Joe squeezed her arm. 'Burst a few of those midnight balloons for me.'

Mick lit a cigarette and handed it over his shoulder to his brother before lighting one for himself.

'What do you think, Hetty, quails' eggs on the buffet or pork pies? How grand is The Grand these days?'

'I don't know.' She stumbled beside them, her shoes pinching. Mick exhaled sharply.

'Patrick. Please, it's not a race.'

Patrick slowed a little.

Hetty had often imagined holding her wedding reception in The Grand Hotel. She had thought carefully about the reception, the cold hams and salad, the trifle bobbled with whipped cream. There would be roses in tall vases and a cake with four tiers. Lately she'd imagined Patrick in a morning suit, a carnation in his buttonhole, brilliant white against feathery green fern, matching her trailing bouquet.

They stopped at the hotel steps. There weren't many; Hetty counted each one as she stood beside Patrick, five in all. Patrick drew on his cigarette heavily as he too seemed to count the steps like an athlete gauging the size of the challenge. Turning the wheelchair around so that Mick faced away from them he said, 'Ready? Here we go.'

That afternoon, for the first time as a married man, Paul had visited Adam. They'd gone to bed at once, Adam leading him wordlessly up the stairs. Afterwards Adam held him too tightly. Paul could feel his breath against his shoulder as Adam whispered, 'Do you love me, still?'

He hesitated a fraction too long because he felt Adam's body stiffen and knew that he was holding his breath. For a moment he felt as though he could kill him simply by remaining silent and so he said quickly, 'I love you, of course I do.'

'Of course?' Adam's laugh was strained. 'Your marriage hasn't changed anything?'

'No.'

Adam hugged him even closer. 'I've been so jealous these past few days, thinking of you and her.'

Paul struggled from his arms and turned on his side to face him. Desperate suddenly to reassure him and ease his own guilt he said, 'Don't be jealous. I don't want you to think like that.'

'Like what? It's normal, isn't it? My lover sleeps with someone else every night, therefore I'm jealous.' He sighed, taking off his glasses and rubbing his hand across his face. 'I thought this Christmas we'd be together. For the first time in years I thought we could spend Christmas together.'

'I'm sorry, Adam.'

'Yes.' He sat up and put his glasses back on. Sitting on the edge of the bed he glanced at him over his shoulder. 'You're sorry, I know.'

Paul reached out, placing his palm flat against his back. Adam's skin was soft as a child's, and so white it was almost translucent. In the summer the freckles on his arms would darken and auburn would show in his hair. In the sun he would burn easily and if they placed their arms side by side his own skin would appear dark as an Indian's in comparison. Moved to tenderness, Paul sat up and slipped his arms around his waist. He kissed his shoulder and Adam turned to look at him.

'Remember our first Christmas?' Adam laughed shortly. 'God, I was nervous! If it hadn't been for you taking charge … I never could quite believe my luck, you know. 1914. Best Christmas of my life.'

'Mine too.'

'It could be like that again, you know.'

Paul laughed. 'Could it?'

'Yes!' Adam twisted round to face him. Becoming animated he said, 'Make an excuse to her – we could spend a whole day and night together. We could make up for all that time we lost.'

Paul lay down on the bed. He held his arms out. 'Lie down, eh? Let me hold you before I have to go.'

Adam lay down, resting his head on his chest. 'You don't

take me seriously.'

'Things have changed, that's all.' Paul lifted his head to smile at him. 'I'm not sixteen any more, Adam.'

'Don't I know it.' He sighed. 'At least we'll be together at school, eh? At least we have that.'

Paul stroked his hair, thinking of his interview with the headmaster, the sense of panic he'd felt as he'd accepted the offer of a job. Perhaps he'd been too hasty, there had to be other work he could do. Shop work, he thought, and tried to picture himself behind a counter in Robinson's, earning even less money than the school offered. It would be difficult enough to keep a wife and baby on a schoolteacher's salary, impossible on a clerk's. And of course it would be different teaching boys rather than being one of them. At least he wouldn't be entirely at their mercy.

He let his hand rest on Adam's head. 'At school – you'll show me the ropes? Make sure I'm not too much of a new boy?'

'You won't need me to mother you! Standing up in front of a class of twelve-year-olds?' He laughed. 'Christ – it's nothing compared with everything you've been though.' Smiling up at him he said, 'You're not worried, are you?'

'No. I suppose not.'

'I can't wait. Seeing you in the staffroom, being able to talk to you without worrying about what other people might be thinking. I don't think I've ever been in a normal situation with you.'

'Normal?'

'You know what I mean.'

Paul resumed stroking his hair, remembering the first time they'd met and whether that situation could be considered normal. The day he left school for good Robbie and George had met him off the train, bringing Robbie's new friend Adam along for the ride. He remembered being light-headed with the relief of never having to see Jenkins or his gang again, that he'd greeted his father and brother with uncharacteristic joy, like a long-jailed prisoner finally released. Some of that joy had spilled over to Adam, who'd seemed bemused by this manic

boy. They'd shaken hands and for a moment Paul had become
still, the noise of the station retreating. Adam had held his gaze,
his hand dry and cool in his. Paul remembered some detached
part of himself noting how handsome he was.

Adam shifted in his arms, drawing him closer. 'How will I
be able to keep the pride from my face when I introduce you in
the staffroom? Half of the old crocks will fall in love with you
at once, of course.'

'Only half?' Paul gently disentangled himself from his
embrace and got up. Beginning to dress he said 'I think you
have a skewed idea of my attractiveness, Adam.'

'No. I just think you're the most gorgeous boy that ever
lived.'

Buttoning his flies Paul looked up at him. 'You'll be all right
tonight, won't you?' Hesitantly he said, 'You could still come
with us, if you want. Margot's friends will be there, you
wouldn't be out of place.'

'Yes I would. Besides, I hate dancing. And dancing with her
friends … Christ! I'd rather have my toenails pulled out.'

Dressed, Paul leaned over the bed and kissed him.
'Goodbye, Adam.' He kissed him again, drawing away as
gently as he could when Adam curled his fingers into his hair.
Paul remembered how much he'd looked forward to this
afternoon in his bed. Now the sex was over with he couldn't
wait to get away, wanting only to be alone. He thought of
Margot waiting for him to take her to the hotel's dance and
sighed miserably.

Adam caught his hand. 'When you're dancing with her
remember I adore you.'

The dress Margot had worn for her birthday party didn't fit any
more. She had tried it on but the buttons along the side seam
wouldn't fasten, the material stretching obscenely across the
bump even when she breathed in. Now the dress lay in a blue
silk puddle on the floor and she realised she had nothing else to
wear for the dance that night.

She stood aimlessly in front of her open wardrobe, staring at
clothes she had riffled through again and again as if a suitable

dress might magically appear. At last she reached for the old-fashioned long black skirt and pale green blouse she had worn to the memorial service. The skirt would have to be held together at the waist with a safety pin.

Laying this dismal outfit on the bed she sighed. She was twenty and would look forty. Paul, wearing the evening jacket now hanging alongside her clothes, would look young and dashing and all heads would turn towards him. They would wonder what he saw in such a dowdy girl.

It was easy to imagine that there had been a sophisticated, older woman in his past. Paul had a gentleness that she imagined could come only from experience; that night in the pub he was slow and careful, making her feel she was as much in control as he was. Robbie, on the ground beside the Makepeace tomb, had acted so quickly that the shock had made her frigid. Although his kisses had softened her, even though she instinctively opened her legs, no one had explained the mechanics of it, that penetration had to be forced to overcome her body's resistance. She'd felt something give inside her and heard Robbie's gasp of triumph. Frightened, she'd laid still and stiff beneath him, hating the way he screwed his eyes tight closed as though he was the one being hurt. It was over quickly, that one and only time with Robbie. She had bled a little and in her innocence the idea of pregnancy hadn't even occurred to her until she'd realised she hadn't bled since.

After that night in the seaside pub, Paul had moved into her room, although he hadn't made love to her again. Lying beside him as he slept his troubled, talkative sleep, she worried that he might be repelled by her pregnancy; she felt huge beside him, fat and unlovable although he treated her with the type of kindness that could easily induce self-pity. She had an idea that Robbie would have been sterner with her. She wondered if Paul would be easier to love than his brother, suspecting that he might be.

Going to the window she looked out on to the street, straining her eyes against the dusk to see him. She had expected him home an hour ago and she began to worry. He still seemed frail to her; he may have fallen or fainted, he may have stepped out blindly in front of a tram. She exhaled sharply, afraid all over again for her future.

He appeared then, as though she had conjured him, walking quickly. Margot stepped back from the window. She would pretend not to have noticed the time. Drawing the curtains she began to dress for the dance.

Chapter Eleven

IN THE HOTEL LOBBY Patrick looked around, trying to guess which corridor would lead them to the ballroom. It would be too bloody easy for the bastards to put up a sign. But then this whole expedition was a crazy idea. They probably didn't even allow wheelchairs into the hotel. There was bound to be some regulation excluding them. He breathed deeply, trying to control the anger that had been building inside him all day.

Evenly Mick said, 'Patrick, perhaps we should ask that porter over there.'

'People are going in that direction.' Hetty smiled at Mick, her pinched little face white with cold and nervousness. 'I'm sure it's that way.'

Mick began to wheel himself along the corridor that Hetty pointed at. He smiled over his shoulder. 'Come on, you two. Looks like they've started without us.'

Outside the ballroom a table had been set up. A girl sat behind it. Ignoring Mick she turned to Patrick. 'Tickets?'

Patrick rummaged in the pockets of his dinner jacket, disturbing the smell of mothballs. At last the three squares of thick, jagged-edged card were found and handed over. Inspecting them as though they might be forgeries the girl said, 'If you want to hand your coats in, the cloakroom's along there.'

'Do you want to hand your coat in, Hetty?'

'Of course she does!' Mick laughed. 'And so do we.' To the girl who was adding their tickets to a small pile he said, 'Thank you.'

She ignored him. 'It's two pence for each coat.'

Handing in their coats, Patrick looked back at the girl.

'Miserable little bitch.'

Mick frowned, glancing at Hetty who was preoccupied with peering into a tiny hand mirror taken from her bag. 'Don't talk like that in front of her. And cheer up. We're meant to be enjoying ourselves.'

'She didn't even look at you. Bloody rude!'

'I don't care! You're just making it worse by going on about it. Now smile, you're upsetting Hetty.'

Tables were arranged around a dance floor, a candle flickering on each one. Above the floor a net was suspended, captured balloons bumping against each other in the rising draught. On a stage at the far side a five-piece band played American Ragtime.

Mick grinned at Hetty. 'I'd ask you to dance, but ...'

Hetty smiled back. 'I think we should find a table first. Catch our breath for a bit.'

'Good idea.' Manoeuvring his way towards the tables Mick looked back at them. 'What are you waiting for?'

Quietly Hetty said, 'It's nice to see him so happy.'

'Isn't it?' Patrick looked at his brother grimly as Mick pushed a chair out of his way, apologising to the party whose table it belonged to. No one moved to help him – they all seemed too shocked. Surprisingly, Hetty laughed.

'Come on,' she said. 'The cavalry's cleared a route for us.'

I look all right, Hetty thought. I look nearly pretty and I'm sitting with the two most handsome men in the whole place. She smiled to herself and surreptitiously glanced at Patrick. He was staring at the dance floor, his face as poker-straight as his back. She wouldn't worry that he hadn't smiled this evening, he was obviously concerned about his brother. They'd overheard a woman tut-tutting that such people really shouldn't be out in public places. Mick had pulled a face at the woman's back and she had laughed out loud.

Mick leaned a little closer to her. 'Has it lived up to your expectations?'

'I think it's lovely.'

He laughed. 'I'm pleased. I would have to complain to the

manager if the hotel had let you down.'

'Have you been here before?'

'Once. A cousin's wedding.' He lit a cigarette. Tossing the spent match into the ashtray he smiled at her. 'Have you been here before?'

'Me? No, never.'

'But you knew about the balloons.'

'Our Albert used to work here. He told me.'

He nodded, keeping his gaze fixed on her face as though trying to memorise her features. She found herself gazing back at him and he smiled slowly before looking down at his cigarette. 'Why don't you ask Patrick to dance?'

She laughed awkwardly. 'He should ask me.'

'He should.' Leaning across her he tapped his brother's arm. 'Patrick, dance with Hetty.'

As though he had been given an order, Patrick stood up and held out his hand, wordlessly leading her on to the dance floor.

The Grand Hotel was just as Paul remembered it when George would take him and Robbie for lunch on the last Sunday before the start of a new term. His father imagined this was a great treat. Neither he nor Robbie could bring themselves to tell him they were both dreading the return to school too much to enjoy it.

The porter remembered him, asking after his father as he took Margot's coat and led them along a corridor. They by-passed what looked like a queue to hand in tickets and another queue for the cloakroom and were ushered into the ballroom. The porter grinned as though he had shown them into the Palace of Versailles. He shook Paul's hand, 'Very glad to have you safely home, sir.'

Margot scanned the room. When the porter had gone Paul asked, 'Have you seen someone you know?'

'Edith Briggs. You remember her from our wedding? And Catherine Taylor. She said Ann would be here too.' Smiling suddenly, she pointed at two girls dancing together. 'Yes. There's Ann and Winifred.'

Paul lit a cigarette, taking his time so she wouldn't notice that his hands were shaking. Watching the two girls dancing together he realised with a sinking heart how few men there were to partner the women and that he'd be expected to dance with all her friends. His hand went to the glass eye and he drew on his cigarette deeply.

Margot smiled at him, her eyes bright with excitement. 'Shall we go and sit with them?'

Hetty said, 'This is nice, isn't it?' She'd been concentrating on her dance steps, looking down at her feet. Now she looked up at him, smiling anxiously.

She smelt of violets, sickly as cheap sweets; even her hair, a frizz of mousy curls, smelt of violets. She wore a dress of brown crushed velvet, reminding him of the skin of small rodents; he could feel her bones though its thin pile and imagined that he could hear her heart pounding fast as a vole's. He had forgotten how tiny she was, or perhaps he hadn't realised; in the shop she was quick and capable, larger than life in that enclosed space behind the counter. Here, on this half-empty dance floor, he felt like a giant dancing with a small child.

He looked up at the balloons. They would float down and be burst under foot with deliberate violence. It would take all his courage not to hide from the explosions under the table. He imagined cowering behind the cover of the starched white tablecloth. Mick would pull him out by the hair.

Smiling, Hetty waved at Mick. Mick waved back and went on watching them through a haze of cigarette smoke, his hand beating time to the music on the arm of his chair. Patrick remembered that dancing the waltz had always been one of the few things he could do better than Mick, that and slaughtering pigs.

Hetty laughed, still smiling at Mick. 'Mam said he could be charming when he wants to be, when he's not getting upset.'

'He treats your mother badly.'

'You heard about the liver and onions, then?'

'He told me. I'm sorry.'

'It's not your fault.' She smiled at him. 'No onions, next

time, eh?' He laughed and her smile broadened. 'That's better. You've looked ever so worried since we got here.' Very briefly she put her finger on his lips. 'And don't say sorry again. It's all right. I was worried, too.'

'About?'

'Showing myself up. Not being posh enough.'

'Posh enough?' He laughed. 'Posh enough for what?'

Nodding her head towards a group of young women giggling amongst themselves she said bitterly, 'Them. I bet none of them ever worked a day in a shop. See that one laughing? She's just moved in a couple of doors down. Newly wed and at least four months gone. She's nowt to be snotty about, that one.'

Patrick frowned at the girl. 'Is she snotty? She looks like a good sport.'

'Good sport?' Hetty snorted. 'You sound like one of them.'

He looked again at the girl. She stood next to a young man, only slightly taller than she was so that her head rested easily on his shoulder as she leaned into him. They held hands, he supposed that's what newly weds did, but then the girl snaked her arm around her husband's waist, drawing him closer. It was a sensual display for such a public place and Hetty laughed.

'No wonder she had to get up the aisle double-quick.'

The girl's husband looked around, as though he sensed they were watched. He stared straight at Patrick.

Later Patrick wondered how he managed to find his voice but at that moment he heard himself say, 'I know him. He was an officer in my platoon.'

'Oh? Should you say hello?'

He barely heard her. He was staring at Paul, a taste like gunmetal on the tip of his tongue, that sweet softening of his guts already starting.

Margot was saying, 'Oh, the new curate's awful! He has *red* hair!' She laughed, showing off, making him want to lead her away somewhere quiet so that she might calm down. 'Most curates are dismal, but *Martin!*' She laughed again. 'Martin's just awful.'

Edith said, 'What a pity,' and blushed.

Paul smiled at her absently, still shocked at seeing Morgan. He forced himself to watch him walk off the dance floor. It was definitely him: not many men carried themselves like Sergeant Morgan. He walked as if he owned the world.

Jenkins had said, 'Have you seen the new sergeant, Harris? I think we should send his photograph to the Kaiser. Immediate German surrender.'

Lying on his bunk Paul said, 'He's surly.'

'Surly, eh? Just your type, I'd say.'

Margot and her friends laughed, startling him back to the present. He lit a cigarette from the butt of the last, remembering Morgan lying beside him, still as stone as German voices joked in the nearby trench. His face, like his own, was covered in mud, like a blacked-up minstrel, only the whites of his eyes showing. A shell exploded and the minstrel eyes had fixed on his, mirroring his own fear. As the earth rained down he felt Morgan's arm on his back, his huge hand protecting his head by pressing him down further into the stink of those killed before them.

He looked up to see Morgan leave. Excusing himself to Margot, he followed.

Morgan sat on the hotel steps, his hands clasped together between his knees. Standing a few feet away, Paul hesitated. Shock had made him forget what his Christian name was. All he had ever called him was Morgan or Sergeant. Using either would make him sound like a prig.

He took a step down so that his feet were at the same level as the other man's thighs. After what seemed like a long time Morgan said, 'Hello, sir.' He got up. Even standing on the step below Paul, he still towered over him. He took out his cigarettes and lit one, tossing the match down. Seeming to make a great effort to look at him, only to look away again, he said, 'How are you?'

Paul cleared his throat. 'Fine. You?'

Quickly Morgan said, 'What do you think about all those balloons?'

'Balloons? Oh … I suppose they'll make a few bangs.'

Morgan sat down on the steps again. 'It's too hot in there, I felt sick.'

Paul sat beside him, judging a careful space. 'Do you feel all right now? You look a bit green.'

Morgan laughed shortly, flicking cigarette ash at the space between his feet. 'I'm all right. Pulling myself together.'

He hadn't changed very much over the months. His hair was a little longer and he was cleaner and more closely shaved. He was the type that could shave twice a day, the type that would always have the shadow of a beard. Types like Hawkins cursed him as a ruffian. The fact that the army couldn't find a uniform big enough to fit him properly only added to the look. Now, however, his evening suit appeared to be tailor-made, cut so that it showed off his broad shoulders and narrow waist. He'd undone his collar stud as though about to undress and the bow-shaped ends of his black tie lay flat against his starched white shirt. The cloth of his trousers strained across his thigh and Paul's cock hardened despite himself. He remembered how attracted he'd been to this astonishing man, how difficult it had been to be around him and the tension in the air whenever he, Jenkins and Morgan were together. Jenkins's innuendoes had never let up; he'd felt like smashing his teeth down his throat.

After a moment he said carefully, 'When did you get home?'

'June.' Morgan dragged his eyes away from the middle-distance to look at him. 'I heard you got married. Congratulations.'

'Thank you.'

Morgan hesitated, then, 'I'm glad you're all right, sir. Recovered. After that business with Lieutenant Jenkins we thought …'

Paul stood up quickly. The shock of hearing Jenkins's name spoken after so long set his heart pounding. His voice broke as he said, 'I have to get back to my wife.'

Morgan stood up too. Facing him he said, 'Don't rush off.' He touched his arm and Paul flinched. Smiling slightly Morgan said, 'Sorry. You followed me out – I thought …'

'I have to go back inside.'

'Yes, of course.' He stood aside. As Paul was about to go in,

Morgan said, 'I sometimes have a drink in the Castle & Anchor. Sunday lunch times.'

Paul nodded, and walked back into the hotel.

Margot sat alone at the table, watching her friends dance with each other. Flushed from the single glass of dark, sweet sherry she'd drunk earlier, blotches of red spread over her face and neck and she fanned herself ineffectively with her hand. Her waistband cut into her and she tugged at it, wondering if she dared unfasten the safety pin holding it together. Beneath her fingers the baby stirred, a faint rippling response. She pulled her hand away.

She had wanted to dance. She had wanted Edith and the others to watch her dancing with Paul and she had wanted them to be jealous. Instead, she watched her friends dancing, forcing herself to smile as they passed by. If they were jealous, they weren't going to show it. Ann had told her how good she was for not minding about Paul's glass eye. They all agreed on how delicate he looked, like an invalid. St Steven's asylum was mentioned – madness alluded to in questions dressed up as concern. From the corner of her eye she saw them exchange sly smiles. She had become the butt of their joke, and she'd looked away, searching for Paul.

Alone at the table she found her gaze drawn to the striking-looking man in the wheelchair two tables away. He talked constantly to the girl beside him, using his hands eloquently. Throwing his head back he laughed and the people on the table between them turned to stare. He stared back. After a moment he said loudly, 'I'm sorry – did you miss the punch line? I'll tell the joke again, if you like. *What's the difference between a nun on a bicycle and a whore on ...*' He stopped, frowning at the girl beside him. 'You know, now *I've* forgotten it!'

A man got up from the other table, outrage making his voice quaver. 'Can't you see there are ladies present? If you weren't in that chair I'd ...'

'You'd what?' Motioning at the man with his cigar he said evenly, 'You're making a fool of yourself. Sit down.'

He sat, blustering, as the man in the wheelchair caught

Margot's eye and smiled. She looked away quickly.

Behind her Paul said, 'Margot, I'm sorry … if I'd known you were on your own …' Margot turned to look at him. Sulkily she asked, 'Where have you been?'

Paul sat down and lit a cigarette, forgetting to offer her one. Eventually he said, 'I needed some fresh air.'

Bitterly she said, 'You missed all the excitement. That man over there nearly got into a fight with the man in the wheelchair. The crippled man was very rude.'

'Was he? Perhaps he had cause.'

Margot frowned at him. 'Are you cross with me?'

'No, of course not!' He got up, crushing his cigarette out. She noticed again that his hands were shaking. 'Come on. Let's show them how to dance.'

Chapter Twelve

EACH SUNDAY MORNING PAUL walked Margot to church, kissing her goodbye at the churchyard gates before crossing the road to Parkwood. This was the fourth Sunday of their marriage. Already a pattern was emerging, a structure to his life of work, home and weekends spent working in Parkwood's garden, neglected since he joined the army. Outside this respectable structure was the occasional evening he spent in Adam's bed. Further outside the boundaries were his thoughts of Patrick Morgan.

Digging out a diseased rose bush, Paul exhaled sharply. He'd been afraid of seeing Morgan again, knowing that one day he could turn a corner and he would be there. He'd always imagined that if he did see him he would walk away in the opposite direction, terrified of the memories that would be stirred up. But, of course, reality was different. In reality he lay awake at night imagining seeking him out at that pub he'd mentioned. He imagined taking him to some quiet place, Parkwood, perhaps, when his father was out, somewhere safely private where Morgan could do just what he wanted with him.

The first time they'd met Morgan had saluted him, bringing himself smartly to attention and making him feel small and weedy, unwashed and stinking after four days and nights in the front line trenches. At that first meeting he'd been too exhausted to notice just how staggeringly beautiful he was. Only later did his skin bristle whenever he stood close to him. Whenever they lay together in the waste of no-man's-land, beneath the once all-consuming fear, he felt protected.

Back in the relative safety of the trench he tried to believe that Morgan was only a competent sergeant, a hard man who cracked filthy queer jokes behind his back just as the other men did. In his heart, though, he knew what Morgan was; he gave himself away, at least to him. And to Jenkins, of course: Jenkins had an unwavering nose for queers.

Paul pulled at a dead rose and a thorn sliced through his gloves and into his finger. He cursed, tossing the glove down and sucking at the bright jewel of blood.

In Parkwood's kitchen George cleaned the wound, tut-tutting as he dabbed on stinging iodine. He glanced up at him. 'You should be more careful, I don't want you getting a blood infection.'

'It's nothing.'

'Oh, I know. No doubt you've seen worse. *Had* worse.' He sighed. 'It doesn't stop me worrying.'

Paul drew his hand away from his father's inspection. 'Don't worry. You don't need to any more.'

George made a pot of tea and set a large slice of cake in front of him. 'Mrs Calder made it. It tastes better than it looks.'

To please him Paul took a bite and surprised himself by finishing it. George smiled. 'I'm impressed. Another slice?' Watching as he ate he said, 'You're getting your appetite back, good. Only normal, in a boy your age.'

Paul laughed through a mouthful of cake. 'You make me sound like a child.'

'You are my child.' George sipped his tea. After a while he said carefully, 'Does Margot mind you not going to church with her?'

'No. I think he minds, though.'

'Whittaker's a fool.'

'Oh?' Surprised, Paul said, 'I thought you liked him.'

'I don't like the way he looks at you.'

Paul grinned. 'Neither do I.'

'I'm glad you think it's amusing.'

Paul got up and went to the window looking out over the garden. The lawns sloped down to the summerhouse, bordered on both sides by flower beds and high brick walls. Behind the summerhouse, sycamores and horse chestnut cast shadows over the kitchen garden where brambles and dock had taken over, strangling the gooseberry and currant bushes. Some of the glass in the greenhouse had been broken and the ashes from his last bonfire were a blackened, solid mass.

Certain he would be killed, Paul had burnt Adam's letters on that bonfire during his last leave. Calm, he threw the letters into the flames one by one. The wind blew charred fragments straight up into the sky and scattered endearments across the neighbours' tidy gardens.

Coming to stand beside him George said, 'The garden was too much for me when you and Robbie were in France. I hated seeing it go so wild knowing how much you loved it, the care you took with it when you were home. I just never seemed to have any time.'

'Perhaps it needed a fallow time.' He smiled at his father. 'A rest from my fussing.' He turned back to the garden. 'You don't mind me taking it over again, do you? I'm not intruding?'

'Intruding? For goodness sake, Paul! This is your home!'

'It's *your* home, Dad.'

He heard his father sigh, knowing what was coming next. At last George said, 'Why don't you and Margot come and live here? It seems silly spending your money on rent when I've so much room.'

'We're happy where we are, Dad.'

'Tanner Street isn't the best place to bring up a baby.'

'You sound like Whittaker. I'll find somewhere better, in time.'

'On a teacher's salary?' He hesitated before saying quickly, 'Paul, please change your mind and finish your degree. You wouldn't be away from home for that long and if you wanted to you could see Margot at weekends …'

'If I *wanted to*?' He frowned at him. 'I don't want to go away again. I've been away from home all my life.' He turned from the window. 'I have to go. I told Margot I'd meet her after the service.'

He was early; hymns were still being sung. Paul sat down on a bench outside the church to wait. He lit a cigarette, staring down at the gravel path, promising himself he would think about Patrick Morgan only for a little while, until the next hymn finished. The congregation drew breath and launched themselves into *Jerusalem*.

He thought about Patrick in evening dress, his tie loose, his cigarette held nonchalantly between his knees as he sat on the hotel steps. He could see that he had cut himself shaving; he could smell his beer breath, see that his teeth were white and straight and put his own to shame. There was a slight kink in his jet-black hair – with a gold hoop in his ear he would be a gypsy. He wore a signet ring on his little finger. He had always despised men who wore rings.

Paul flicked cigarette ash at the ground, remembering. They lay together in no-man's-land, Morgan's arm and hand heavy on his back and head, causing his helmet to cut into the back of his neck. He could hear him breathing, deep and steady as a fit man running, and he was afraid the Germans would hear. Their patrol was almost over. In a few minutes he would be drinking tea laced with rum, trying not to shake too obviously in case it disturbed the child sent to replace the last Second Lieutenant to have been killed. His teeth would chatter uncontrollably, causing Jenkins to make some bloody remark. Eventually the shaking and chattering would stop. The rum would make him feel light-headed. He had all this to look forward to, in a few minutes.

Morgan whispered, 'All right, sir?'

Paul nodded into the mud. The weight on his back and head lifted. He signalled that they should move on.

There wasn't any rum. Instead Hawkins saw to it that he was served tinned peaches and condensed milk, a reward for not being dead. Wide-eyed and silent, the replacement watched him eat until Paul paused, his spoon halfway between his mouth and bowl and dripping peach juice. Meeting the boy's gaze Paul said, 'I've forgotten your name.'

'Davies, sir.'

'Stop staring at me, Davies.'

'Sorry, sir.'

Behind the boy's back Jenkins laughed. 'Don't mind Harris,

old man. He's aloof with everyone. I've been trying to crack a smile from him for weeks now – he's just too serious-minded for ordinary chaps like us.' He looked at Paul, eyebrows raised. 'Can't seem to see the joke, can you, Harris?'

'Maybe you should explain it to me.'

'Oh, I don't think you're that slow, Harris. You'll catch on in your own time.' He'd looked at Davies. 'By the way, don't call him *sir*. It rather goes to his head.'

In the churchyard Paul frowned. Of course it was inevitable that in remembering Morgan he should also remember Jenkins. A rook hopped and flapped across a grave and he watched it, telling himself he must stop thinking about both.

Jerusalem ended.

'So, what next?' Mick looked out over the park lake. Closing one eye he made a pistol of his hand, taking aim at a swan swimming towards them. As if it really had been shot, the swan dived into the water. He turned to Patrick. 'Are we going home or are you going to go on staring into space like a love-sick girl?'

Patrick went on watching the birds on the lake. Thinking of Paul he said, 'We'll go home. It looks like rain.'

Mick began to wheel himself along the path. Over his shoulder he called, 'You could always knock on his door, you know. Knock knock. Oh, hello, Mrs Harris. Is your husband at home? It's just that I want to fuck him so badly I think I'm going to burst.'

Patrick had to run to catch up. Taking hold of the chair he swung it around so Mick faced him. 'Why don't you keep your filthy mouth to yourself?'

'It's only the truth, isn't it? Bugger the boy and forget him. You're beginning to get on my nerves.' He held his gaze for a while before manoeuvring the chair round and wheeling himself away.

Pushing the wheelchair along the street towards home, Patrick thought back to the time when he'd first realised he loved Paul. He remembered crouching close to a brazier as he brewed tea at the end of the trench furthest from the officers' dugout with Collier huddled beside him, his baby face blank from exhaustion. The shelling had kept up all day; Lewis, Anderson and Smith had been killed. He'd liked Smith. Pouring tea into a tin mug he handed it to Collier who cupped it in both hands. Tea slopped over his boots as the mug rattled against the boy's teeth. Patrick remembered thinking it would be better in a baby's bottle – less would be spilled.

He'd looked up to see someone emerging from the officers' dugout, adjusting the strap of his helmet tighter around his chin. Patrick stood very still, squinting into the darkness. From this distance all the officers looked the same. After a moment another emerged. The first officer turned to the second and adjusted the other man's helmet, too. Patrick watched more carefully. The first officer could only be Paul; only Paul would care enough to do such a thing.

The two began to walk towards the brazier, stooping slightly to keep their heads below the sandbags. He watched as Paul turned and smiled reassuringly at the other man, Davies, the new Second Lieutenant. He looked down at his tea. The two passed by with only the briefest acknowledgement. A shell exploded. Paul shoved the boy against the sandbags, shielding his body with his own.

He wondered if he'd loved him from that moment, or earlier as he'd watched him adjust the boy's helmet, if it was his tenderness or his bravery that made him feel as he did. Whenever he saw Paul he felt soft and sentimental, as though pity and desire had become confused. Perhaps it wasn't even love he felt but something far more basic: an overpowering desire to fuck him. Lieutenant Paul Harris was by far the most fuckable man he'd ever seen. He wanted to keep him safe so that he might have him all to himself.

Mick said, 'Why have you stopped?'

'I need a cigarette'

'Here. Give it to me. I'll light it.'

'I can light my own.' His hands were shaking and he dropped the box, scattering matches over the pavement. He scrambled over the freezing flags, chasing matches that jumped away from him or fell between cracks. His fingers were clumsy, numb with cold, blotched pink and red and white like raw sausage.

As he stood up straight Mick held out his hand. 'Give them to me.' Lighting two cigarettes at once he handed one to him. 'Do you want to know what I would do if I were you? I'd forget him.'

Patrick laughed harshly. 'Would you? Fancy!'

'All right – what are you going to do? It's been weeks since that dance.'

'Three weeks, that's all.'

'Three weeks. He knows where you work, Pat. He knows where you *drink*. Don't you think if he was interested …' He exhaled sharply, exasperated. 'Jesus – I can't believe I'm even talking about this, as if he was some coy bloody girl playing hard to get! For Christ's sake, why can't you just forget him? Carry on like this and one of us will end up in the condemned cell.'

Patrick turned his back on him. They had stopped outside the Church of the Blessed Virgin. Beside the porch was a statue of Mary cradling the crucified Christ in her arms, a larger-than-life-sized portrayal of misery. The sculptor had concentrated on the agony of Christ's dying, his back arched so that each rib strained against the blue-veined marble skin. His arm stretched long fingers to the ground as his head lolled against his mother's thigh. Mary raised her face to heaven, betrayed.

Sighing, Patrick said, 'Do you want to go in and light a candle for Mam?'

Mick nodded, tossing his half-finished cigarette into the gutter.

On New Year's Eve, on the steps of the hotel, he'd had the urge to brag, 'The shop's up and running again now. Of course, it's in a good position – good passing trade, and I'm earning a reputation for quality … *There are rooms above. Empty, private …*' Thank God he'd kept his mouth shut.

Lying on his back in bed, Patrick slipped his hand beneath the waistband of his pyjamas, resting his palm flat over the

105

warmth of his groin. He curled his fingers into his pubic hair, tugging the curls straight. He would allow the fantasy to build slowly. First, Paul in uniform, cap and polished boots, tapping a swagger stick against his thigh. Holding the image for a while he smiled, watching this fancy-dress Paul walk up and down outside the shop, waiting for him, of course, anxious, impatient. Once in the room upstairs he would hold Paul's gorgeous little face between his hands and kiss him roughly, backing him hard against the wall and tugging at the buttons of his tunic as Paul groaned, his eyes big with fear. It would be his first time.

Patrick's fist closed lightly around his cock. Opening his eyes, he stared at the ceiling. Of course Paul wasn't interested in him, Mick was right. He thought of him, dancing with his pretty wife, smiling into her eyes as though he loved her. Rolling on his side he cursed and brought himself to a quick, unsatisfactory climax.

Chapter Thirteen

HETTY SAID, 'ME MAM'S poorly. She won't be able to see to Mr Morgan this dinnertime.'

She watched as Patrick went on jointing the pig. Its head sat on the counter beside him, its soft, dead eyes watching her above its broad grin. Wondering if he had heard she started again.

'I'm not deaf, Hetty.' He glanced at her. 'What's wrong with your mother?'

'A bad cough – she didn't want Mr Morgan catching anything.'

'No, of course.' He sighed, laying the cleaver down gently. 'He's expecting her. I don't like leaving him on his own all day.'

As she'd planned to she said, 'I'll go, if you like, the shop's quiet.' Even to her own ears she sounded reluctant and she expected him to dismiss the idea at once.

Instead he asked, 'Are you sure?'

Already anxious, she managed to smile. 'As long as you can spare me.'

'I'll pay you the same rate as your mother, on top of your normal wage, of course.' He turned back to the carcass as though the matter was settled. 'Twelve thirty, then. The key's underneath the lion. Let yourself in.'

Between outbreaks of coughing her mother had said, 'If he's left soup for him see that it's piping hot. He'll only make you heat it up again if it isn't. And he likes his tea strong, almost black. Don't chatter – he hates it. Set his tray with the good silver and a serviette. You'll find them in the third drawer of the dresser in the back room, all starched and ready.'

'I won't remember all that.'

'Yes, you will. He'll soon tell you, anyway. Soon lets you know when it's not right.' She smiled a rare, soft smile. 'He's a gentleman. Such good manners.'

'Except when you serve him liver.'

Her mother sighed. 'Aye, well. We can all lose our tempers sometimes.'

Crouching beside the hideous lion, Hetty fumbled for the key, shuddering at the woodlice that scattered in panic from her fingers. Nervously she opened the front door, squinting into the gloom as she stepped into the hall. 'Hello? Mr Morgan ...?'

A door at the end of the hallway opened, banging against the wall as Mick wheeled himself towards her. He frowned, stopping a few feet away. 'Hetty? What are you doing here?'

'Mam's poorly. I've come instead. If that's all right?'

For a moment he seemed lost for words. He took off the glasses he was wearing, folding them into his shirt pocket and closing the book on his lap. Taking out his cigarettes he lit one, exhaling a long plume of smoke before finally looking up at her. 'Shouldn't you be at the shop?'

'He's spared me.'

'Right. Well, good ...' He wheeled himself towards her, awkwardly pushing open another door and waving her through. 'Please, come in. Sit down.'

This was a different room from the one she'd been shown into last time. The other room was cramped, busy with wallpaper and furniture and bric-a-brac. This room was empty except for a desk, a bookcase and a single armchair. There were no pictures or photographs, only the spines of books to look at, rows and rows so that the bookcase was full and still more were stacked on the mantelpiece and floor. Despite her nervousness Hetty asked, 'Have you read all these?'

'There were one or two I couldn't finish. Take your coat off, Hetty – sit down. Would you like a drink? Is it too early for a drink?'

He looked younger. His hair was washed but not combed

and there was a stain of something that looked like jam on his collarless shirt. The tartan blanket that usually covered him from the waist was missing, the legs of his grey flannels neatly folded and tucked beneath his thighs. Realising she had been staring she looked away quickly, unbuttoning her coat and draping it over the back of the armchair. 'I'd best get on, Mr Morgan, you'll be wanting your dinner.'

'I'm not hungry. Look, sit down. There's no hurry for any of that. Sit down and tell me what you've been doing today.'

She sat down on the edge of the chair, feet and knees together, hands folded in her lap, making herself as neat and demure as possible to hide the awkwardness she felt. She promised herself that in a moment she would make her excuses and escape to the kitchen.

He laughed self-consciously. 'I don't bite, Hetty.'

She made to get up. 'Mr Morgan, Mr Morgan told me I should see you get something to eat …'

'Too many *Mr Morgans*, Hetty. It might be less confusing if you call me Mick, as you did at the dance. We had a good time, didn't we? I didn't expect to enjoy it so much.'

'It was lovely.'

'Have you kept your balloon?'

'It's shrivelled up quite a bit.'

'I know the feeling.'

Noticing her blush he looked at his cigarette. 'Sorry. Always was hopeless in mixed company.'

She smiled. 'You've jam on your shirt.'

'Oh?' He frowned down at himself. 'Blast it, so I have.'

'Is that why you've no appetite? Filled up on bread and jam?'

Picking at the stain he said. 'Just the jam, actually.' When she laughed in disbelief he said, 'Don't tell Pat. He thinks it's decadent not to spread it on bread first. So,' he cleared his throat. 'Was the shop busy today?'

'Mondays are quiet.'

'Then he won't want you to rush back?'

'He didn't say.'

Patrick hadn't said anything, only nodded curtly as she

called goodbye, raising the meat axe to bring it down hard on a carcass. He'd been silent all morning. Earlier she'd dropped a tin tray on the tiled floor and its clatter made him jump so badly a woman in the queue had mouthed, 'Nerves. They're all bad with their nerves.' The rest of the queue had nodded sagely.

Hetty glanced at Mick. Nerves didn't seem to affect him very much. She wondered how he had lost his legs, imagining the horror of it. Ashamed of her gruesome thoughts she said quickly, 'Would you like me to make you a cup of tea?'

'No, thank you. Father Greene made me some earlier. I get the feeling he only ever makes tea when he comes here. He seems so keen to do it I haven't the heart to tell him I'm capable of boiling a kettle. Pat doesn't like me to, of course. He worries I'll scald myself reaching up.'

'I'd worry, too.'

He looked down at his cigarette, burnt almost to nothing between his fingers. Tossing it into the fire he said, 'Don't worry about me, Hetty. Waste of time. Now, tell me how you came to work for Pat.'

'I fancied a change from Marshall's.'

'From sugar pigs to real pigs? I would have thought the sugar pigs were pleasanter.'

'I like the shop.'

'Do you?' He lit another cigarette, frowning. 'I hated it. Dad made me work there every minute I wasn't at school, helping with the slaughtering out the back. Patrick and I were the only boys from Thorp Grammar who knew how to wield a meat axe.' He looked at her through a grey screen of smoke. 'As soon as I left school I joined the army to get away from it. Dad called me all the names he could think of. I told him I'd be a general. Shame he got himself killed before I was even a major – I would've liked to see his eyes pop one last time.'

'Don't you miss them?'

'I miss my mother.'

'I remember her. She was always so lady-like in her lovely clothes, so tall and elegant. I could never look like that.'

'Yes you could.' He held her gaze, just as he had at the dance. As she was about to look away he said, 'I think you're

110

very pretty. And you looked so lovely at New Year. I was proud to be with you.'

She blushed.

After an awkward silence he cleared his throat. 'You know, I've been stuck in this house for days. If Pat isn't expecting you back at the shop perhaps we could go out? The park is just at the end of the road ... we could take a turn around the duck pond.'

'Oh, I don't know ...'

He grinned. 'I look pale, don't I? As though I need some fresh air? And Father Greene said I'd go blind reading so much.'

'Did he?'

He nodded solemnly. 'Terrible blind. Now you don't want that on your conscience, do you?'

She stood up, taking her coat from the back of the chair. 'Once round the pond then straight back.'

Patrick locked the shop door, turning the sign to *Closed*. He'd had enough of customers, their grumbles and inane chatter, the way their fingers scrambled secretively in their purses like misers begrudging every dirty penny. The last one had wanted three sausages. Three bloody sausages. Her hands had been filthy.

He took the day's takings from the till and walked along the High Street to the bank where the grey-faced little snob of a clerk counted the pennies and half pennies as though they stank. Patrick stared at him, willing him to say a wrong word as the queue shuffled impatiently behind him. He noticed that the bag of copper had speckled the counter with grains of sawdust. He smiled to himself, gratified.

As the clerk weighed the coin he found himself thinking of Paul, remembering the first patrol they went on together. His beautiful face had been daubed with mud and all badges, all indications of rank, stripped from his tunic. Snipers shot at officers first. Paul had smiled at him encouragingly and he remembered having to look away. Lust, on top of such fear, was too much. He wouldn't look at him directly again until they were safely back.

Hawkins always sent Paul on these patrols because Jenkins was such a useless little get. Patrick had suggested once he would go alone with one of the corporals, no need to risk an officer. The man laughed his terrible, braying laugh. It was as if he believed Paul enjoyed these expeditions into no-man's-land.

The clerk was saying, 'Sign this, please.'

A slip of paper was pushed under the grille. Patrick signed it absently, thinking of Paul's slow, practised squirming through the ruts and furrows, how he kept his face close to the mustard-gas stink of churned earth. He had wanted to protect his body with his own as they crawled, covering his full length. He screwed his eyes closed.

Shoving the empty cloth bag under the grille, the clerk said pointedly, 'Good day, Mr Morgan.'

Patrick started, opening his eyes. He glanced over his shoulder and the next in line glared at him. Bundling the bag up he pushed it into his pocket and walked out.

Patrick wandered the maze of narrow alleys that ran off the High Street and were lined with second-hand bookshops and pawnbrokers and poky, beer-only pubs. Stopping outside a junk shop he gazed through its grimy window. Amongst the battered furniture and bric-a-brac a hollow elephant's foot bristled with crutches. Next to it stood a wheelchair, a luggage label displaying its price. He wondered what had become of its owner and found himself staring at the suggestion of an indent on the chair's seat, as though whoever it was had only recently been lifted from it. He shuddered.

He walked on until he came to the high walls embedded with shards of glass that shielded Marshall's sugar factory from sweet-toothed burglars. The factory backed on to the railway line. He could hear the trains rumbling their way west to Darlington or north to Newcastle. If it weren't for Mick he would steal a ride; he would lose himself in a larger place than Thorp, if it weren't for Mick.

He remembered the army doctor watching him as he signed Mick's discharge papers, his cool, condescending voice as he said, 'I hope you understand the enormity of what you're taking on.' This dapper little colonel in his pristine white coat and polished riding boots, and himself, a rough, awkward sergeant who imagined he could look after such a severely disabled man. Smiling the doctor said, 'Major Morgan isn't the easiest patient.' He should've told him to stick his stethoscope up his arse.

A train whistle screamed. Patrick stopped on the embankment a little past the factory and watched the train speed north into a tunnel. He'd been to Newcastle once during leave in the middle of the war. He remembered liking its vastness, nothing like the pitiful villages of France and Belgium, or the closed-in narrowness of Thorp. Imagining himself living and working there, he'd strolled along its streets. Girls had smiled at him. He must have looked happy, he supposed.

He walked on towards Thorp Station. Cheap cups of tea could be had from the station buffet where Bath buns sweated under their glass domes and a coal fire burned in an ornate grate. The buns were soft and sugary and delicious. Decisively, he crossed the street and bought a platform ticket from the station's front office.

Leaning into the doorway of the classroom Adam said, 'Well, you look the part, at least.'

Paul turned to him from wiping the blackboard. 'Looks are deceptive.'

'Oh dear.' Adam came in and perched on the edge of his desk. 'Bad day?'

Placing the blackboard duster down Paul said, 'I got through it. I don't think I taught them very much but at least there wasn't a riot.'

'Did you expect there to be?'

'I keep expecting them to spot what a weakling I am.'

'You're not weak.'

'Aren't I?' Wearily he said, 'Are you going home? I'll walk back with you.'

'I was thinking we could ...' Adam laughed awkwardly. 'You know ... if she's not expecting you I could squeeze you in before Henderson arrives for his Latin tuition ...'

'I'm tired, Adam. All I want to do is crawl home, eat and go to bed.'

Adam followed him out of the classroom. As they walked along the corridor he said, 'How about after supper, after Henderson?'

'Not tonight, Adam.'

'It's been a while, that's all.'

'Less than a week.' Paul looked at him. 'I don't want Margot to become suspicious.'

'Why should she? We're friends, aren't we?'

They walked out of the school and into the yard. Boys still milled about. A football rolled at Paul's feet and he kicked it back in a curving arc. Adam raised his eyebrows. 'Impressive. Tell the boys you were a football player and all your worries will be over.'

Paul frowned at him, knowing from the brittle edge to his voice the mood Adam was slipping into. 'I'm sorry if you're disappointed.'

'Disappointed! Don't flatter yourself.'

They walked almost to Tanner Street without speaking. Finally Adam said, 'I suppose she'll be waiting with a meal on the table, little house all spic and span.'

'I doubt it.'

'Oh? She looks like the domesticated type to me. So, will you have to fry yourself an egg, or something? Christ, if I had a wife ...'

They stopped outside Paul's door. Hesitantly Paul said, 'I'll see you tomorrow.'

Adam ignored him and went on walking towards his own house five doors away.

There were no Bath buns, just a few rock cakes, yellow as sulphur and studded with dead-fly raisins. Patrick carried his cup of tea to a table by the window, rubbing a view-hole in the condensation to look out at the platform. Two sailors were waiting, their huge kit bags lolling at their feet. He watched them, jealous of the easy way they stood and talked together.

114

He had never been easy around other men, only Mick, and Mick didn't count.

After he had signed the papers in the doctor-colonel's office, a nurse had showed him along a corridor. He remembered glancing inside the open doors of the first ward he passed, catching a glimpse of five or so men playing cards around a table. All of them were double amputees, like Mick. All of them turned to look at him as he passed, defiantly dismissive of visitors with legs.

When the nurse left them alone together Mick said, 'Have you come to take me home?'

Patrick nodded. He sat down beside the cumbersome, institutional wheelchair that took up too much space in the bare little room deemed suitable for visitors. They hadn't seen each other for two years. Mick reached out and touched his face, sweeping his thumb under his eye.

'Don't cry, Patty. I'm all right.'

'I felt it, when you were wounded, the pain …'

'No.' Mick leaned closer. Taking his hand he ducked his head to look up into his downcast face. 'You only think you did, afterwards, when you found out. The shock … it must have been the shock.'

'It was terrible.'

Mick smiled slightly. 'They gave me morphine so quickly, and then the doctors put me to sleep … the pain was in your head, Pat. It wasn't real.'

'I thought I was going to die.'

Mick sat back in his chair. 'I'm so sorry, Patty. I tried not to think of you. I couldn't help it.'

The sailors climbed aboard their train. His tea had gone cold but he drank it anyway. Lighting a cigarette he thought of Paul again, idle, unfocused thoughts: Paul in dress uniform or in black tie and dinner jacket, a doll to dress up as the fancy took him; Paul as bridegroom, a yellow rose in his buttonhole. He saw again the girl on his arm and fought against the sudden surge of jealousy.

The tea finished, he walked out on to the platform. Suspended on a chain outside the waiting room a large clock face showed five o'clock. Patrick watched as the minute hand jerked past the Roman numeral twelve. He looked along the platform, anxious now even as his cock stirred in anticipation. Taking a deep breath he walked purposely towards the public toilets.

The man said, 'Not here.'

Boldly as he dared Patrick said, 'Where, then?'

'Follow me.' The man turned away from him. 'It's not far.'

He followed him out of the station toilets, keeping a few steps behind. They walked through the dark back streets, the man's furtiveness acting like a magnet, drawing him along. He didn't once look back. He's a fool, Patrick thought. Only a bloody fool would put himself in such danger.

The man pushed open a back yard gate and beckoned him inside. As soon as Patrick was in the yard the man shut the gate quickly, and hurried to unlock the door into the house. Even then he didn't stop. Patrick saw only a brief glimpse of a chaotic kitchen, pans in the sink and on the stove, their contents left to congeal. He breathed through his mouth against the smell of cold grease and damp.

The stairs creaked and he felt he should tiptoe to avoid the noisiest boards and that he should've taken off his shoes. He knew these poky terraced houses – the neighbours could hear a dog fart through the walls. At the top of the stairs the man glanced at him before pushing open the bedroom door. He went at once to the bedside table, picked up a photograph frame, and slipped it under the bed. Patrick almost smiled; the man had a sweetheart, then. He didn't want her pretty little face smiling out at him as he was fucked.

Neither spoke, only undressed by the light of a full moon shining through threadbare curtains. Naked, they lay down on the bed. Patrick stared up at the cracks in the ceiling and gently rested his hand on the man's thigh.

'Maybe you should take your glasses off,' he said.

'I'm blind without them.'

'Take them off.'

He sighed, taking off his spectacles and placing them on the floor.

Patrick rolled on to his side. Propping himself on his elbow he looked down at the skinny, hairless body beside him. The man smiled slightly and for the first time Patrick saw that he was handsome, perhaps even a little younger than himself. The smile stayed in his eyes, wry and intelligent, as though he understood the absurdity of their situation.

Kneeling now, the man bowed his head and closed his mouth around his nipple, biting gently as Patrick drew a sharp, surprised breath. His hand moved down Patrick's body, past his leaping, greedy cock, to rest on his thigh before pushing his legs apart. Lifting him slightly, he pushed a finger inside him, biting down harder on his nipple as Patrick arched his back and clenched his fingers into his hair. He would come too soon. Twisting away he sat up, leaning back on his elbows.

The man looked up at him myopically. 'Relax.'

'Sorry.'

'You're married, aren't you?'

'No!'

'You're being unfaithful to someone.'

'No. There's no one.'

'Then relax.'

'I'm sorry.'

The man laughed. 'Jesus.' Taking Patrick's hand he closed it around his cock. 'I've been hard since I first saw you. You don't have to apologise to me.'

His penis was small, like a boy's, its skin smooth and soft as fine kid. Patrick held it gently, his fingers reaching down to stroke his balls. The man groaned, a deep, sexy noise full of that knowing smile, and he kissed Patrick deeply, his hands moving over his body. After a while he broke away, sitting on his haunches beside him. 'Ready now?'

Patrick nodded.

The man took one of the many pillows and placed it beneath his groin as he rolled on to his belly. He laughed a little. 'Be careful. I've not seen many as big.'

He'd imagined he would think of Paul. Instead he thought of nothing but the effort of pushing himself inside this stranger's body. As he tried and failed the man reached back, taking hold of his cock to guide him. Finally he said matter-of-factly, 'You'd best use some spit.'

Patrick spat on his fingers, rubbing the spittle over his cock before trying again. The resistance gave. Beneath him the man cried out, bracing himself against Patrick's thrusts. His head banged against the metal bars of the bedstead, which in turn banged against the wall. Patrick gritted his teeth, holding back from the release of orgasm, wanting to go deeper and deeper as hard and as fast as he could. Eventually the body beneath his lost its tension and collapsed down on to the mattress. Patrick's own orgasm followed quickly.

The man rolled on to his back, throwing his arm over his face and panting heavily. He laughed. 'Christ.'

Patrick lay still, closing his eyes against the sound of his breathing. In a moment he would get up and dress. He wouldn't touch him or look at him again. Now though he felt too drained to move. The familiar despair crept over him and he covered his face with his hands.

'Are you all right?'

Patrick heard the bed creak and tensed, not wanting to be touched. He knew the man was leaning over him. Forcing himself to speak he said, 'Yes.'

'What's your name?'

From downstairs came the sound of someone knocking on the door. Patrick glanced at the man but he only frowned as though he might have something to do with the caller. When he made no move Patrick said, 'Answer it.'

'I'm not expecting anyone ...' He frowned again. 'Jesus! I forgot about Henderson!' He got up, pulling on trousers and shirt. Buttoning the shirt swiftly he said, 'Stay here. For God's sake stay out of sight.'

Patrick began collecting his clothes from the floor. Feathers tumbled across the bare boards, the small, white and brown feathers used to stuff pillows. He wondered how anyone could live like this. The rosebud-patterned wallpaper was peeling from a damp corner, the bedding was stained with mildew and the feathers collected in balls of dust. On the bedside table was a teacup containing half an inch of cold, muddy cocoa, and he remembered the picture frame the man had hidden under the bed. Curious, Patrick knelt down, stifling a sneeze caused by the thick layer of dust. His fingers closed around the frame and he picked it up, peering at the photograph in the dim light.

Paul gazed back at him. Dressed in cap and trench coat, its collar turned up to frame his face, he was unsmiling, as beautiful as ever. Patrick placed the picture down gently on the bed and stood staring at it before lifting it up again. He turned it over, easing out the cardboard holding it in place. On the back of the photograph Paul had written, *Adam, I really think I should have smiled – don't you? (What a prig I look!!) My love always, your Paul.*

Your Paul. Setting the picture down on the bedside table, Patrick looked towards the door and the sound of voices in ordinary conversation carrying from the kitchen. He remembered the man as the one who had stood beside Paul outside the church. How could he not have recognised him? Of course they were lovers, the two of them. On the back of the photo another hand had written *January 1916.* They were lovers and had been for years. Anger rose inside him. Sweeping his arm across the table he scattered its contents across the floor.

The glass in the picture frame cracked in two. Next to the broken cup a puddle of cocoa sat proud, too glutinous to soak into the bare floorboards. An old shoebox that had been behind the cup spilled its contents of bundled letters. Patrick crouched beside them, recognising Paul's handwriting on the torn envelopes.

He crouched there for what seemed like minutes, the voices downstairs a low, background drone as he imagined reading each letter. To his eyes each envelope seemed thick, each letter pages long, nothing like the short notes he'd sent and received. He reached out and picked up one of the bundles. Seven or eight letters weighed heavy in his hands. He held the bundle to his nose, wanting to smell Paul on the stiff envelopes, but there was only a faint smell of dry earth. The bundles felt gritty, the blue and gold cord they were tied with fraying at both ends.

The cocoa had soaked into the floor. Patrick stooped and

picked up the broken cup, slipped the picture back under the bed and put the letters in their box, before beginning to dress. He put on his jacket and chose a bundle of letters, thrusting it into his inside pocket. One bundle among so many wouldn't be missed.

The man appeared in the doorway. 'I heard a crash.' He smiled awkwardly, glancing over his shoulder towards the stairs. 'I had to tell my visitor I have a cat.'

'I knocked the cup over.'

'Doesn't matter … you don't have to run off because of a broken cup.' He smiled that same wry, condescending smile, making Patrick want to punch him. He turned away. Touching the letters to make sure their bulge wasn't obvious he heard the man, *Adam*, laugh. 'Well, perhaps we'll meet again?'

Brushing past him Patrick ran from the house.

Chapter Fourteen

January, 1918
DEAREST A – THANK YOU for the chocolate, and the socks – I gave the marmalade away to one of the poor kids they've been sending us recently. He tells me it was delicious and sends his very best wishes. (He hopes for strawberry jam next time).

Remember I told you about Captain Hawkins? Today he showed me a photo of his wife and baby. She is called Agnes and the baby is called May and we both stood looking at their photograph and smiling like fools for what seemed ages. I told him she was very handsome and the baby very sweet and felt sorry for him as he put the picture away. He's only just back from England and baby's first Christmas.

Dad sent me my copy of Robinson Crusoe. *Do you remember how I told you Granddad read it to me when I was eight and was sent home from school with whooping cough? George thought the story too difficult for me but Granddad said I was just like my mother and nothing was too difficult for her. Reading it now I find that it is too difficult. I find myself thinking about Robinson and Friday too much for my own good. The pages are becoming damp as it hasn't stopped raining for days – already there is mildew on the cover. I know Dad meant well but I'm afraid the book will be destroyed by this bloody weather.*

How is school? The boy you told me about, Brownlowe, I do remember his brother from Christmas parties and such. I was sorry to hear what happened. Rob knew him quite well, I think. I'll let him know, as he'll want to send condolences to the family. I agree it's unlikely he's alive if they've listed him as missing, but being out here makes you pessimistic – they may be right to hope.

Remember the shrine I told you about on the side of the road? We passed it today, blown to smithereens. Later Smith said what a pity it was because the little statue of the Virgin had such a pretty face. Jenkins laughed so much the poor man took offence. I tried to apologise to him, but it was difficult with Jenkins crying with laughter. It wasn't that funny really – it was just the sad, serious way Smith said it.

We're having a quiet time of it at the moment. I read Crusoe *and think of you (and Friday). I sleep a great deal, and dream all kinds of idiotic things. Last night you were here with me. Hawkins gave you a dressing down for not having the right kit. You asked if I had a spare pistol you could borrow. It all seemed very normal but then I woke up missing you so much I couldn't go back to sleep. I walked out into the trench and ended up drinking tea with Smith and Sergeant Thompson, although I wouldn't normally bother the men. Thompson with his gold-tooth-grin sees right through me and I can't decide whether his smirking behind my back bothers me or not. Mostly not, I think. His tooth is fascinating. It makes his breath smell of gun metal, as though he sucks on the barrel of his rifle. Am I smirking behind his back, now? Yes, definitely.*

Write soon, won't you? My very best love – P

PS: I've suddenly realised that I don't have a photograph of you. I thought you could go to Evans's studio in your Sunday best and have your picture taken beneath the artificial rambling roses. Look pensive. Don't smile. Right profile would be best, I think. Next time Hawkins shows me his wife and family I can produce you from my wallet, my own true love.

Patrick folded the letter back into its envelope and placed it beside the others. He remembered the demolished shrine, the Virgin lying in a ditch amongst splinters of wood, her hands still clasped to her chest, her head a few feet away. It had made him remember the statuette of Saint Francis kept in his mother's dressing table drawer because its head had broken off. Whenever the drawer was opened the bearded face rolled towards the light, exhaling the stink of lavender.

At the French roadside Paul had hurled the Virgin's head into the sky. Watching him, Patrick had crossed himself. Rain came down in sheets, blurring Paul into a grey smudge as he stared after the head's trajectory. The cobbled road ran with water, the countryside disappearing under the flood. He thought of the head drowning.

Mick's voice shouted up the stairs. Patrick jumped, expecting him to burst into his room just as he used to. Gathering the letters together he left them in a pile by his bed and went downstairs.

Sitting at the bottom of the stairs Mick said angrily, 'I've been shouting for you for ages. What were you doing up there?'

'I must have dozed off.'

'Liar!'

'Don't call me a liar.' He edged past into the kitchen. 'Do you want some supper?'

Mick followed him, banging his chair on the door; he damaged it in exactly the same place every time so that a groove had appeared. He glared up at Patrick. 'Where were you this afternoon?'

'You were all right. You were with Hetty, weren't you? I didn't think you'd miss me.' He began looking through cupboards, finally bringing out a tin of corned beef. 'Will this do? I'll make you a sandwich.'

Mick knocked the tin out of his hand, sending it scuttling across the floor. 'I asked you where you were today!'

'Nowhere.'

'Seeing Harris?'

Patrick laughed bleakly.

Taking a fistful of his shirt, Mick yanked him down so that their faces were level. 'The fire in my room went out – do you know how cold it is in this morgue?'

Patrick pulled away. 'Hetty should have …'

'Well she didn't! You had no right to send her here like that.'

'I thought you'd be pleased.'

Mick gazed at him as though he couldn't believe his ears. 'I don't want her skivying for me! I can look after myself!'

'Then go and light the fire in your room.'

'I would if you left some fucking coal in the scuttle!'

'You know where the coal is, Mick. Down the cellar steps, first door on your left. Remember? We've always kept it there.'

'Piss off.' Mick turned the chair round, banging it against the door again. The book that had been on his lap slid to the floor and Patrick stooped to pick it up, then followed him into his room.

The cold came as a shock after the warmth of the kitchen. Placing the book on the hearth he squatted in front of the dead fire and cleared the ashes from the grate.

'Give that book to me. It'll get filthy down there.' Without looking up Patrick handed it to him. Snatching it Mick barked, 'Now get out.'

Patrick sighed. 'I'll light the fire first.'

'I want to go to bed. I don't need a fire if I'm asleep.'

'It's early yet.'

'I'm tired. And I don't need your help, either, so just get out.'

Patrick straightened up, dusting ash from his hands. 'You haven't eaten today, have you?'

'So?'

'Why don't I make you a sandwich? I'll bring it to you in bed.'

Mick bowed his head, fumbling in his pocket for his cigarettes. After a while he said, 'She didn't light the fire because we went for a walk. To the park. We had a nice time, really. The kerbs were a bit difficult for her, but she's quite strong. Didn't complain.' Lighting the cigarette he said, 'I asked her to visit me again.'

'Did she say she would?'

'Yes.'

'So what's wrong?'

'Nothing.' He laughed bitterly. 'Everything's tickity-boo.'

'I'll light the fire, shall I? Then get you something to eat?'

'Do you think she said yes out of pity?'

Crouching in front of the fire Patrick looked at him. 'I don't know, Mick.'

'If it's pity I'd rather she didn't bother.'

Patrick turned back to the grate. 'Maybe pity will become something else.'

Mick exhaled as though he'd been holding his breath. 'Maybe. Corned beef sandwiches then? I'll go and make a start in the kitchen.'

Margot made supper of eggs and bacon and black pudding and Paul ate it without comment. He was always quiet when he came home from the school, as though he was too exhausted even to make conversation. She would have liked to hear about his day, to talk about the other masters and their wives and families. All day she tried to think of things they could discuss over supper, ordinary gossip that would make their marriage seem normal, but nothing very much happened to her. She cleaned the house, she shopped with the little money he gave her and from time to time she visited her mother, short, stilted visits in an atmosphere still crackling with her mother's anger. Since New Year's Eve and that disastrous dance, she had felt friendless. As she went about her chores, aware of the baby moving inside her, she tried to be proud of the fact that she'd out-grown the girls she'd been at school with.

So far their neighbours remained strangers, although she could hear their children's cries and shouts through the walls. Often she left the house just to get away from the nagging feeling that the women in the street were deliberately snubbing her. She'd go window shopping, avoiding the haberdashery with its display of lacy Christening gowns, and wished she'd saved even a little of the weekly allowance her father used to give her.

She knew that soon she would have to ask Paul for money to buy clothes and underwear, replacements for items that were becoming too tight or too threadbare. She had begun to worry about this, of being even more of a burden, noticing that Paul's cuffs were becoming frayed and that he spent nothing on himself apart from the cheapest cigarettes. She thought of her father, who wouldn't settle for anything but the best pipe tobacco, a little treat that had always seemed unremarkable;

now, compared to Paul, he seemed like a spendthrift.

She cleared the table of the supper dishes. Unable to stand the silence any longer she asked, 'How was school?'

'Fine.' He looked up from the *Evening Gazette*. 'It was fine.'

She rinsed a plate under the single cold tap. 'And Adam, is he all right?'

'Yes.' He returned to the newspaper. 'He's fine, too.'

She felt compelled to persist. Making her voice light she asked, 'Is he courting?'

Paul flicked over a page. 'No.'

'No? That's a pity, he could bring his girl to supper, if he had a girl, of course.'

'He hasn't.'

'Oh well. It was just a thought. You know, I realised today that he lives next door to that girl, the one who was with that crippled man's brother at the dance.'

He looked up at her, frowning. 'His brother was with a girl? Are you sure?'

'Yes!' She laughed. 'I thought I recognised her when she was dancing with him.'

He turned back to the paper. After a while he said, 'I don't remember a girl.'

Sighing, Margot scrubbed at the greasy frying pan. She thought of the slight, sharp-faced girl she sometimes passed in the street. She looked about her own age and sometimes she felt that she should introduce herself but so far she'd been too afraid; the women who lived in the terraces seemed unpredictable, too quick to make friends and enemies.

Paul stood up. 'I'll dry, shall I?'

'No. You should sit down, you've been working all day.'

He took a tea towel from the drawer and began to wipe the plates. Earlier he had taken off his jacket and tie and unbuttoned his collar so that the dark hair of his chest was just visible. There was ink on his hand. As usual when he stood close to her, she was surprised by how much she wanted him.

He smiled at her and she looked down into the grey washing-up water. Summoning courage she said, 'I may need a few shillings extra, soon.' She felt herself blushing. 'There are

126

some things I need.'

'Of course. How much would you like?'

'I don't know … not very much.'

He began to put the plates away. 'You must tell me if I'm not giving you enough housekeeping.'

'Things *are* expensive.' Awkwardly she said, 'How much more could you give me?'

'Enough to go mad and buy you a new dress? I'm sorry, I didn't realise you were worrying about money. Tomorrow make a list of everything you need, for the baby as well. I'll draw the money out on Saturday.'

Relieved, to her horror she began to cry. At once Paul drew her into his arms, kissing the top of her head as she pressed her face to his chest. 'Oh, Margot, hush, please don't cry over money. Money doesn't matter.'

She drew away from him, hurriedly wiping her eyes. 'Yes it does … you work so hard.'

He laughed. 'I've worked harder.'

'You always look so exhausted.'

'Well, that's just me – pale and interesting, I can't help it.'

She blew her nose, then stuffed her handkerchief into her pocket, avoiding his gaze. 'I know you don't sleep well.'

'I can't help that, either.'

'I'm never sure whether to wake you or not.' Her voice rose and she tried to fight back the tears, remembering how frightened she was when Paul woke shouting in the night. Last night she had found him crouched in the corner of their bedroom, his arms covering his head as though protecting himself from blows. Managing to meet his eye she said, 'What happened last night, for instance …'

He frowned. 'Last night?'

'You got out of bed, you were shaking.'

'I don't remember.' He sat down at the table and lit a cigarette. Exhaling smoke he said, 'I'm sorry. I'll sleep in the other room, if you like.'

'No. I don't want you to do that.' She blushed again because she said the words too hastily, making herself sound brazen. 'You wake me anyway. It's better if I'm there with you.' Sitting

127

down beside him she said, 'Don't you think it's better?'

He laughed, looking down as he rolled his cigarette around the rim of the ashtray. 'I think it's much better. I don't want to scare you, that's all. I know how horrible it is, being woken like that.'

'It's all right. I don't mind.'

He smiled, reaching for her hand and squeezing it gently. 'Try to wake me, next time it happens. Give me a good kick.' Still holding her hand he stood up. 'Shall we have an early night?'

Paul stared at the bedroom ceiling and lit a cigarette. Beside him Margot snored quietly, soft little rasps of breath that made him feel protective of her. A moment ago he had covered her more snugly with the eiderdown, watching her for a moment to make sure she slept on. He considered getting up and spending the night in the spare room to save her from the horror of his nightmares, but the thought of that monastic, freezing little room filled him with dread. He closed his eyes, torn by his need for the comfort of Margot's presence and the guilt that he might wake her.

They had made love and afterwards she had held on to him, smiling sleepily. She seemed to enjoy sex, although they were both made awkward by the feeling that sleeping together was somehow illicit. That first time, in the room above the pub, he'd conquered his nervousness by losing himself in the kind of foreplay he practised on Adam during those long Sundays spent in bed together before he left for France. It was the kind of sex he liked best: no penetration but slow, engrossed caresses and long, deep kisses, lips and tongue and fingers all intent on one purpose. He could make time stand still that way, he could make the whole world recede until all that was left was touch and taste and he'd press his fingers to Adam's lips so that even the silence would be pure. It only took concentration, a single-minded forgetting.

That first time with Margot had been his first time with any woman and he'd been afraid of hurting her, afraid, too, of his own reactions. In the end it seemed he'd wanted her too badly;

after the foreplay, the silent, astonishing exploration of her body and her own shuddering climax, he'd entered her with what seemed too much force against too little resistance and he'd come too quickly. Only afterwards did he think about the baby and for a moment he was swept by a terrible sense of guilt. She would miscarry; the baby couldn't survive such violence. He'd talked himself down from the sickening height of fear, trying to convince himself with rational arguments. Still he remained afraid, and it became another reason why he hadn't made love to his wife again until tonight. And there was Adam, of course, and the pestering voice in his head reminding him of his faithlessness.

He stubbed his cigarette out and rolled over on to his side. Unable to sleep, he remembered what Margot had said about Morgan being with a girl at the dance. He knew he shouldn't be so surprised – it would be normal, sensible even, to put on a front and take a girl dancing. All the same, he felt jealous, a bitter feeling none the less real for being irrational. Patrick Morgan was the one person he could retreat into fantasy with: a strong, gorgeous man uncomplicated by all the disappointments and compromises of reality. In his fantasies Morgan had eyes only for him and never thought of hiding behind a fearful front of heterosexuality. In his fantasy world he believed that Patrick Morgan was invincible, a compelling superstition he'd held since the first day they'd gone on patrol together.

Jenkins had said, 'You know, Harris, some battalions don't send men out. Not even to inspect the wire.' After a moment he went on, 'You always go, too. You and Morgan – our own David and Goliath – there must be quite a feeling of comradeship out there, between you and the mighty sergeant.'

Writing a report at the dugout table, Paul made himself look up. 'What would you know about it?'

'Nothing, of course, seeing as you keep all the glory for yourself.'

'Hawkins has ordered I take Sergeant Morgan out on patrol tonight. Why don't you come with us, see how glorious it really is?'

He laughed as though astonished. 'Would you really want

me there, spoiling your fun? Surely you want to be alone with him?' Slyly he added, 'And I'm sure he feels the same way – he just can't seem to stand to let you out of his sight.'

Morgan had appeared in the doorway then. He looked from Jenkins to him and back again. Jenkins smirked. 'Well, I'm sure you two have lots to discuss about tonight's jolly. I'll leave you to get on with it in private.'

Paul remembered that Morgan had sat down opposite him and had turned to watch Jenkins step out into the trench. When he seemed certain he was out of earshot, Morgan said gently, 'Are you all right, sir?'

'Why shouldn't I be?' For the first time he had met Morgan's gaze directly. Morgan leaned forward and for a surreal moment Paul imagined he was about to kiss him. Instead he picked up a box of matches from the table. 'May I?' He struck a match, illuminating his face for a second before he lit his cigarette. Paul remembered feeling a sense of melodrama, a sense that he had added to the over-wrought nature of a scene that should have been ordinary, if only for the sake of his own sanity.

Margot shifted beside him, rolling over so that her body nudged his, and he moved away a little. Her belly was hard, the skin stretched too tightly over the life inside it. He expected a tiny fist to break through the thin barrier and punch him. He stubbed the cigarette out and closed his eyes in an attempt to sleep.

Chapter Fifteen

'YOU GOING OUT, HETTY?'

Adjusting her hat in front of the hall mirror, Hetty turned to her father. 'I'm going for a walk.'

'Oh?' Joe smiled. 'Who with?'

'No one.'

'No one called Morgan?'

She turned back to the mirror, the ratty little face under the ugly cloche hat. Harshly she said, 'I'm going for a walk, that's all.'

Joe sat down on the stairs and took a bag of sherbet lemons from his pocket. Holding out the bag to her he said, 'Here. Save me from eating all these myself.'

'No, thanks.'

'No?' He returned the sweets to his pocket. 'I'll keep them for later then, when you get back.' Looking at her he said, 'Your Mam said you had to see to the major the other day?'

'I didn't *see* to him.'

'Then what did you do?'

Talked, Hetty thought. Laughed and talked. She had never laughed so much with anyone. Sighing she said, 'I sat with him, that's all.'

'And then you went for a walk in the park.'

She frowned at him. 'How did you know?'

'Mrs Carter saw you.'

'Nosy old bag. What did she say?'

'What was there to say?'

'Nothing. We went for a walk, that's all.'

'I'll tell you what she said.' He took a sweet from its bag, contemplating it for a moment before popping it into his mouth.

131

'She said you were laughing and joking and carrying on like bairns.'

'We were feeding the ducks.'

'Well, there's no harm in that.'

'Why shouldn't he laugh and joke, anyway?'

'No one's saying he shouldn't.'

'I can just imagine her tut-tutting, all disapproving, thinking he should be in a home, out of sight so he doesn't offend ...' She drew breath and Joe smiled at her.

'Who does he offend?'

'You know what I mean.'

Joe took the sweets out again. Shaking the bag a little he peered into it, selecting carefully. 'He's a handsome lad, though. What happened doesn't stop him being a handsome lad.' He looked up at her. 'Are you going to see him now?' She coloured and Joe exclaimed. 'Oh, Hetty, don't. Don't. Don't get involved. It's all right your Mam doing her bit and helping out, she can take it.'

'Take what?'

'I don't blame him for getting frustrated, any man would. But it's bad enough your Mam having to put up with it. I don't want him taking it out on you an' all.'

'He's lonely.'

'Is he? Well, that's not your worry. And what about his brother? What does he have to say about it?'

She looked at her reflection. 'He doesn't say anything.'

Carefully Joe said, 'Are you trying to make him jealous?'

'No!' She turned on him. 'That would be a terrible thing to do.'

'Yes. It would.'

Hetty laughed bleakly. 'Nothing would make him jealous anyway. He looks right through me.'

'Hetty ...' He sighed. 'Have you thought about going back to Marshall's? You liked it there.'

'I like it where I am.' She took her coat from the hook. 'I'll see you later.'

In the shop Patrick had said, 'Mick enjoyed going to the park yesterday. Thank you for taking him out.'

'It was no trouble.'

'It was very kind of you. He tells me you're going to visit him again?'

'On Sunday.'

He'd smiled as though relieved. 'He's looking forward to it.'

Unable to stop herself she said, 'You don't mind, do you?'

'Mind?' He'd laughed. 'I'm pleased. He thinks a lot of you.'

Now outside the Morgan's front gate, she hesitated. She could go home and tomorrow she could apply to Marshall's for her old job; she could decide never to see either of the Morgan brothers again and it would be sensible and easy, like loosening a too-tight corset. The Chinese lion grinned at her. Sighing, she walked up the path to the door.

Nervously Mick said, 'You are going out, aren't you?'

'I thought I'd play gooseberry.'

'For God's sake, Pat!'

Patrick laughed. 'I'm joking. Don't worry, I'm going to the pub. You and Hetty can have the house to yourselves.'

'Perhaps she's expecting you to be here.'

'She's coming to see you, Mick. She won't want me hanging around.'

'Won't she?'

Patrick sighed. 'Well, if she does and I'm not perhaps she'll get the message.'

'Maybe you should stay. It's not seemly, is it? A young girl alone with a man …'

The knock on the door made them both jump. Patrick smiled at Mick reassuringly. 'I'll go and let her in.'

Lying on the bed Adam watched as Paul took off his trousers and folded them over the back of the chair. 'God, I've missed you.'

Paul glanced at him. 'Aren't you getting undressed?'

'Not yet, I like seeing you naked when I'm still fully dressed.'

'Really?' Unbuttoning his shirt Paul said, 'Get undressed,

133

eh? We haven't got long.'

'And you want to get straight down to it? Christ.' Adam sat on the edge of the bed and began untying his shoelaces. 'Very romantic.'

Naked, Paul climbed beneath the bedcovers. The sheets felt damp and smelt of sex. Unable to help himself he thought about Margot. She would be in church now, listening to her father's sermon. Afterwards, Daniel would tell her again how worthless her husband was. Later still, as he sat opposite him at lunch, the Reverend would make a point of cross-examining him about his prospects as a teacher or ask how much nearer he was to finding a decent place to live. All the time he would look at him as though he was some sub-species of human, an offence to nature. Paul covered his face with his hands, desperate for a cigarette.

Adam knelt beside him. Lifting his hands away he kissed Paul's mouth lightly. 'I have missed you.'

'I know, I miss you too.'

'Do you?' He laughed slightly, sitting back on his heels to look at him.

'Yes. Look, Adam, do you mind if I smoke?' Paul got up and went through his jacket pockets for his cigarettes.

Adam said, 'What's the matter?'

'Nothing.' He exhaled smoke, looking down at the tip of the cigarette. 'Lunch with Margot's parents.'

'Oh. Well, do you have to think about it now?' Adam lay down and held out his arms. 'Come here. Let's have you thinking about something more entertaining.'

Paul lay down and rested his head on Adam's chest. He felt Adam's fingers curl into his hair and begin to massage his scalp. Paul closed his eyes, trying to concentrate on his touch. Instead he saw himself facing Whittaker across the vicarage table. He drew deeply on the cigarette.

'Get up.' Adam pushed him away. 'There's ash all over the bed, all over *me*.' Grasping Paul's wrist he frowned. 'You're shaking. What's the matter with you? It's lunch with your in-laws, not some dawn raid! For Christ's sake, Paul, grow up.'

Paul got up and began to dress. Aware of Adam watching

him he said, 'The sheets need changing.'

'So you're going home in a sulk?'

'I don't think either of us are in the mood now, are we?'

'Come back to bed.'

'They're expecting me there at one o'clock.'

'Then we have a couple of hours. Please, Paul. I've waited all week for this.' Adam held out his hand. 'I just want to hold you. You can smoke all over me if it helps.'

Half-dressed, Paul lay down beside him. 'Whittaker really hates my guts.'

'You got his daughter pregnant, Paul.'

'And I married her.'

'Shotgun weddings tend to be a bit embarrassing, especially if the bride's father is a vicar.' Adam squeezed his hand. 'He'll get over it. And if he doesn't, so what? You don't *have* to go there for lunch.' He pulled Paul into his arms and kissed him. After a moment he took the cigarette from him and stubbed it out before rolling him over on to his front. Paul was still wearing his shirt and Adam pushed it up, exposing his backside. Paul heard him sigh and felt his lips on the base of his spine. He closed his eyes as Adam entered him, counting the strokes until he climaxed.

Adam fell on to his back, breathing heavily. Finding Paul's hand he kissed it. 'Sorry. Sometimes all you need is a quick, hard fuck.' He looked at him, smiling. 'Not shaky any more?'

'I shake all the time.'

He laughed. 'No you don't. You're over all that now.'

Paul lay on his stomach. He went over the process of dressing, of going out into the street and walking to the church. In the graveyard Margot would come out to meet him, kissing his cheek and taking his hand while her father glowered and her mother smiled. Her parents should unite against him and have done with it, but they had taken sides, making it worse.

Feeling Adam's hand on his back he rolled away and got up.

'What are you doing now? Don't rush off. I want to make love to you.'

'You just did.'

'Not properly ...'

'It felt properly to me.' On impulse he said, 'Do you want to go for a drink?'

Adam laughed, astonished. 'A drink? Where?'

'The Castle and Anchor's closest.' He thought of Patrick. He might be waiting for him at the bar at this moment. Tempting fate, he decided to press Adam into going with him. 'Come on, just one pint.'

'The Castle and Anchor's a dive. We can't go in there.'

'Why not?' Paul looked at him from buttoning his flies. 'Why shouldn't we go in there?'

Adam shook his head. 'We'll get such a warm welcome, won't we?'

'It's not stamped on our foreheads, Adam.'

'Isn't it?'

'I'll go on my own.'

'Do that. The smoke in those places brings on my asthma.'

Dressed, Paul leaned over the bed and kissed him.

Adam caught his wrist. 'Try and come back tonight?'

'I'll try.'

Patrick had always liked the look of the Castle & Anchor public house. He liked the way its double doors straddled the corner of Tanner Street and Skinner Street, its shape like the prow of a ship sailing out over a cobbled sea. He liked the gothic script etched into its opaque windows: *Fine Wines & Spirits. Snug & Private Rooms.* Snug. He liked that word best.

Patrick crossed Tanner Street, glancing at Hetty's house as he passed by. He thought of the photograph of the dead boy on their mantelpiece and tried to remember what he had looked like. Something like Hetty, he supposed.

Before he reached the pub he could hear the piano playing. As he pushed the door open the playing stopped and into the sudden silence a voice called, 'It's the big man himself! On your own today, Patrick?'

Patrick nodded at the group of men playing dominoes. The one who had spoken said, 'The major's all right is he? It's marvellous how you cope with him.'

The others nodded, their eyes fixed on their game. One of

them looked up briefly. 'You're a saint, Patrick. Not many would do what you do ... Oh, look at that! I'm knocking.'

The first man laughed. 'And I've won. There. Another game?'

The dominoes were turned over and shuffled; the piano started up again. Patrick imagined taking a couple of heads in each hand and banging them all together. The din from the piano would drown out the cracking of thick skulls.

At the bar a pint was already pulled and waiting for him. Maria smiled. 'All right, Patrick?'

He made to get his money out but she shook her head. 'Already paid for.'

To his right a voice said, 'Patrick. Hello again.' Paul smiled at him. 'Did I give you a start? I'm sorry.'

Patrick exhaled sharply. 'Sir ...'

Paul took a cigarette case from his pocket. He opened it and held it out. 'I really did startle you, didn't I?' As Patrick took a cigarette Paul said, 'Do you want to sit down?' He caught his eye, holding his gaze for what seemed like an age before Patrick broke away. Patrick picked up his drink and carried it to an empty table.

Sitting opposite Paul took a long drink from his own pint. Lighting a cigarette he said, 'So, this is your local?'

'Yes.'

Paul looked around. 'It's different from The Grand Hotel, anyway.' He blew smoke down his nose. 'How's your brother?'

'He's fine.'

'Did he enjoy himself at New Year?'

'Yes, thank you.'

'Good.' He took another long drink, almost draining his glass.

Patrick stood up at once. 'Let me get you another.'

'Thanks. I'll have the same again.'

Maria raised her eyebrows in Paul's direction. 'Who's that, then?'

'One of the officers I served with.' So she wouldn't notice the tremble in his hands Patrick gripped the edge of the bar, turning his knuckles white. When he'd seen Paul he'd thought his knees would buckle, that he'd collapse on the floor. His heart was pounding even now.

Maria was smiling at him quizzically. 'An officer, eh? I thought he sounded posh. Slumming it, is he?'

'Something like that.' Fumbling with the coins he paid her quickly and carried the two pints back to the table, slopping beer over his shoes. He sat down, watching as Paul took another long drink. Nervously he said, 'It's strong stuff, the beer they serve here.'

Putting his glass down Paul said, 'Isn't it?'

'You should go easy.'

Paul lit another cigarette. 'Was that your fiancée, the girl you were with at New Year?'

'No. She works for me.' Patrick voice quavered and he cleared his throat. 'I have my own butcher's shop. It's on the High Street.'

'I know – Morgan's, the butcher's with the happy pig in the window.'

'Happy pig, eh? I suppose it is. I always thought it was sinister.'

'Then why do you keep it?'

'I don't know … people recognise it, I suppose.'

Patrick tried to ration himself to looking at Paul for only a few seconds at a time. All the same he noticed that the glass eye was a shade darker than it should be and there was a faint white scar below it where the shrapnel had cut. He was thinner than he remembered and less boyish. In the army he'd been serious, weighed by responsibility. Now he smiled and the smile changed him, made him more attractive, if that were possible. Hardly able to believe he was sitting across a pub table from him, Patrick stole another look.

Paul's hand went to his face and he laughed awkwardly. 'I lost the eye.'

'Yes.' Patrick looked down at his drink. 'Sorry.'

'Worse things happen.'

Forcing himself to meet his gaze he said, 'It's the wrong shade of green.'

Paul smiled. 'I rather like that. It draws attention.'

'What does your wife think about it?'

He stubbed his cigarette out. 'She likes it, too.' Finishing his pint, he put the empty glass down. 'Another?'

Patrick watched him at the bar, allowing his eyes to linger on his neat little backside until the beginnings of a hard-on made him look away. He wondered if he would be drunk enough to take back to the shop. Three pints of beer in quick succession might make a man his size just pissed enough. He looked down at his own half-finished drink. In all his fantasies Paul had always been stone-cold sober, an awkward, vulnerable boy, not this self-assured man. Perhaps a dingy room over a butcher's shop wouldn't be good enough for him. Thinking of the soiled mattress left behind by the last tenant, his hard-on shrivelled.

As he sat down Paul said, 'Cheers.'

'Cheers.'

Paul lit another cigarette, offering him the open case. When he shook his head Paul laughed. 'I smoke too much. They wouldn't let me smoke in the first hospital and I nearly went mad. One of the nurses used to take pity on me occasionally, but Matron caught her and gave us both a frightful row. I couldn't see at the time and I thought this Matron was enormous, a real battle-axe. She wasn't, of course.' After a moment he asked, 'Do you know what happened to Sergeant Thompson?'

Patrick nodded. 'He stayed on. I told him he was mad.'

'Didn't you ever consider it?'

'Never. Did you?'

'Sometimes.'

Patrick stared at him incredulously. 'You'd have stayed in the army?'

Paul stared back. He smiled slowly. 'I liked the uniform.'

'It suited you.'

'Heads turned.'

'I'm sure.'

Holding his gaze Paul said, 'So, you have your own pork butcher's shop. Do you sell everything, right down to the squeal?'

'Everything.'

'Drink up.' Paul drained his glass.

'Where are we going?'

Standing up, Paul said, 'You're going to show me round your shop.'

Chapter Sixteen

'THIS IS INEXCUSABLE.'

Daniel went to the dining room window, lifting aside the lace curtain to look again for Paul. Turning to Margot he snapped, 'Did you tell him to be here for one o'clock?'

'Yes.' Anxiously she said, 'Can you see him?'

Iris sighed. 'He's probably staying at home until this rain stops. Lunch can wait a few minutes.'

'He's half an hour late, Iris, half an hour.' Daniel looked at his watch. 'Almost forty minutes, now.'

Standing beside her father, Margot looked out at the path leading from the vicarage to the churchyard. Rain bounced off the ground, hammering on the roof of the bay window and running down the glass. 'Perhaps I should go and look for him.'

'You'll do no such thing!' Daniel frowned at her. 'Go out in your condition in weather like this simply because he's forgotten the time? We'll eat without him.'

'I'm worried, I've never known him be late.'

'You hardly know him at all. I should imagine this is typical behaviour.'

Her mother laughed sarcastically. 'Typical.'

'I suppose you think this kind of thoughtlessness is acceptable? That it's all right to keep everyone waiting?'

Iris snapped, 'I'm surprised he agrees to come here at all the way you treat him.'

'How do I treat him? How does one treat a person who hasn't the grace to meet one's eye or make even the smallest effort at conversation?'

'You should make allowances.'

'Allowances!' Daniel snorted. 'He should pull himself

together.'

Her mother laid down her knitting and stood up. 'I'll go and turn the oven down.'

'No, we'll eat now.' He turned back to stare out of the window as though keeping a vigil. 'Margot, go and help your mother.'

The rain began slowly, a few fat drops that gradually became a downpour. Patrick turned his collar up, shivering as rain trickled down his back. Halfway along the deserted High Street he stopped at the entrance to an alleyway. To Paul he said, 'It's down here, the back door to the shop.'

Paul smiled at him, the rain plastering his hair flat. 'So what are we waiting for?'

'It's not much …'

He laughed. 'Patrick, I'm getting wet.'

Once again Patrick checked for the shop keys in his pocket. His fingers closed around them, the key to the back yard gate already warm from his touch. Exhaling he said, 'All right. Let's get out of this rain.'

The bones were massive, their bulbous ends pink and white and shiny as newly shelled pearls. Standing in the doorway at the back of the shop, Paul turned away from them quickly, breathing through his mouth to avoid their cold-iron smell. On the wall above them hung knives and cleavers, their metal dull in the grey, rain-soaked light. Everywhere was scrubbed and stung with the smell of bleach, a smell that mixed with that of the bones and was impossible to ignore. Soaked to the skin, Paul shuddered.

Opening the door to a flight of stairs, Morgan turned to him. 'It's up here.' He hesitated. 'As I said, it's not much …'

Brushing past him, Paul began to climb the stairs. He glanced back at Morgan who was hesitating still, dripping rain from the hem of his trench coat. For a moment Paul saw him in cap and puttees and he smiled slightly. 'There's no time like the present, Sergeant.'

At the top of the stairs Paul found himself in a room that was empty apart from a mattress covered in blue and white striped ticking, a large, brown stain at its head. Above it was a window that was too high to see from, a grill of wire mesh covering it. Pictures had been torn from a magazine and stuck to the wall above the fireplace: a fat baby in a tin bath advertising *Pears Soap* and a soldier with a girl on his knee. The smell of bones and bleach was overlaid with mustiness. Behind him a floorboard creaked and Paul turned round.

'It's been empty for a while,' Morgan said. Awkwardly he added, 'There's a kitchen, and another smaller room ...'

Paul took off his coat and folded it on to the floor. 'You should rent it out.'

'Maybe.'

'But then you wouldn't be able to show me around.'

'No. That's what I thought.'

'So you've been thinking about it?'

'A bit.' He glanced over his shoulder as though expecting someone else to walk in. Distractedly he repeated, 'A bit.'

Paul stepped towards him. Touching his arm he said, 'You're soaking.'

'So are you.'

'Do you want to get out of those wet things?'

'Do you?'

Paul looked towards the mattress. 'Do you have any blankets?'

Morgan reached out and cupped his face. Surprised by his tenderness, Paul stood very still. Morgan's long fingers were dry and hard; as he pressed his palm to his cheek Paul could feel its calluses and he remembered the weight of it, pressing his head down into the mud of no-man's-land. He closed his eyes. The memory was vivid and he laughed shortly, appalled to find that he was crying.

Softly Morgan said, 'Hush now. It's all right.' Still holding Paul's face he wiped the tears away with a careful sweep of his thumb. 'You're all right now. Safe.' Morgan pulled him into his arms. He rocked him, stroking his hair, repeating over and over the same quiet words. At last he whispered, 'Lie down. I'll hold you. I'll make it all right. Lie down.'

Wiping away snot and tears with his hand, Paul gasped for breath. Morgan kissed him, a soft, dry kiss. His hand cupped Paul's face again and he kissed him more forcefully until Paul responded.

Morgan led him to the mattress and they lay down. He pulled Paul into his arms, his hand slipping beneath his clothes to rest over Paul's heart. 'There,' Morgan said. 'Almost calm.'

Paul closed his eyes, his head on Morgan's chest rising and falling as he breathed. For a while they stayed like that and he imagined he would sleep listening to the sounds of the other man's body, as though he was a shell pressed against his ear. He thought of the nightmares he wouldn't have, the memories drowned out by the thud of his heart.

'I remember the first time I saw you.'

Paul opened his eyes, startled from drowsing.

Quietly Morgan went on, 'I wasn't afraid until then. I couldn't stand that you might be killed.' He shuddered, holding him still closer. 'It was all I thought about, how terrible it would be to lose you.'

The rain pounded on the roof. A drop of water appeared on the ceiling and began a steady beat to the floor. The room grew darker and cold seeped from the damp mattress. Warmed by Morgan's body, Paul began to drift into sleep again, finding himself at sea. There was no land on the horizon. Both England and France were far away. Waves crashed the decks, soaking him. The ship rose from the high sea again and again, riding the storm.

Patrick watched Paul sleep, half sleeping too, going in and out of dreams of ditches and trenches and stone-cold cellars where dead men lounged nonchalantly against green-moss walls. He saw Very lights dazzle the dark sky and illuminate the ragged stumps of trees, and he focused on the rain dripping from the ceiling so that he wouldn't see more. Beneath Paul's body his arm went to sleep. The rain stopped. Watery winter sun slanted through the high window and he closed his eyes against it.

They must have slept for an hour or more. Paul murmured,

frowning as he looked up at him. 'What time is it?'

'Three o'clock.'

'Oh Christ!' He struggled to stand up, going at once to his coat on the floor. Searching through its pockets he took out his cigarettes. Patrick watched from the mattress, saw that his hands trembled as he attempted to strike a match. He got up, took the matches from him, and lit one.

'I had to be somewhere.' Paul laughed bleakly, accepting the light. 'It's too late now.' Glancing at him he said, 'Did you sleep?'

'A little.'

He looked down at the cigarette. 'I'm sorry. Crying like that … I'm sorry.'

'It's all right.'

'Feeling sorry for myself …'

'It doesn't matter.'

He held out the open cigarette case. 'Sorry, I should have offered you one.'

'No, thanks.'

'I smoke too much.' Bowing his head he said, 'I'm really sorry. I shouldn't have come here. When I saw you at that dance … Anyway. I'm an idiot.'

'No. No you're not.'

'I have to go.'

'Paul …' He'd never used his name before. For the first time in his life he felt himself blush.

Gently Paul said, 'I'm married, Patrick. My wife is pregnant.'

'Then why did you come here?'

'I don't know.' Patrick looked at him and laughed painfully. 'I was thinking about you, the last patrol we went on, before …' He exhaled a long breath of cigarette smoke. 'Before all that other business. I suppose I thought seeing you again would put it all in perspective.'

'No other reason?'

He laughed again, looking away.

Quickly Patrick said, 'I don't want anything from you. Just to see you from time to time … We could meet here. I could

145

make it nicer.'

'Fix the leaky roof?' Paul smiled. 'I've been fucked in worse places.'

'It's not just about that.'

Paul looked down at the cigarette. After a while he said, 'When I first saw you … in France when we first met …' He hesitated then went on quickly, 'I tried not to think about you, to look at you, even. I just wanted you safely out of my sight.'

'I think about you all the time.'

Paul tossed his cigarette stub into the fireplace. 'And I went to that pub wondering if you really would be there, half hoping you wouldn't be … then you walked in.' He laughed shortly. 'I'm still getting over the shock.'

Attempting to smile, Patrick said, 'I'm not so shocking.'

'You are to me.'

He forced a laugh. 'Why?'

Paul gazed at him. 'Because you make me feel like a fey little queer when you look at me? I don't know.'

'I don't mean to make you feel like that.'

'It's all right. I am a fey little queer.'

Patrick stepped towards him. 'Paul, let me see you. It's safe here – no one will suspect anything.' He tried to make his voice lighter. 'Who would suspect two old comrades meeting up from time to time?'

'To re-live the past?'

'No! It's finished, all that. I just want you. Since I first saw you …'

Paul put his coat on, glancing at him as he fastened the buttons. 'I really have to go.'

'Next Sunday, I'll be here. I'll be here all day.'

'Wednesday evening would be better. About seven o'clock?' Paul pulled on a pair of gloves. 'Is that all right?'

'Yes.'

Paul smiled. Briskly he said, 'Good. I won't cry and you can fuck me as much as you want. I'll look forward to it.'

'Paul …'

About to go downstairs Paul turned. 'It's what you want, isn't it?'

Patrick wondered if he was blushing again. 'You want it too.'

'Of course. I'm up for anything. Seven o'clock, Wednesday. Don't worry if I'm late.'

Chapter Seventeen

IN THE PARK, HETTY and Mick took shelter from the rain in the bandstand.

Breathless and laughing Hetty said, 'Look at us! Two drowned rats.'

Mick frowned at her. 'You're soaking. I don't want you to catch cold.'

'I'm all right. Besides, what can we do? We'll just have to wait here until it stops.'

'I'm sorry. I shouldn't have suggested going out.'

'It wasn't raining when we set off.'

'All the same.'

She smiled. 'Did you watch the bands play here?'

Lighting a cigarette he said, 'Sometimes. I came here once when I was on leave. I remember the band was playing *Keep The Home Fires Burning* as a girl handed me a white feather.'

'Silly cow.'

He laughed, looking down at the cigarette. 'I think it must have been a swan's feather. It was huge.'

'I hated the girls who did that. Our Albert was given one and he was only sixteen.'

Clamping the cigarette between his lips, Mick wheeled himself to the edge of the bandstand. Looking out over the park he said, 'Do you think it rains more than it used to?' He glanced at her over his shoulder. 'In France I used to think that the whole country would be washed away. I had a sergeant who believed the bombardments caused it to rain … I forget what his theory was now. Mad as a hare. I had him sent home, poor bugger. Sorry.' He smiled slightly. 'Pardon my French.'

Hetty smiled back, thinking of Patrick and trying to see the likeness between him and this frail, dark-eyed man. Their similarity seemed insubstantial to her. She thought of Patrick's silences, his unpredictable moods, and her familiar disappointment in him made her sigh.

'What are you thinking about?'

Hetty shook her head. 'Nothing.'

'I'm sorry I've kept you out so long. As soon as it lets up we can go home.'

'I don't mind being here with you.'

'No? It's cold, isn't it? It's cold and wet and the wind sounds as though it's going to blow the roof off and you're stranded with a cripple whose chair will probably sink into the mud as soon as we leave here.'

'There's a path.'

He snorted. 'Well, that's all right then.'

Laughing, she said, 'You sound like Patrick when you get cross.'

'I sound like him all the time.'

'No you don't. You sound posh all the time. Patrick sometimes forgets to.'

'Posh eh? My father used to tell us we sounded like …' He stopped and looked away.

'Like what?'

'Nothing. It doesn't matter. He was a pig of a man.'

'That's a hard thing to say. He must have loved you.'

'I wonder why people say that?' He wheeled himself back to the centre of the bandstand, turning the chair round to look at her. 'Why do they presume such a thing? Probably because their own fathers and mothers love them. My father was a drunk who beat us with a leather belt. I don't think love was important to him.'

'Wasn't he proud of you?'

'Should he have been?'

'Of course! My father's proud of you and he hardly knows you.'

'Is he proud of Patrick, as well?'

'Patrick wasn't a major.'

'No. Patrick just did all the hard work.'

'I suppose for the whole of the war you just sat around giving orders?'

'I suppose I did.' He smiled at her. 'And then they had the temerity to drop a great big shell on the nice cosy dugout I'd set up for myself. Unbelievable.'

'Is that how it happened?'

'It? You mean this?' He looked down at himself. After a moment he laughed. 'I remember a second lieutenant finding me. He was covered in mud, from head to toe, but his face was so pale he looked like a ghost. He asked me if I was dead so I asked him if he was dead and he said no, he didn't think so. He wandered off then. I wanted to believe he'd gone to fetch help but he didn't come back. Two stretcher-bearers dug me out a couple of hours later.'

'How could he leave you like that?'

'He *was* dead, I think. In a way.'

'You lay all that time?'

'My legs were only broken … it wasn't as if … well, you know. All that came later.' He smiled. 'Anyway. Now you know. You're the only one who does.'

'Except Patrick.'

'Pat's never asked.' The rain stopped. Throwing his cigarette down he said, 'Let's go home.'

Back outside the house Mick said, 'Come in and get warm before you go.'

'I should get back, really.'

'Do you have to?'

She hesitated, thinking of the dull Sunday afternoon stretching ahead of her, her mother asleep behind the *News of the World* and her father retreated to bed. She wondered if Patrick was in the house and glanced towards its dark windows.

Mick laughed slightly. 'I bought a cake. *Pat* bought a cake, actually. But it's cake, all the same. I was hoping you would share it with me.'

'What kind of cake?'

'I'm not sure, to be honest.' He smiled slowly. 'Your favourite?'

'Well, if it's my favourite.'

The cake was ginger, dry and crumbly, the kind of shop-bought cake her mother treated with contempt. Watching her eat it at the kitchen table, Mick said, 'Perhaps it was the only cake left in the whole shop.'

She frowned at the half-eaten slice on her plate. 'Now you've made me feel sorry for it.'

He laughed. 'Then you shouldn't have such a soft heart.'

'I haven't really.'

'No? I think you have.'

She sipped her tea. Placing her cup down on the saucer she said, 'There's a young couple moved in a few doors down from us. Really young they are – well, she is. They only got married a few weeks ago and she's pregnant – showing – you know.' Hetty sighed. 'I asked her when the baby was due.'

Mick exhaled softly, 'Oh.'

'I know. I don't know what came over me to be so nasty …'

'Don't worry, Hetty. She's newlywed, she'll be walking around with her head in the clouds no matter what anyone says to her.'

'Harris, they call them. He's odd-looking, the husband.'

He gazed at her. 'Is he? I heard that girls swoon when they see him.'

'He's too thin. And he has a glass eye.'

Mick laughed. 'That is quite horrible, isn't it? Poor thing.' Still smiling at her he said, 'So, he isn't beautiful?'

'That's a funny word to use about a man.'

'His brother was beautiful. Now, if you'd seen Robbie Harris you would have swooned. All the girls did.'

'I don't swoon.'

'No. You're too sensible. Robbie and I were invited to a ball, once. Both brand new first lieutenants, fresh from the front, Christmas 1914. We were glamorous in those days – Rob was, anyway. He was fighting the girls off with a stick.'

'I bet you were, too.'

'Oh, I just stood close to him, basked in his glory.' He lit a cigarette, shaking the match out slowly. 'He wrote to me when he heard I was wounded. Didn't stop writing until he was killed.' He laughed shortly. 'And it wasn't as though I was swamped with letters from Patrick. I think the nurses thought I hadn't anyone in the world apart from Rob Harris.'

'I would have written to you, if I'd known.'

'Then it's a shame we didn't know each other. I could have put your picture by my bed and all the other men would've been jealous of me.'

She laughed, embarrassed, looking down at the cake crumbs on her plate. 'They'd wonder why you didn't have someone prettier.'

The front door slammed. From the hallway Patrick called, 'It's me.'

Mick rolled his eyes. 'Who else?' He looked at her. 'Before he comes in, tell me you'll come and see me next Sunday?'

Standing in the kitchen doorway Patrick smiled at her broadly. 'Hetty! I didn't think you'd still be here.'

'Well she is.'

'You've had some cake. Good.'

Sharply Mick said, 'The cake was awful.'

'Was it, Hetty?'

'Are you drunk?'

'Am I? What do you think?'

Mick glared at him. 'Perhaps you should go and lie down.'

'No, I'm all right. I'll walk Hetty home; it's nasty out there. Are you ready, Hetty?'

'There's no need.'

Patrick grinned at her. 'Now, are you sure?'

'I'm sure.' She edged past him but he followed her into the hallway.

'Have you had a nice afternoon, Hetty?'

'Yes, thanks.' About to go, she said, 'Goodbye, Mr Morgan. Tell Mick I'll see him on Sunday.'

Patrick closed the door and returned to the kitchen.

'I'm *Mr Morgan* now and you are *Mick*. Now, what does that tell us?'

Mick sighed. 'Do you want to tell me what's happened?'

Patrick sat opposite him and hacked off a piece of cake. Through a mouthful of dry crumbs he said, 'You tell me what's happened.'

'I wouldn't like to guess.'

Patrick laughed, spraying ginger cake. 'You usually do.'

'You went to the pub. You drank too much then went to the toilets behind the Parish Church and buggered some poor, furtive bastard who's now trying to hide his shame from his wife and children. There. How accurate was that?' He pushed himself away from the table and manoeuvred his chair to the door. 'I'll be in my room.'

Alone, Patrick sat down. He could still feel Paul's weight across his arm, still smell and taste him. He thought of the hole in the ceiling and the mattress's damp stink. Tomorrow he would start on the job of making the room presentable. He smiled to himself. For the first time in his life he felt truly happy.

Into the darkness Paul said quietly, 'Margot, would you like me to fetch you a glass of water?'

'I'm all right.'

'You're crying.' He touched her shoulder and she jerked away from him.

'Go to sleep.'

'I can't. Not when you're upset like this.'

She sat up suddenly, pulling the covers away from him and clasping them to her chest. Through her tears she said angrily, 'You still stink of beer. Breathing beer all over me. How could you get drunk like that?'

'I wasn't drunk.'

'Well, Daddy thought you were! He could smell it, too. And you lit a cigarette in front of him when you know he hates it!'

'And I put it out again, as soon as he asked.'

'I've never seen him so angry … I thought he was going to hit you.'

Paul laughed despite himself. 'So did I.'

'It's not funny. Why couldn't you just be on time? Why did you have to go to a pub and get drunk? You're just making him hate you.' Tears ran down her face and he sat up and put his arm around her shoulders. She shrugged him off. 'He hates you and now he thinks you're a drunk as well.'

'I'll go and see him tomorrow, after school. I'll tell him …'

'What? What will you tell him?'

'I don't know. That I'll never do it again?'

Wiping her eyes she said, 'He wants you to come to church with me on Sundays.'

'No, Margot.'

'Why not?'

'I'd feel like a hypocrite.'

'That's just a fancy word for saying you can't be bothered.'

He lay down again, groping for his cigarette case and matches on the bedside table. As he lit one he thought of Patrick Morgan refusing to chain smoke like him. He thought it almost pointless to take or leave cigarettes like that. Closing his eyes he inhaled deeply, picturing Morgan's face as he kissed him.

'Paul?' Hesitantly she said, 'If you came to church with me it would make things easier. It would show Daddy that you respect him.'

Daniel had seemed calm. He had stood up when he walked into the room, seeming to assess his breathlessness and his still soaking clothes as proof only of his stupidity. Then he had caught the smell of brown ale on his breath and the colour left his face.

'You've been drinking,' he'd said, and his voice had quaked with anger. 'What kind of a man are you?'

Paul felt Margot's hand close tentatively around his. After a while she said, 'Would it be hypocritical to sing a few hymns and close your eyes during prayers?'

He got up. Shrugging on his dressing gown he said, 'I'm going to make a cup of tea. Would you like one?'

'No.' Pulling the covers over her she turned her back on him.

Downstairs, waiting for the kettle to boil he smoked another cigarette and thought about Morgan, just as he had thought of him all afternoon. All afternoon he'd been aroused by thoughts of him, even as Daniel ranted and Margot wept. He thought of Wednesday and smiled in anticipation.

Chapter Eighteen

April, 1920
*FORGIVE ME, FATHER. IT'S been six months since my last
confession ...*

Patrick sighed. He could begin with small sins and work up
or he could begin and end with Paul. He glanced towards the
confessional box and the few waiting penitents. In the aisle the
younger priest genuflected and walked quickly from the church.
At least he wouldn't be hearing his confession. He smiled,
imagining the boy's jug ears burning crimson.

Paul had laughed at him. 'You'll be on your knees flogging
yourself from now until Christmas. Are you sure you've
thought this through?'

'No one gets flogged.'

'Pity. Well, do what you have to. It seems pretty pointless to
me.' He frowned. 'Unless you don't intend to fuck me again.'

'Don't call it fucking.'

'Patrick, the priest will say go and sin no more or whatever it
is they say. If you won't take any notice of him why bother
unless you want to end it?'

'Of course I don't want to end it! I love you, for Christ's
sake!'

Paul had sighed, covering his face with his hands. The sheet
had gathered at his waist, exposing his chest, and Patrick had
reached out, circling his nipple with the edge of his thumbnail.
Paul lowered his hands. 'Will you keep going back to
confession, week after week? Turn me into a sin you need
absolution from?'

Patrick had kissed his mouth gently. 'No. You're not a sin.'

'A sinner, though.'

'No!' Exasperated, he'd held Paul's face between his hands and forced him to meet his eyes. 'You're the best person I know. Have known. Ever.'

Paul had grasped his wrists to lift his hands away. 'Ever and ever, cross your heart? How many people have you known, Patrick?'

'Armies of them.'

Paul gazed at him intently. 'Tell me again.'

'What? That I love you? You know I do.'

'No …' He'd laughed a little. 'I know you *love* me.' At last he'd added softly, 'I love you, too.'

The narrow door to the confessional opened. Realising he was next in line Patrick got up and walked out into the spring sunshine.

The day after their meeting in the Castle & Anchor, Patrick had fixed the leak in the shop roof and thrown the old mattress away. He had taken the brittle, yellowing posters down and painted the walls the colour of milky Camp coffee. From Ellen Avenue he had brought his parents' feather bed and covered it with a Paisley silk shawl. The chimney was swept. Every Wednesday afternoon, after Hetty had gone home, he would light the fire and lie down on the bed to wait, his fingers worrying the shawl's silky tassels as he watched the shadows lengthen on the ceiling. Paul always arrived on time. After three months of Wednesdays his heart still raced when he heard his light, quick steps on the stairs.

Walking back now to the shop through the Wednesday market, Patrick stopped at the sweet stall. Remembering that his lover had a sweet tooth, he bought half a pound of chocolate caramels.

Paul said, 'What are you giggling at, Wilson?'

'Nothing, sir.'

It was the end of the school day, the boys noisily jostling one another to get out of the classroom as quickly as possible. Stepping in front of Wilson, Paul held out his hand. 'Show me.'

'It's nothing, sir. Honestly.'

Paul snatched the folded piece of paper from his hand. Looking at it he crumpled it and threw it in the waste paper basket beside his desk. 'You can go.'

'I didn't draw it, sir.'

'Get out of my sight.'

The boy dodged past Adam who smiled at Paul from the classroom door. 'What was all that about?'

'Do you want to see? It's not a very good likeness, but I think the huge, dead, staring eye will give you a clue who it's suppose to be.'

'Oh. Well, we can all expect that kind of thing. Best to rise above it.' Stepping inside the classroom he closed the door behind him. 'So, how are things? Are they behaving themselves, apart from that? There's nothing you're concerned about?' He laughed, embarrassed. 'No advice needed?'

'There is one thing you can tell me – how do you get through the day without a very stiff drink?'

Adam sighed. 'Look, Paul. As head of the English department, the headmaster's asked me to have a word with you.'

Paul glanced at him while packing exercise books into his briefcase. Adam smiled awkwardly. 'He told me that he passed your class the other day and had to come in.'

'Yes, he did. I had no idea he could shout so loudly.'

'Apparently he had to, because of the noise your class was making. He told me you'd lost control.'

Paul looked down at the briefcase: twenty essays on *The Merchant of Venice* to be marked. Shylock's pound of flesh seemed nothing; it would be easy to survive such a wound. He felt Adam's hand light on his arm. 'Yes, he's right. I lost control of the little bastards.'

'And it wasn't just that lesson, was it?'

'Adam, what has the head told you to tell me?'

He coloured. 'That I'm to keep an eye on you.'

'Nice choice of words. Anything else?'

'Paul …' Sighing, he said, 'I know you're not happy.'

'Do I have to be happy? Are any of the old duffers in the staffroom happy? There's not much sign of life in there, let alone happiness.'

'All I'm saying is perhaps you need to think about what you really want to do. Teaching is a calling, after all.'

'And no one called me, eh?' Snapping the briefcase closed he made to pass.

Adam caught his arm. 'I miss you, you know.' Awkward still, he repeated, 'I miss you.'

Paul avoided his gaze. 'I have to think about Margot. And it's not as if we never meet.'

'Three, four times a month if I'm lucky? She should let you out more.'

'She's my wife, not my bloody jailer.' He fought down his irritation, desperate to get out of the school gates so he could have a cigarette. Two cigarettes, one quick after the other. He felt for the case in his pocket, rubbing his thumb over the smooth patch his fingers had worn in the silver.

'Adam, I have to go.'

'Right, of course. I'd walk home with you, but I have work to do.'

Paul touched his arm as he brushed past. 'Goodnight, Adam.'

Lighting a cigarette as soon as he got outside the gates and the possible sight of the head, Paul hesitated, imagining going back inside the school and finding Adam. Adam's new Head of English office was tiny but it had a lock on the door and a window with a thick, dark blind. The fucking could be over in a matter of minutes, the holding and reassuring would take half an hour or less. It would save having to tell more lies to Margot; it would save an evening in Adam's bed, listening to talk of timetables and staffroom gossip. For a little while it would save him from the constant guilt. He drew deeply on the cigarette, thinking about throwing it down to the ground and returning to the dank atmosphere of the school. He thought about Patrick, of being held in the warm, quiet peace of their room, and the cigarettes he could smoke without any guilt at all. He glanced at the barred windows of the school and walked away.

* * *

Hetty swept the shop floor, thinking of Mick. Tonight, as she did most Wednesdays and Sundays, she would tell her mother she was going to the picture house with Elsie and walk instead to Ellen Avenue, letting herself in with the Chinese lion's key and calling his name into the gloom. He would come out from his room, smiling his dazzling smile and she would have such an urge to kiss him it was indecent. He would take off his glasses, folding them into his pocket, and push his fingers through his unruly hair as though he was transforming himself into someone else for her. He would say her name gently, as though surprised that she should have kept her promise and turned up to see him again, as if she could stay away. He was all she thought about; he made weighing sausages and scrubbing bloody trays and standing on her feet all day bearable, because at the end of it all she could go and see him and he would smile as if she was the most beautiful girl he'd ever seen. In his room she was always aware of his bed behind them, so conscious of it her skin tingled. She wondered if there was something wrong with her to want him so badly.

Sweeping up the bits of mince and sawdust she looked up as Patrick walked through from the back of the shop and turned the sign on the door to 'closed'.

'There. They're too late for pork pies now.'

'We've sold out anyway.'

'Have we? Good.' He smiled absently over his shoulder as he opened the till and began counting the takings. 'You can go now, Hetty. I've left some ham and bread in the pantry for Mick's supper. There's an egg custard, too, if he wants it.'

She carried the dustpan outside to the yard. From the shop she could hear Patrick humming under his breath. She frowned, picking up the tune at last – *The Boy I Love*. It played in her head as she fetched her coat and walked home.

The baby had kicked and punched all day. Kicked and punched and danced on her bladder so that it seemed she had spent most of the afternoon watching spiders dart from the corners of the outside lavatory. Sitting in the kitchen, her hands fumbling with knit one, purl one, Margot watched the clock on the dresser, waiting for Paul.

Her mother had spent the morning trying to teach her to knit, just as she had tried at the beginning of the war. Then there had been a misshapen balaclava her mother had unpicked and now there was this half-finished bootie, trailing grubbily from its needle. Paul would ignore it unless she said something and then he would kiss her and say it didn't matter. Nothing mattered to Paul, the price of food, the rise in their rent, the unrelenting contempt her father held him in – nothing. She sighed, looking down at the knitting and pulling at it in a desperate attempt to give it shape.

Paul came in through the back door and kissed the top of her head. She caught his scent of outside and cigarettes as he placed his briefcase on the floor beside her. He went into the pantry, coming out with the tin of biscuits. Beginning to eat his way through them, he frowned at her. 'What are you doing?'

'Mummy's teaching me to knit.'

'You haven't forgotten I'm going out tonight?'

'I don't usually forget, do I?' She looked up at him. There were shadows under his eyes, contrasting darkly against the pallor of his skin. During his nightmares last night he had cried out so loudly the neighbours had hammered on the wall. Laying the knitting down she reached out and squeezed his hand. 'I don't mind you seeing your friend. He should come here, one evening, and then you wouldn't have to go out in the cold. I could meet him … is he married? He could bring his wife.'

'He's not married.' Paul drew his hand away from hers. 'I'll make a start on supper, shall I?'

Outside the discreetly anonymous door at the back of the shop, Paul glanced up and down the alley before taking out his key and turning it in the lock. He locked the door behind him quickly and walked through the yard. Inside, he ran up the stairs. As always, he felt like a criminal.

Patrick was smoking on the bed, his left hand trailing to the floor, his fingers twisting at the dull colours of the rag-rug. As Paul walked in he turned slowly to smile at him and Paul's insides softened with the familiar mixture of love and lust. His

160

beauty was astonishing. It always made him smile.

'Hello, *sir.*'

Paul knelt beside him and kissed his mouth. 'Sergeant.'

Touching his face Patrick brushed his thumb gently beneath his good eye. 'You're all right?'

'Are you?'

'I am now.' He made room on the bed and they lay side by side, passing the cigarette between them until it was finished. Eventually Patrick said, 'I was thinking just now, I don't know when your birthday is.'

Paul laughed. 'Why? Are you planning a party?' He stood up. As he took off his jacket he said, 'Your birthday's in June. I remember you were sent a cake and you shared it amongst the men.'

The men had sprawled in the long French grass, their faces lifted to the hot sun as they licked cake crumbs from their fingers. He had approached them, curious about their laughter, jealous of it. Wanting to be included, all he had done was kill the atmosphere as effectively as if he'd thrown a grenade amongst them. Patrick had scrambled to his feet and brushed the unseemly crumbs from his tunic. The sun behind his head had created a halo for him.

Tugging at his tie Paul said, 'Why do you want to know when my birthday is?'

'Because I don't know and I feel I should. There are all kinds of things I don't know about you.'

Paul began unbuttoning his shirt. 'All right. My birthday's in October. I'll be twenty-four. I hate tripe and suet puddings but other than that I'll eat anything. What else? Oh yes. Wednesday is my favourite day of the week.'

'That's funny. Wednesday is my favourite, too.' After a while Patrick said, 'You haven't told me anything yet.'

Paul thought of all the things he might tell him: that he had made a better soldier than he had thought he would, or that he was terrified of being blind again. He could confess that he was afraid he would make a bad father, or that every day when he went into school he was sure he would be sacked. He could tell him about Jenkins, of course, although Patrick knew all about that. When he'd first started visiting him in this room he'd imagined he would find the courage to talk about what he'd done, but the time he spent with him had become too precious to be ruined by the past.

Aware of Patrick waiting for a reply he said, 'My earliest memory is watching my grandfather planting roses in our garden. He died when I was twelve and I still miss him. When I'm gardening I imagine he's there with me.' He smiled. 'There you are – I like gardening. You didn't know that.'

He finished undressing and lay down beside Patrick. Taking his hand Patrick said carefully, 'When did you realise you were different?'

'Different? Is that what we should call it?' Paul smiled at him. 'I can't remember. I always knew, I think. What about you?'

Patrick was silent for a long time. At last he squeezed Paul's hand tightly. 'There was a man my father called a nancy-boy in the shop where he bought our school uniforms. He was so arch, you know? Flapping and mincing about.' He laughed shortly. 'I was fifteen and I knew I wasn't anything like that. I wasn't like him and I wasn't like Mick. I didn't seem to fit at all.'

Standing up Patrick began to undress. 'I used to tell myself that I'd change, get married, eventually, putting the idea off until some time in the future when everything would be all right. I even went to a prostitute, once.' He smiled at Paul over his shoulder. 'Seeking a cure, I suppose. I didn't think much about marriage after that.' He took off his shirt and tossed it down. 'Then I saw you. I saw you and I thought – he's like me, a queer who's not a flapping, mincing nancy-boy.'

Naked, he knelt beside Paul, his hand going to cup his face. 'Tell me about the first man you went with.' His eyes were dark and unreadable and Paul frowned, grasping his wrist to lift his hand away. Patrick said softly, 'What was he like?'

Paul got up and fetched his cigarettes from his jacket. Lighting one he heard himself say calmly, 'He was my French teacher. He buggered me on the floor of his study. He didn't bother to undress me. He didn't try to make it easy. He just fucked me. Afterwards he couldn't look me in the eye. I speak

162

French well, though, my French is pretty good.'

Patrick gazed at him from the bed. 'I'd like to kill him.'

'The Germans saved you the bother.'

'I wanted there to be someone who did undress you, who was tender and careful.'

Paul thought about Adam, that first time when they had undressed each other. Adam's eyes had never left his as though he was afraid he was about to be stopped. Paul drew heavily on the cigarette. Looking at Patrick he said, 'There was one boy. He was the same age as me, nineteen, a Second Lieutenant, like me. We'd both been gassed. The hospital where we were sent was by the sea. We walked through sand dunes, far away where we wouldn't be found. It was July and he was pale as winter. We had to be careful with each other because everything hurt so much – the sunshine, the grass, even the salt in the air. I think we both just wanted to be comforted by someone neither of us had to talk to.'

He tossed his cigarette into the fire and lay down on the bed again. Rolling on his side Patrick pulled him into his arms and held him tightly.

Jenkins's teeth were chattering and he was crying and wouldn't stop and Paul pushed him back against the ladder scaling the side of the trench. All the others had climbed it and were crawling towards the German line. But Jenkins went on shaking and crying and Paul held his face between his hands, forcing him to meet his eyes.

He started and grabbed at the sheets to stop himself falling. He felt Patrick's arms around him, hugging him more tightly. 'I'm here, it's all right.'

'How long have I slept?'

'Not long.' Patrick was silent for a while. At last he said, 'I'm sorry about earlier. I had no right to ask you those things.' He got up and lit the candles on the mantelpiece. In the soft light his honey-coloured skin became flawless. Paul couldn't see the moles on his back, or the raised, white scar that disfigured his thigh and was a permanent reminder of the Somme. He watched the shadow of Patrick's body, his muscular arms and shoulders, fold into the corner of the room, the candles flickering in the draught he caused. He thought of how Patrick was the only person in the world who knew how wicked he was and yet he didn't seem to mind.

He said, 'I wish we hadn't met in France.'

Patrick climbed back into bed. He reached for Paul's hand. 'We wouldn't have met at all if it hadn't been for the war.' He looked at him. 'Unless you'd walked in the shop and suddenly fancied a bit of rough.'

'I think I probably would have been too scared.'

Patrick laughed. He began to kiss Paul and his mouth moved down his body until his lips closed around his semi-erect cock.

Every Wednesday evening after he'd kissed Patrick goodbye, Paul went to Parkwood to bathe. George frowned as he ushered him through to the warmth of Parkwood's kitchen. 'Are you all right? You look exhausted.'

'I'm fine.'

George peered at him anxiously. 'You look awful. Such dark rings under your eyes … are you sleeping?'

Paul went to stand in front of the fire. On the mantelpiece his own face looked out at him from his wedding picture. Avoiding Margot's eyes he glanced at George. 'Don't look so worried, Dad, I'm all right.'

Pouring him a measure of Scotch George handed him the glass. 'Sit down. Drink this while I run the bath.'

The French master had been called Mr Rouse; his fingernails had been too long and his breath had smelt of peppermints. One Friday afternoon he'd kept him back after the class. 'Have you fallen out with the other boys, Harris?'

In the bath, Paul winced at the memory. How could the man not know that masters weren't supposed to notice such things? It had been one of the few occasions he remembered blushing.

Rouse blushed, too. 'I only ask because you always seem to be on your own. It seems quite hard on you.' He laughed, embarrassed. 'Is there anything I can do to help?'

Paul gazed at him, his colour returning to normal. 'No, thank you, sir.'

Hurriedly, Rouse said, 'You know, your French is very good. I have some books in my room that may help you progress even further, if you're interested? If you're at a loose end you could come and have a look at them.'

Paul remembered how the man's voice had quavered a little, how he had cleared his throat and looked away to the window and the fourth form playing cricket on the school field. He heard the thwack of the ball on the bat and the applause as the batsman was caught out. Rouse breathed heavily, waiting.

'What time should I come, sir?'

Paul submerged himself in the water, counting seconds as he concentrated on not breathing. He wouldn't think about the scratch of those long fingernails, or the sweet shop taste of his breath. He wouldn't remember that afterwards the man had wept with shame, or that Jenkins had caught him coming out of his rooms. Jenkins had grabbed his arms, pinning him against the wall.

'Extra tuition, Harris?'

'Let go.'

Jenkins wrinkled his nose. 'What's that smell?' He made a show of disgust. 'Harris, you *stink* of old queer! You disgusting, filthy little pervert. I think we should get you cleaned up, don't you?'

Two of Jenkins's friends appeared from the shadows. Jenkins smirked at them. Pushing Paul ahead of him he said, 'Let's go.'

He remembered that when they stripped him he imagined he actually did stink and a part of him felt that this was one punishment at least that he deserved. The bath water had been freezing; the other two had held him down as Jenkins took a toilet brush to his genitals. He'd been sore for days, imagining everyone could smell the stink of bleach every time he undressed for bed. Jenkins made sure all the boys in their dormitory knew what he'd done. The rumours spread around the school. He'd contemplated suicide.

Paul broke to the surface, gasping for air. The water was becoming cold and he got out of the bath and dressed. Catching sight of his reflection in the steamed-up mirror he turned away quickly, hating the sight of himself.

Chapter Nineteen

THE LIVER WAS ARRANGED on a tray, sprigs of bright parsley tucked between its folds, blood tingeing the tight green curls. Liver was cheaper than chops or ham. Standing outside the butcher's shop window, Margot thought of the few coins she had left in her purse. She watched a bluebottle crawl across the snout of the model pig. If the fly landed on the liver she would buy something else. The fly took off and flew out of sight. Margot sighed. They would have liver for supper, just as the doctor ordered.

The shop was empty and she walked up to the counter decisively, already taking out her purse. The butcher smiled. 'What can I get you?'

'Half a pound of liver, please.'

He went on smiling at her. At last he said, 'It's Mrs Harris, isn't it? Lieutenant Harris and I were in the same regiment. I remember seeing you at that dance at New Year. Are you well?'

'Yes, thank you.' She looked down at her purse again, disconcerted by his steady gaze. 'Half a pound of liver, please.'

As he weighed the liver he glanced over his shoulder. 'Would you like anything else?' He placed the small, neatly wrapped parcel on the counter in front of her. 'Some bacon to go with the liver, or a nice chop, perhaps?'

She fumbled for coins. 'No, thank you. How much is that?'

'Free to new customers.'

'Free?'

He smiled. 'Free.'

She put her purse back in her handbag, thinking of what she could buy with the money saved. Glancing at him she said, 'Thank you.'

'My pleasure.'

She remembered Robbie saying, 'I had a letter from Paul this morning, about a piglet. Apparently his men chased the creature round an orchard, butchered it and then roasted it on a spit. He drew pigs in the margins, all curly tails and snouts.' He'd laughed. 'The letter was all about nothing, really. You'd think he was at a Boy Scout camp.'

Walking home from town, Margot remembered that Robbie said, 'I never thought he'd make much of a soldier. At school he was always such a fearful little thing. Odd, really, how he's turned out.'

Not really interested, she'd asked, 'And how has he turned out?'

Robbie was silent for a while. At last he said, 'Have you heard of Stoics, Margot? Nothing mattered to them, everything was accepted as it was, as though they'd risen above human feeling and emotion and nothing could touch them. Insane, really, if you think about it, but that's how Paul is. Doesn't complain, doesn't question. The perfect junior officer.'

She laughed. 'I think you mean he's brave.'

'It's a kind of bravery, I suppose.' He'd sighed, squeezing her hand. 'I suppose I thought he was more intelligent than to accept it all without doubt.'

At home Margot slipped the liver on to a plate. She touched it gently, thinking of the piglet Paul's men had caught in an orchard in France and imagined its insides slopping on to the grass. The handsome butcher had probably played a big part in the slaughter.

She went upstairs and lay down on their bed. Taking Paul's pillow she held it to her, inhaling the faint smell of him. The baby had been still for a while and she pressed her hand against her side. She felt a tightly bunched fist push against her palm and was reassured. Robbie's baby would be strong like him; she imagined a bold little boy, nothing like Paul – she couldn't imagine he would be anything like Paul.

Closing her eyes she thought of Robbie walking through the graveyard, remembering how she would watch him from her bedroom window, willing him to stop and look back. He never did. He kissed her goodbye cheerfully, called her his sweet girl and didn't look back, making her wonder if he thought about her at all when she wasn't with him. She tried to imagine his body beside her each night, his cries waking her instead of Paul's, but all she could see was his back as he walked away. Soon she would forget what he sounded like and only photographs would bring back his face. Softly she said his name, letting it go into the silence.

From the classroom doorway Adam bawled, 'Quiet! You will all be quiet this instant! Ramsey – sit down at once, boy!'

Ramsey sat. The banging of desk lids stopped and all the boys looked straight ahead, their backs straight as their faces. Adam stepped forward and a few in the front row flinched.

'Mr Harris,' Adam said. 'Would you wait for me outside, please?'

In the corridor Paul leaned against the pea-green wall, the noise still ringing in his ears. It had started quietly at first, soft thuds that could almost be ignored; then Ramsey had stood up and begun to conduct his orchestra of desk lids and the boy's flaying arms had brought the level of noise to a deafening climax. They couldn't hear his feeble requests for them to stop and he knew they would've ignored him even if they had. For those few minutes he was back in boarding school, singled out for special punishment. As the noise became louder it was all he could do to stop himself crying.

Coming out of the class room Adam said, 'Go and have a cigarette.'

'No. I'll go back and face them.'

Adam stopped him by placing a hand firmly on his chest. 'Go and have a cigarette. You're white as a sheet. They shouldn't see you like this.'

'Will you tell the head?'

'I won't have to, Paul. I think the whole school heard.' He sighed. 'Look, have a walk around the yard, calm yourself down, then come and see me in my office. We'll talk.'

'What about them?'

'Leave me to deal with them.' He touched his arm. 'Go on, off you go.'

From the dugout doorway Jenkins said, 'Davies is weeping again.'

Paul looked up from his supper of cold, tinned stew. Unwinding the scarf that covered much of his head and face, Jenkins sat down opposite him. 'Do you ever feel like weeping, Harris?'

A shell exploded. Earth fell from the ceiling on to the table and Paul pushed his plate away. Standing up he said, 'I'll go and speak to him.'

'It won't do any good. Besides, why shouldn't he have a good old blub?'

'I don't want the men seeing him like that.'

'Then off you go and talk to him. I'm sure the poor mite couldn't feel any worse anyway.'

'What do you mean by that?'

'He's scared of you, Harris! Absolutely terrified you'll tear him off a strip for some minor infringement! Maybe you're best leaving him to Sergeant Morgan, now I come to think about it.'

'Morgan?'

'Didn't I say? Morgan's taking care of him. It's quite sweet to see, really, the big man sitting so quietly with the boy. Morgan had one of the men make him a cup of tea. Plenty of sugar, no doubt.'

'Why didn't you bring him in here? He shouldn't be bothering the men. For God's sake, they have enough to put up with!'

'What's really the matter, Harris? Scared you've got a rival for Morgan's affections?' Jenkins laughed. He sat back in his chair and lit a cigarette, flicking the spent match on to the shiny gristle left on Paul's supper plate. 'There's something about the Sergeant, isn't there? Cut above. I don't wonder you can't keep your eyes off him.'

'Why don't you go to hell!'

'Now, I could be trite and say we're all already *in* hell.' He gazed at Paul. 'I had a quiet word with Davies. You know, the boy's so innocent he hardly knew the meaning of the word *pervert*.'

In the schoolyard, Paul drew heavily on the cigarette. He remembered that he couldn't bring himself to stay in the dugout with Jenkins and had gone out into the trench. The men were dark shapes huddled against the sandbags; he could smell the stew they were spooning into their mouths, a stink like over-boiled bones. That morning he had inspected their feet and Corporal Taylor had joked that he was like Christ, about to wash the feet of the disciples. Further along the trench Morgan crouched beside Davies, watching as the boy sipped from an enamel mug. He caught his eye and for a moment they'd stared at each other.

In the school playground Paul closed his eyes, sucking smoke deep into his lungs. The cigarette was finished, burnt almost to his fingers. In a few minutes the bell would ring and hundreds of boys would swarm outside, making him want to find somewhere to hide. Tossing the cigarette down he turned and walked back inside the school.

Adam said, 'Sit down, Paul.' He smiled too brightly. 'Feeling better?'

'I'm fine.' He sat down, aware of Adam watching him from the other side of his desk. Attempting to smile back at him he said, 'I've stopped shaking, anyway.'

'That's good. Right, I've given the whole class detention and the headmaster will cane Ramsey tomorrow. The boy will also apologise to you in person and in writing.'

'That should prove embarrassing.'

'I don't care who's embarrassed. We're trying to instil discipline. Besides, he deserves to be embarrassed.'

'Do I?'

Taking off his glasses Adam pushed the heels of his hands into his eyes. 'I've made myself hoarse shouting at those boys. I don't think I've been so angry in my life. All I could think about was that this is my fault. I should have realised you weren't ready for this.'

'I am ready, most of the time.'

'You should see yourself, Paul. You look worse now than when you first came home. And you *are* still shaking.' Frowning he said, 'Perhaps you should take a day or two off.'

'No. Things will be better tomorrow. I can't put off facing them.'

'I hate seeing you like this. Listen, why don't you come and see me tonight? We'll talk some more.' He stood up and walked around the desk. Holding the door open for him he said, 'Seven o'clock?'

In Adam's bed Paul thought about Second Lieutenant Davies. In October 1918 a sniper had shot him in the head. His had been a quick, painless death – a second's carelessness and then nothing. He had written to the boy's parents and said that their son had always been brave. Reading over his shoulder Jenkins had laughed.

Adam propped himself up on his elbow. 'Do you want to tell me what happened today?'

Paul closed his eyes, remembering how helpless he had felt as the first thuds of desk lids broke the unnatural quiet of the class, increasing in speed until the noise grew louder and louder. All the boys had looked at him, all of them smirking. He wondered if it would have been worse if one of them had looked ashamed. At last he said, 'It was a prank, that's all. Do we have to make so much of it?'

'Yes, if it's the only way I can get you to come and see me.'

'So am I here for a fucking or a bollocking, then?'

'Don't talk like that. God, you're a crude little sod, sometimes.' He sighed. 'You were an officer, Paul. Why can't you cope with a few thirteen-year-olds?'

'I don't know. Maybe because the school hasn't issued me with a tin hat and a machine gun.'

Adam was silent for a while. At last he said quickly, 'The head wants to give you your notice. I've persuaded him to give you another chance.'

'Thanks.'

'For Christ's sake try and sound a bit more grateful.'

'I am. Really.' He managed to smile at him, although the shame of almost losing his job had his heart racing.

Adam laughed bleakly. 'Do you want to *show* me how grateful you are?'

Paul closed his eyes as Adam pushed him on to his stomach and entered him roughly. He wondered when they had stopped making love, when Adam had given up on tenderness for this quick, angry fucking. Adam called out triumphantly and the bedstead rattled against the wall like the clatter of desk lids.

Chapter Twenty

MICK SAID, 'I HATE Sundays. I've always hated Sundays, the way they drag. Patrick looks forward to them, he had quite a spring in his step this morning. Of course, it's his day of *rest*, whereas I rest every day.'

Hetty looked up from the book she'd been reading to him. 'I knew you weren't listening. Do you want to hear how it ends?'

'Not really.' Throwing his cigarette stub into the fire he said, 'Do you ever see your new neighbour? You know that young girl – Mrs Harris. Has she had the baby yet?'

'I see her sometimes, and no, she hasn't had the baby yet. She came in the shop. Patrick gave her free liver.'

Mick raised his eyebrows. 'Did he?'

Hetty sighed. Closing the book she said, 'I think he took a fancy to her. I suppose she is pretty. And it's not as if she'll be a good customer – poor as mice, her and that husband. All make-do-and-mend. She peered into her purse as though it was a big, black, scary hole.'

Mick laughed but his eyes remained questioning. 'Do you see much of her husband?'

She frowned at him. 'Why?'

'I knew his brother, I told you.'

'I did hear one thing about him. Mrs Shipley who lives next door to them told Mam how he makes such a row in the night she has to bang on the wall with her shoe, says he sounds like he's back fighting the war single-handed. She says her Fred is ready to go round there and throttle him, one eye or not.'

Mick lit another cigarette. 'What did *her Fred* do during the war? Don't tell me. Reserved occupation.'

'He was too old to be called up.'

'Lucky him.'

'It can't be easy being woken night after night.'

'No. It's not easy.' He stared into the fire, his mouth set in a thin, angry line. After a while he said, 'It must be hard on the boy's wife.'

'I suppose so.'

'You suppose so? Can't you imagine how frightening it must be for her? For God's sake, can't you empathise even a little?'

Returning his angry gaze Hetty said, 'Maybe I just think she's lucky to have a husband and a baby on the way.'

'Even a husband whose screams wake the neighbours? Will any husband do, Hetty?'

'Not any, no.'

He flicked cigarette ash at the hearth. Without looking at her he said, 'I'm tired. Perhaps you'd better go home.'

'I thought you wanted to go for a walk in the park?'

'I hate that park, it's full of bloody women who can't keep their little brats from staring.' He looked at her at last. 'I think you should go, now. Thank you for coming to see me.'

'I don't want to go.'

'No? Do you want to read me another chapter of that terrible book? Or we could play cards. There's such a lot to keep you here, isn't there?'

'There's you.'

'Me?' He manoeuvred his chair back, turning it round to face the window. Staring out over the garden he said, 'You shouldn't let me keep you, Hetty.'

'Why not?'

He looked at her. At last he said, 'Because I think I'm in love with you. I *am* in love with you – and that's terrible because what business do I have falling in love? A great bloody useless lump like me?' Turning back to the garden he said, 'I thought your company would be enough. It isn't. It's too bloody painful.'

'What if I was in love with you?'

'Are you?' He frowned.

'Yes.'

'But what's the point in that? I'll never be any good for

175

you … and people look at me and think … they think …'

'I don't care what they think.'

'I do! They think I don't have normal feelings, and if I do …' His face twisted into an angry smile. Bitterly he said, 'Well, no one likes to think about it, do they?'

She crouched beside him. 'I do love you. I have for ages now.'

He gazed at her. 'You love me?' He searched her face, his eyes intense. Cupping her cheek with his hand he said, 'I can't have you love me, Hetty.'

She kissed him, gently at first, until she felt his resistance give. He groaned softly, his hand going to the back of her head and his fingers knotting in her hair as his tongue searched out hers. As he pulled her closer to him the arm of the wheelchair pressed against her and she drew away. She laughed a little, frustrated. 'I can't get close enough.'

He pressed his hand against her cheek. 'Maybe you should go.'

'Do you really want me to?'

'No. But if you stay …' Desperately he said, 'I just want to hold you so badly.'

'I know. I want that, too.'

'I don't want you to do anything you might regret.'

'I won't.'

'If we just hold each other, that's all.'

She nodded, impatient with desire. 'That's all.'

He laughed as if he couldn't believe the passion in her eyes. Softly he said, 'Help me on to the bed.'

Margot watched Paul shave at the kitchen sink. Earlier, he had taken his eye out and cleaned the socket while the eye watched from a glass of water. The eye didn't produce tears and throughout the day he would drop water into it to prevent the socket from becoming dry. Usually he did all this in private but this morning it seemed he had forgotten she was there.

The *Sunday Post* was spread out on the table in front of her. She had been pretending to read the same article for the last ten minutes. Turning the page she said, 'You promise you won't be late?'

He glanced at her, razor poised. There was a line of soap on its blade and he rinsed it off. 'I promise.'

'Because you know what Daddy's like. And it is his birthday.' After a moment she said cautiously, 'You'll make an effort, won't you?'

Looking in the mirror he'd propped up on the window ledge, he dragged the razor across his cheek.

'I know you don't want to go, Paul.'

He smoothed back his hair with both hands. Catching her reflected gaze he said, 'I'll be there, don't worry.' He shrugged his jacket on. 'Are you sure you don't want me to walk you to church?'

'I'm sure. Go and see your friend, have a nice time.'

After he'd gone Margot went into the front parlour and lifted the lace curtain away from the window to watch him walk towards the High Street. Letting the curtain fall, she thought of thin French actresses and looked down at her own mountainous body in despair.

Paul walked to the Red Lion pub where he had promised to meet Patrick. There was a group of young lads on the corner of Tanner Street and he felt his heart beat quicken. He wished often he didn't look so obviously like a frail little queer. He tried to walk a little taller and resisted quickening his step as he passed the youths. Not one of them looked twice at him and he wanted to laugh at his paranoia but it was too depressing. He thought of the boys at school and wondered what they had in store for him next. He knew he was completely at their mercy, just as he had been at Jenkins's.

Last night he'd dreamt of Jenkins again and woke in a sweat to find Margot standing over him, her hair dishevelled from sleep and her eyes wide with fright. 'You were swearing!' She gazed at him in disbelief that he could use such terrible words. 'And who's Jenkins?'

'No one.' He held out his hand to her. 'No one, come back to bed.'

No one. Paul lit a cigarette as he turned the corner on to

Skinner Street. If only.

Jenkins crouched beside him and sang softly, 'The boy I love is up in the gallery, the boy I love is …'

Paul had been asleep on his bunk. Startled, he'd sat up, fumbling in his haste to fasten his tunic buttons. He searched his pockets for a cigarette, appalled to see that his hands were shaking as he struck a match.

Jenkins laughed. 'Lord, you're uncivil! Aren't you going to offer me one of those? Isn't that the done thing?'

As Paul made to get up, Jenkins placed a hand on his chest, pushing him down again. 'Hawkins asked me this morning if I knew what was wrong with you. Said you'd been behaving strangely. I wonder if he knows just how strange you are. Perhaps I should have a quiet word with him, put him in the picture.'

As if on cue, Hawkins came in. He frowned from Jenkins to Paul. 'Harris, have you told him yet?'

Paul scrambled out of his bunk, trying to avoid brushing against Jenkins who, as usual, stood too close to him. Straightening his tunic he said, 'No, sir, not yet.'

Hawkins grunted. 'All right, I'll do the honours.' He looked at Jenkins. 'You and Harris and twenty of the men are going on a little raiding party. Top brass want us to catch a Fritz prisoner.' He grinned at Paul. 'They imagine we can find out a few of their secrets, eh, Harris?'

'Yes, sir.'

To Jenkins he said, 'I wouldn't normally send the two of you but I think you can learn from Harris's experience. So mind you take notes, Jenkins – you'll be doing it on your own next time.' Hawkins sat down at the table. 'Be a good chap and go and tell Johnson to fetch me a cup of tea, would you, Jenkins?'

When he'd gone, Hawkins looked at Paul. 'Do you think he'll manage?'

'I don't know, sir.'

Hawkins frowned at him. 'I'm worried about you. I hope you're not coming down with something.'

'No, sir, I'm fine.'

'Fine! You always say you're fine, thank God!' He sighed.

'I'm sorry I've had to foist Jenkins on you, Paul. But he has to start pulling his weight some time.' After a moment he laughed. 'The bugger went very white, didn't he?'

Crossing the High Street close to Patrick's shop, Paul remembered just how white Jenkins had gone. He had wanted to feel gratified but instead he had felt sick at the thought of having to rely on him if anything went wrong. The only comfort was knowing that Patrick would be with him. Later that night as they prepared for the raid, he'd caught Jenkins watching him as he cleaned his pistol.

'Morgan's going on the raid.' Jenkins grabbed his arm, forcing him to turn to look at him. 'If Morgan's going you don't need me – you can tell Hawkins you don't need me!'

Jenkins's face was twisted with fear and anger. Unable to cope with his fear as well as his own Paul shook off his grasp and turned back to his gun.

'Did you hear me, Harris? Tell Hawkins you'll do it on your own – you and bloody Morgan!'

'He won't listen to me.'

'He will! You're his blue-eyed bloody boy! He will listen!'

Paul stared at him. He felt as though he was seeing him properly for the first time in his life. He had only ever looked at him obliquely and always with a creeping sense of his own cowardice for not facing up to him. He saw how ordinary he was, rather plain and pasty-faced beneath his veneer of arrogance. For a moment he felt sorry for him. 'Listen, you'll be all right. It's really not as bad as you think it's going to be, once you're out there. Just stay close to Morgan and me –'

Jenkins had laughed so harshly he sounded like a mad man.

Paul stopped along the alley that led to the Red Lion. He leaned against the coal-blackened wall and breathed in deeply in an effort to manage the panic rising inside him. In St Stevens, when he'd allowed himself to remember that raid, a nurse had found him curled into a ball on the floor of the common room, fellow patients gazing at him with mute acceptance. A doctor was fetched; there was the usual carefully suppressed exasperation with him when despite their coaxing he couldn't speak, although he'd wanted to tell them that the guilt felt like a terrified animal trapped inside him. If he didn't stay still enough to keep it contained its panic would kill him. Eventually they had carried him to bed. An injection was administrated.

He pushed himself away from the wall and steadied himself. Taking another deep breath he walked inside the pub.

In The Red Lion Patrick looked around for a familiar face and was relieved not to find any. Tucked away in one of the back alleys that ran off the High Street, the Lion was used mainly by the market traders and its Sunday afternoon trade was quiet. Two men stood at the bar; in the far corner a middle-aged couple nursed two halves of stout. From a room above the pub he could hear scales being practised on the piano, the same flat notes repeated over and over, jarring the pub's sullen silence. At the bar the barmaid smiled at Paul as she handed him their drinks. Patrick watched her curiously and tried to work out if the interest she showed in Paul was merely professional friendliness or something more appreciative. The way others looked at Paul had always preoccupied him; whenever they were in public together his jealousy made sure he was never quite at ease.

Paul sat down. He set the two pints of beer on the table and immediately lit a cigarette. He placed the open case between them. 'I'm pleased you came.'

Patrick took a long drink. Wiping his mouth he said. 'Did you think I wouldn't?'

'I wasn't sure. I thought you might be wary.'

'Wary!' He laughed dismissively. 'Those two at the bar. Are they queer, do you think?'

'I doubt it.'

'So why should they think we are?'

'They might think I am.'

'Of course they don't.' He frowned. 'Don't say things like that. You're just like any other man.'

'Am I?'

Patrick looked away. The woman with the stout was rummaging in a large handbag and he watched her, wondering what might appear. A handkerchief. She blew her nose noisily.

180

The man sitting next to her sighed.

Patrick took one of Paul's cigarettes, a cheaper brand than the one he smoked. He picked up the silver case, touched by the irony of something so expensive containing such rubbish. Turning the case over he read the inscription on the back, squinting at the ornately curling script.

Paul said, 'My father gave it to me for my twenty-first.'

He read the inscription aloud. '"To Paul with my fondest wishes and love."' Weighing it in his hand he looked at him. 'Your father?'

'You don't believe me?'

He placed the case down gently. 'Yes. I'm sorry, I believe you.'

Paul trailed his finger through the condensation on the side of his glass. Without lifting his gaze he asked, 'How's Mick?'

'All right. He's with his girl, Hetty.'

'Does he know who you're with?'

'No!'

Paul frowned at him thoughtfully. After a moment he said, 'You're lying. You do it so badly I can tell. He knows you're with me.'

'He doesn't know anything about you!'

'He was great friends with Robbie, did you know that? They served together at the beginning of the war. I think he confided in him.' After a moment he said, 'Rob could hardly ever bring himself to confide in me. At school he avoided me like the plague. Didn't want to be tarred with the same brush.' He smiled at Patrick, only to look down at his pint again. 'I couldn't blame him, really.'

'He should have looked out for you – if I'd been your brother –'

'He did – once or twice, when I was getting my head kicked in.'

'Christ!' Patrick shook his head. 'I would have made sure no one even touched you!'

'What does Mick say about you seeing me?'

Patrick considered lying to him again but found himself saying, 'He says what you'd expect him to. He thinks you've corrupted me, of course.' He sighed in exasperation. 'I don't take any notice! I don't care what anyone thinks.'

The piano practice stopped and Paul glanced up. 'Every good boy deserves favour.'

'What?'

'It's a scale, the first letter of each word represents a note, e, g, b, d, f.'

'You play piano as well as all your other talents?'

'Very badly.'

Patrick smiled at him, holding his gaze for so long that Paul looked away, glancing quickly at the two men at the bar. 'Perhaps this wasn't a good idea.'

'You wanted to come here.'

'I like pubs. And I don't have any other drinking partners. Besides, I feel cooped up in the house, in school, in your little room. I needed a change.'

Paul became silent, drinking steadily and smoking with his usual fixed concentration. In their room Patrick welcomed his quietness, it felt calming and easy knowing they would talk only if they wanted to. But today his silence had an edge to it, as though there was something preoccupying him that he didn't feel he could share. Patrick shifted uncomfortably. There were times when he felt he would never know Paul properly just because of the difference in their class; he suspected that Paul behaved differently around the men he'd shared the officers' mess with and that different Paul was out-going and talkative. He imagined if he had been a doctor's son rather than a butcher's Paul wouldn't be so silent.

Determined to make him understand that he wasn't just a thick, taciturn butcher, Patrick cleared his throat. 'Is there something wrong, Paul?'

Paul jerked his head up to frown at him. 'Why do you ask?'

'You're quiet.' He laughed awkwardly. '*Quieter*.'

'So? You're all right with that, aren't you?'

'Yes –'

'For Christ's sake, Patrick, don't you start too! Why does everyone feel that I should be talking all the time? What is there to say, anyway? Bloody words – they don't make the slightest bit of difference to anything!'

'All right. I'm sorry.' He looked so agitated that Patrick had the urge to take his hand. Instead he said gently, 'Do you want another drink?'

Paul shook his head. 'No. I have to go. I have to go and *talk* to my father-in-law over lunch. Talking proves that you're a good sort, apparently.' Exhaling cigarette smoke he said, 'I'm sorry. I shouldn't lose my temper with you – you don't deserve it.'

Patrick smiled. 'Is that you losing your temper, then? Blink and you miss it?'

'Pathetic, isn't it?'

'A bit. We should have a ride out up on to the moors – you could practise having a good shout at some sheep.'

'Is that all I'm fit for?'

'No! It was a joke – are you feeling sorry for yourself now?'

Paul drained the dregs of his beer and stood up. He touched his brow above his glass eye as though straightening an imaginary patch. It was a habitual, reflexive gesture that Patrick guessed he was hardly aware of performing, and as ever he felt soft with pity. He picked up the cigarette case and handed it to him, discreetly brushing his fingers. 'I'll see you on Wednesday.'

Paul nodded.

Patrick watched him walk out, wishing that he could leave with him and that they could walk through the streets without any dirty-minded bastard suspecting anything. But they had to be careful, Paul was insistent on the amount of care they took. 'Look at me,' he'd once said to him, 'and imagine what men like Thompson would think if they saw us walking down the street together.'

He knew Paul was right. Despite what he'd said earlier he knew it was a risk just sitting together in this pub. Patrick glared at the backs of the two men at the bar. Suddenly he hated everyone as much as they must surely hate him.

Chapter Twenty-one

WALKING THROUGH THE CEMETERY from church her father asked, 'Have you thought of any names for the baby?'

'Grace, if it's a girl.'

'That's nice, I like that. Grace.' He smiled. 'It's pretty.'

Margot glanced at the stone angel a little further along the path. 'It was Paul's mother's name.'

'Oh.' He laughed emptily. 'What about boys' names?'

Robert, she thought, Robert after his father. She would call him Bobby. Her father looked at her. 'Margot? Did you hear me?'

'We haven't thought about boys' names.'

'No, well, perhaps when you see the baby a name will suggest itself. It's often the way.' He cleared his throat. 'Where is Paul this morning?'

'Seeing a friend. Someone he knew in the army.'

'And what's his name, this friend of his?'

'I can't remember.'

'Really? Haven't you met him?'

'No. He's allowed his own friends, isn't he?'

'Well, they weren't very much in evidence at your wedding. I've never known a groom with so few guests.'

'I think most of them are dead, Daddy.'

He was silenced and she hoped that she had shamed him. As they passed Grace Harris's grave a magpie flew low over the path in front of them, followed swiftly by its mate. Her father laughed a little. 'The male magpie never lets his mate out of his sight, did you know that? They're extremely jealous creatures, magpies.'

She looked at him. 'Are you saying I should never let Paul

out of my sight?'

'That would be rather difficult, wouldn't it?'

'Yes.'

He sighed, stopping to face her. 'Are you happy, Margot? If I thought you were happy then I wouldn't mind him so much.'

'I'm happy.'

'Then why do I never see you smile? Heaven knows the last time I heard you laugh.'

'I'm tired. The baby makes me tired. And sometimes there isn't a lot to smile about, but that's nothing to do with Paul.'

'Then what is it to do with? That dreadful little house?'

'No! It's not dreadful!'

'You're very loyal. I just wish he could do better for you.'

'He works hard.'

They reached the vicarage. From the open kitchen window came the smell of roast beef and the clatter of pots and pans. She turned to her father. 'Please, please don't be horrid to him over lunch.'

He looked surprised. 'Am I horrid? Then I'll try not to be.' He smiled half-heartedly. 'I'll make a special effort on my birthday.'

The Reverend said grace and Paul closed his eyes and bowed his head and said Amen when it was over, and when he looked up Margot smiled at him, pleased. Beneath the table she ran her foot up his shin and he imagined spending the afternoon in bed with her, as they often did on Sundays.

The Reverend said, 'So, Paul, who is this friend of yours Margot has told us about? An army friend, she says?'

He wondered if he should lie, make up a fictional character – a lieutenant he'd known since 1915, a fellow officer he had fought side by side with, through thick and thin. He could have a slight limp from an old wound; he would be easy to construct – a composite of all the second lieutenants he had ever seen killed. Swallowing a mouthful of roast potato he said, 'You probably know him. He owns a shop on the High Street. Patrick Morgan, of Morgan's Butchers?'

The Reverend raised his eyebrows. 'A butcher? And he was

an officer, was he?'

'No, a sergeant.'

'I didn't think officers and sergeants mixed.'

'Well, we're neither officer nor sergeant, now.'

'Morgan …' Margot's mother frowned thoughtfully. 'Wasn't it the Morgans who were killed in that dreadful accident?'

Paul glanced at her. 'Their car was hit by a coal wagon.'

'That's right! Dreadful, quite dreadful. And their sons were away in France, weren't they? I remember reading about it in the paper. So sad.'

Daniel said, 'If it's the man I'm thinking of he was a rogue. The council wanted to close his shop as a danger to public health – the place was absolutely flyblown. Always seemed to have money, though. Something underhand going on, no doubt.'

Evenly Paul said, 'You don't know that, sir.'

'Common knowledge.'

Paul thought of Patrick's fierce hated of his father and wondered why he was defending him. All the same he said, 'But you don't have any evidence.'

Daniel snorted. 'When a man whose only visible means of support is a disgusting butcher's shop dresses his wife in mink and drives a fancy little car, then I would say the evidence is staring one in the face.'

'Perhaps he inherited money.'

'Don't be naïve, boy.' He looked at Margot. 'I hope you don't shop there. I don't want your and the baby's health risked by tainted meat.'

Margot blushed. 'It's really very clean, now.'

'All the same. Old habits die hard – there are plenty of other butchers on the High Street.'

Paul placed his knife and fork down. Turning to Daniel he said, 'He's a friend. Are you suggesting I shouldn't trust him to sell my wife decent meat?'

'I am, yes.'

'For God's sake!'

'Don't dare blaspheme at my table! I know you don't

believe in anything beyond your own comfort and convenience, but the rest of us do.'

Iris sighed. 'Oh please, you two. Must you bicker every time you meet?'

'Asking him to show a little respect isn't bickering, Iris.' Daniel frowned at Margot. 'Are you all right?'

'No!' Tears stood in her eyes. 'Why can't you just try to get on! Why can't you just be quiet!' Pushing herself away from the table she ran from the room. Paul got up to follow her but Iris motioned that he should sit down.

'I'll see to her. Finish your meal.' She looked at Daniel. 'Try not to fight.'

As she closed the door behind her Daniel said, 'I have never known my daughter to be so unhappy. She was happy with your brother, but you knew that, didn't you? As soon as I set eyes on you at that wretched party I could see how jealous you were of their happiness. You must have hated Robert. You must have hated him as much as you have contempt for my daughter. You pretend to Margot that you love her but that's all it is, pretence – men like you don't love anyone. You can't!'

Paul laughed, astonished, even as his stomach contracted with fear. 'Men like me?'

'Do you honestly imagine I don't recognise what you are? I'd rather Margot gave the baby up than be married to a creature like you.' Whittaker was staring at him. He leaned across the table, bringing his face up close to Paul's. Exhaling a sharp, sour breath he said, 'When I think of all the decent boys killed …'

Paul looked down at his plate, his fingers going to the glass eye. He thought of the decent men, the ones he could remember, those who had stayed alive long enough to make an impression on him. Then there was Jenkins, of course.

He heard Daniel laugh contemptuously. 'You should look in a mirror before you set foot in my house again. Take a good, hard look at yourself.'

The door opened and Margot's mother came in. To Paul she said, 'Margot would like you to take her home.'

Paul got up too quickly and swayed dizzily. His legs were

shaking and he leaned against the table for a moment. Iris said, 'Are you all right, Paul?'

Daniel snorted. 'He's fine, Iris. Nothing for anyone to worry about any more.'

Paul looked at his father-in-law; he was gazing at him evenly, his eyes still dark with anger. Robbie had admired this man, in his letters he'd called him compassionate. *Nothing gung-ho about the Reverend,* Robbie wrote. *He seems to understand what's going on out there.*

Returning to his meal Daniel said, 'Take Margot home. Make sure you look after her.'

Margot woke from a dream about the baby in which Paul had stood in her father's pulpit and announced to a packed church that the baby wasn't his. He'd only been pretending to be married. He would rejoin the army, he said, the war wasn't over. He had two eyes again.

Lying still on her back she stared at the ceiling, listening to the Sunday silence. Earlier Paul had drawn the curtains against the afternoon sun and now a pale grey light filtered through the thin material. In the corner of the room was the crib Paul had bought from Parkwood. Made from dark oak, it had rockers and a canopy carved with Tudor roses. It was very old, he said. It smelt of empty churches and was too big for their little room. This afternoon she'd told him it was ugly and threw her hairbrush at it. She had wept and hadn't allowed him to comfort her.

Her throat still felt raw from crying. By her side was the crumpled, snotty handkerchief she'd clasped in her fist as she drifted uneasily to sleep. On the bedside table a cup of tea had formed a milky skin; a sandwich curled its corners to reveal a creamy sliver of fatty ham. He'd thought she might be hungry because she had left most of her lunch. She had resolutely ignored this small act of peace-making.

Thinking about the dream Margot remembered that all the faces in the church had been those of strangers and that Paul had been in uniform. She'd thought how handsome he was as she stood at the back of the church. He'd looked straight at her

188

and smiled as he disowned their marriage.

Margot closed his fist around the sodden hanky, afraid that she was about to cry again. Her mother had said it was the baby that made her cry, her body playing rotten tricks. Things would seem so much better when the baby was born. Stroking her hair, hush-hushing her, Iris had told her to be brave.

From the bedroom doorway Paul said, 'May I come in?'

'It's your room, too.'

'I thought you might not want to be disturbed.' He came in and sat at the foot of the bed. Reaching out he set the crib rocking gently. 'I'll take it back to Parkwood. You can choose a new one.'

'We can't afford a new one.'

'I have a little put by. Don't worry about money.'

'How much is a little? It would have to be more than a *little* if I'm not to worry.'

Looking at the crib he said, 'My father will help us.'

'So we have to go running to him, now?'

'Robbie had savings.' He turned to her. 'In his will the money was left to Dad. Now he wants us to have it. Is that running to my father? Or is that claiming what's rightfully yours?'

Ashamed, Margot looked away, unable to meet the pain in his face. Not only had she told him she hated the crib, but that she hated him, that she wished she'd never married him and why did it have to be Robbie who was killed? Her face burned as she remembered and she closed her eyes, trying to keep her tears in check.

Quietly Paul said, 'Don't start crying again, Margot. I don't think I could stand it.'

'I'm sorry. I try not to.'

He lay down beside her on his back and took his cigarettes from his pocket. Lighting one he said, 'Dad thought you might hate the crib. He said he always did – he said it reminded him of something out of a Grimm's fairy tale. My mother liked it, though. She thought it romantic.'

Trying not to cry she sniffed, 'Do you think it's romantic?'

'Dad said when I was born he couldn't bear to put me in it. I slept in a drawer by his bed. It had meant a lot to her so he hid it away, out of sight. Is that romantic?'

Hesitantly she said, 'It must have been hard for you, growing up without her.'

'Harder for Rob, I think.' There are photographs of her with Rob. I used to be jealous of him for knowing her. Jealous of him for all kinds of reasons.'

'Such as?'

He smiled slightly. 'He was taller than me.'

'Not very.'

'Enough. Heavier, too. Not such a weed.'

'You're not a weed.' She turned on her side to look at him. Often she felt she could spend hours looking at him; she had decided that his face was perfect, that no other man even came close to his perfection. It seemed wrong, sometimes, that he should be with someone as ordinary as she was. She laid a hand on his chest, wanting him suddenly.

He glanced at her. 'I'm sorry I made you cry.'

'You didn't. It was Daddy's fault. *My* fault. I shouldn't be such a baby.'

He took her hand from his chest and held it at his side and absurdly she felt rejected by this small gesture. Wanting to regain a closeness she felt she had squandered she said, 'I love you.'

He was silent for so long she thought he hadn't heard her; her heart beat faster as she imagined repeating it. At last she said, 'I'd understand if you don't love me, but I love you.'

He turned on his side to look at her. For what seemed a long time he searched her face as though looking for signs that she might not be telling the truth. He pulled her towards him. The baby kicked and she pressed his hand hard against her belly as he kissed her.

Chapter Twenty-two

One Month Later

A DOUBLE BED HAD appeared in Mick's room. Hetty stared at it.

Gently Mick said, 'I was tired of sleeping in a child's bed.'

She glanced over her shoulder, almost expecting to see Patrick watching her from the doorway. 'Did Patrick …' Words failed her. Mick wheeled his chair closer and took her hand.

'I told Patrick the other bed was uncomfortable.'

'So he went and bought this?'

'He didn't have to buy it. The bed was upstairs.' He smiled awkwardly. 'My mother used to call it the guest bed. It was never used.'

'What must he think?' Pulling her hand away from his she stared at him angrily. 'What must he think of me?'

'Why should he think anything?'

'Because of that bed! Doesn't it tell him what to think?'

'I told him the other bed was uncomfortable.'

'So you say! I bet he had a right good laugh.'

'A laugh? Is it funny?'

She looked away from his angry gaze. 'It's humiliating.'

Mick snorted. Manoeuvring his chair around he said, 'For God's sake, sit down. I'm not asking you to test its springs just yet.' He lit a cigarette and wheeled himself towards the open French windows. 'I was thinking we could go out, later. It's a lovely day and there's a band playing in the park.'

'Have you told Patrick about us?'

'No.'

Going to stand in front of him she said, 'Promise me.'

'I promise.' He looked down at his cigarette. 'What do you

take me for?'

'I know how close you are.' She heard Patrick moving about in the room above them and glanced up. 'Maybe he's guessed, anyway.'

'Maybe. Would it really matter? Are you ashamed of us, now?'

'No …' She sighed. 'It was seeing that bed. It's as if you're taking it for granted.'

'It?' He smiled slowly. 'I wouldn't take it for granted, Hetty. I'm far too amazed.'

'Amazed? I'm amazing now, am I?'

'You, *it*. Come here.' He cupped her cheek, drawing her down so that their faces were level. Kissing her he murmured, 'The bed *is* very comfortable …' He kissed her more deeply. 'We could test it, if you wanted.'

'I thought you wanted to go out?'

'We've all afternoon.' His eyes searched hers, smiling. Above them Patrick's footsteps sounded heavily and Mick grinned. 'Lock the door.'

She remembered the first time, how she had helped him on to the narrow single bed before taking off her blouse and camisole and kneeling beside him. As he tentatively touched her breast she kept her eyes fixed on the wall, shy of him now, afraid to glimpse below his waist. She knew that he had unbuttoned his fly, that his hand was moving frantically to bring himself to climax. She heard him cry out and felt his hand fall away from her breast; she lay down and rested her head on his chest, listening to the dramatic thud of his heart and breathing in the soft, musk scent.

After a while he'd said, 'I'm sorry.'

She looked up at him. His eyes were closed and he'd covered his face with his forearm. Reaching up she took his hand. 'We were both scared, I think.'

He made a noise like a laugh. '*Scared*. I'm still shaking.' Lowering his arm to look at her he said, 'That was horrible, wasn't it? For you, I mean. I'm sorry.'

'It's all right.'

'Let me hold you.' He moved on to his side so that they faced each other, their noses almost touching. Pressing his hand against her cheek he said, 'Your breasts are beautiful. I knew they would be. *You're* beautiful, my beautiful, sweet girl. How did I live without you?' He kissed her. 'I love you.' After a while he said hesitantly, 'It really wasn't that you felt sorry for me, was it?'

'No!' She frowned at him and he touched her mouth as if to silence any further protest, smiling in relief.

Lying in his arms now, in the new big bed, Hetty kissed his chest. 'You're so handsome, you know? The most handsome man I've ever seen.'

He laughed. 'What brought that on?'

'I've always thought so.'

'Have you? Astonishing.' He rested his hand lightly on her head. 'Hetty, on my desk there's a letter addressed to me. Would you fetch it?'

She got up, padding naked across the room, aware of his eyes on her. Smiling to herself she picked an envelope up from the desk and turned to him. 'Is this it?'

'Yes.' He held his hand out. 'Now come back to bed. I want to read it to you.'

She weighed the letter speculatively in her hand. 'It feels important.'

'It is. Now come here.'

As she climbed into bed again he sat up and reached for his glasses from the table. Hooking the frames around his ears he cleared his throat and for a moment he looked embarrassed. 'I've been keeping something from you.'

Anxiously she said, 'Oh? What?'

'It's nothing to worry about. It's foolish, really. Well, not foolish, exactly … I've been writing …'

'Writing? Who to?'

'No, not letters. Poetry.' He coloured. 'I've been writing poetry. I sent some poems away to a magazine.'

'Oh …' She smiled at him uncertainly, relief mixing with surprise. 'And they've written back to you?'

'Yes. They've written back to me.' He glanced at her from the letter. 'Several times. They wanted to see more, so I sent more.' After a long pause he laughed. 'They're talking about publishing a volume, a *slim* volume, but a volume, nevertheless.'

'Of your poems?'

'Yes.'

'Well … that's good. Lovely …'

'They're going to pay me, Hetty. I've actually earned some money!'

'Well done. I'm really pleased.'

Taking off his glasses he looked at her. 'Well, I think it's exciting, anyway.'

'So do I!'

'Then you might act as though you do.'

'I'm surprised! You never mentioned anything, not even that you wrote.'

'I wanted to keep it to myself … if I'd failed …'

'Failed?'

'If no one had wanted them … anyway, now I've told you. Now you know. I write. It keeps me sane when you're not here.'

'What do you write about?'

'The war.'

'Oh.'

'I tried to write about other things but it was all terrible, sub-Wordsworth stuff. And it's all I know, isn't it? War. And butchering, I suppose. Not too many good poems in a pig's innards, though.'

'But there are in men's?'

'Yes.' He gazed at her. 'You think I shouldn't exploit it? I'll write about how lovely the spring flowers are, shall I? Not upset anyone.'

'Are your poems upsetting?'

He was silent, reaching for his cigarettes and lighting one. Hetty watched him until he met her eye. At last he said, 'I didn't write them to upset people. I know you lost your brother …' After a while he said, 'I wrote things as I remembered them.'

Hetty lay down. She tried to imagine him writing, settling himself at the desk with paper and pens and realised she didn't even know what his handwriting looked like. She imagined poets as dishevelled and eccentric, their desks littered with papers. Mick's desk was almost bare. She imagined he kept its drawers locked.

'I knew you liked to read, but writing poetry …'

'It's quite common, really. Lots of men scribbled away – the trenches were chock-a-block with poets.'

'Did you write then?'

'I've always written.'

She thought of the poetry she learnt in school, lines learnt by rote that left her feeling hollow with boredom. She remembered the empty hours staring at the strange formation of words on paper, listening to the drone of her teacher's voice, the beat of his ruler on his desk as he kept time. Agitated by the recollection she got up suddenly and began to dress.

Mick said, 'Don't you want to hear what the letter says?'

'It says they want your poems, doesn't it?'

He tossed the letter down on the bed. 'That just about sums it up, yes.'

'Do you want to go out?' She buttoned her skirt. 'I think it's a good idea. The fresh air will do you good.'

She felt his eyes on her as she finished dressing. At last he said, 'I thought you'd be excited. Pleased, at least.'

'I am. I'm pleased for you.'

'It's the most exciting thing that's ever happened to me.'

She laughed without thinking. 'Is it?'

'Apart from you.'

Turning to him she said, 'Do you want to wear your suit? If the band's playing everyone will be out in their Sunday best.'

'Hetty, don't be like this.'

'Like what?'

'I don't know … brittle.'

'Brittle? What does that mean? Is that a poet's word?'

'You know what it means.'

'No. I'm not as clever as you.'

'Oh Hetty, you're brighter than anyone I know.'

'Bright! I left school when I was thirteen.'

'So?'

'So? I don't understand poetry, Mick. I don't understand it and it makes me feel stupid. So there. Now *you've* learnt something about me.' Snatching his clothes from the floor she tossed them on the bed. 'Here. Let's get you dressed.'

'Hetty.' He caught her hand, holding it tightly as she tried to pull away. 'Hetty, I haven't changed into someone else since this morning. I still love you. The only thing that's changed is that now perhaps I can be more independent financially. I'll have a little bit more than just my army pension …' Taking her other hand he held them both between his own. 'Do you still love me?'

'I should, shouldn't I?'

'Should?'

Looking away she felt herself blush. 'If I didn't I couldn't do what we do … and you don't just stop loving someone, just like that.'

'Not even if they tell you they write poetry?'

She smiled. 'Not even then. Come on, get dressed up in your suit and let's go and see this band.'

From his bedroom window Patrick watched Hetty push his brother along the street towards the park. In the distance he could hear the brass band playing a marching tune he felt he should know the name of but didn't. The tune reminded him of square-bashing and he drew the curtains in an attempt to muffle the sound. It made no difference and he went to lie on his bed, wondering how he would kill the hours until Mick came home. Looking at the box of Paul's letters by his bed he reached out and trailed his fingers across the ragged tops of the envelopes.

Choosing one at random he switched on his bedside lamp and turned the letter over in his hands. He'd read them all, many times, and recognised this one from the way it had been opened: a ragged tear ran through *A*'s surname, disfiguring the letter *s*. *A* must have been desperate to get to the letter inside; there were greasy fingerprints along the bottom of the envelope, as though he had interrupted his breakfast to open it. Patrick thought of *A* standing in that filthy kitchen, pausing briefly before tearing the envelope almost in half in his haste. Closing his eyes, Patrick tossed the letter down.

He thought of asking Paul about *A* every time he saw him and every time the question wouldn't come. Usually they made love almost at once, Paul slow and sensual, calming him, making him take all the time they had. During this long, sweet process there could be no question of talking.

He could have asked about *A* in the pub, he supposed. Dropped it casually into the conversation between the plink, plink, plinks of the piano. He had thought about it, thought of asking, *Who was best man at your wedding?* He imagined Paul's quizzical look, that smile of his that still brought on the stirring of a hard-on even while making him feel stupid.

Often he told himself that Paul couldn't possibly be seeing this man. He had a wife he seemed to love, and he had himself, enough sex for anyone. More often he believed that Paul did see him and the jealousy kept him awake at night. He would turn on the light then and re-read the letters because oddly they were reassuring. When he wasn't writing about what was going on in France Paul wrote like an adolescent with a crush on his teacher. His words seemed to clamour for *A*'s attention, suggesting to him that *A* could barely summon the interest to write more than a few lines in reply. It made him want to smash the man's face in for his callousness but it also made him believe that the relationship was doomed. He thought about *A* outside the church on Paul's wedding day. He'd looked as though he'd rather be a thousand miles away.

Restlessly he got up and went to the window, drawing back the curtains and opening the sash. He leaned out, listening for the band and trying to pick out the tune. Eventually he recognised it: *The Merry, Merry Month of May*. He smiled to himself. With sudden decisiveness he closed the window. He'd follow Mick and Hetty to the park – a normal, Sunday thing to do.

Chapter Twenty-three

MARGOT'S ANKLES WERE SWOLLEN and her wedding ring cut into her finger. The midwife had told her the baby's head was engaged and she pondered this odd expression as she walked slowly, arm in arm with Paul, along past the cemetery and Parkwood towards the park and the sound of the brass band. She wished she didn't feel so ponderous, like a great seedpod about to burst.

Behind them a voice called, 'Paul! Margot! Wait for us!'

Adam Mason smiled as he walked towards them, a young woman following closely. Breathlessly he said, 'We thought it was you two!'

She had seen Adam only once or twice since the wedding and had hardly spoken more than a dozen words to him since. Now he was smiling at her as though they were the closest of friends. He turned to the girl behind him. 'Emma, you know Paul, don't you, from school? This is his wife, Margot Harris. Emma is one of our French teachers, Margot.'

'Pleased to meet you, Margot.' Emma linked her arm through Adam's. 'It's a lovely day, isn't it? Adam and I thought it was perfect weather for a stroll in the park.'

The girl was slight as a boy, neat in a grey two-piece and a matching hat. Her skirt skimmed her calves fashionably and Margot noted that her shoes and handbag matched and that she wore the slightest suggestion of lipstick. She looked severe and clever at once and she felt huge beside her. Self-consciously she moved even closer to Paul as though he might shield her from the girl's condescending smile.

Paul said, 'We're going to the park, too, if you'd like to join us.'

'But we're slow.' Margot laughed awkwardly. 'You'd have to drag your feet …'

The girl said, 'Oh, we don't mind, do we, Adam?'

'Of course not. It will give us more time to enjoy the air.'

Paul stopped to light a cigarette, allowing Margot and Emma Hargreaves to walk a little further ahead of them. He smiled at Adam who looked away sheepishly. 'So, what's this about, then?'

'It isn't about anything. She lives in one of those bleak boarding houses on Jesmond Terrace. I felt sorry for her spending every weekend alone, she's homesick.'

'You're not courting, then?'

'No!'

Paul smiled at Adam's look of horror. Because he was so easy to tease he said, 'She's a lovely girl. You could do a lot worse – should I be thinking about buying Margot a new hat?'

'What?'

'For your wedding.'

'Do you think that's funny? Is that your idea of a joke?'

'No – I only thought …'

Adam shook his head angrily. 'You think I'd get married? You really think I could be as immoral and faithless as you are?'

There was such venom in his voice Paul stepped back. Adam was glaring at him. 'I'm sorry,' Paul said. 'I didn't mean to upset you.'

'*Upset me?* You think you still have the power to upset me? You don't know anything about me! So, I'll tell you some home truths, shall I? I'd never marry! I wouldn't treat women as you do – I wouldn't be so bloody cruel!' There was a thread of spittle hanging from Adam's mouth and he wiped it away with the back of his hand, his eyes blazing. 'You know – *you're* the joke! You're the one who can't decide whether he's fish or bloody fowl! You should grow up and realise you can't have all the sweets in the fucking sweet shop!' All at once he turned away and ran to catch up with the two women.

Hetty parked Mick's chair at the end of the last row of deck chairs. 'Here will have to do.'

'Here's fine. Sit down and stop fussing.'

'I'm not fussing.' She sat down gingerly, never fully trusting of folding chairs. 'It would've been nice to get closer to the bandstand, that's all.'

A family of children turned to stare at Mick. Hetty poked her tongue out at them then said loudly, 'There should be places reserved for veterans. Veterans should get special treatment.'

'Be quiet!' Mick glared at her. With quiet intensity he hissed, 'Don't call me a veteran. You make me sound like some decrepit old soldier.'

A man in front hushed them and Mick stared at him angrily. As he turned away Mick tapped him on the shoulder. 'Are we bothering you?'

'What?'

'I know you heard me because you've got extra sensitive hearing, but I'll ask again: are we bothering you?'

'Yes, so shove off.'

'Say that again.'

The man laughed. 'Shove off, you bloody freak, you're frightening the kids.' He turned away and Hetty watched anxiously as the colour drained from Mick's face.

She touched his hand. 'Ignore him, he's ignorant.'

Mick leaned forward in his chair and hooked the man around the throat with his right arm, dragging him backwards. The man's deck chair collapsed and he gasped in shock as Mick hauled him up by the neck, bringing his face close to his own. 'What did you call me?'

The man's children began to cry. Pulling uselessly at his arm, Hetty said, 'Mick, please, let him go!'

'Major, can I help, at all?' Paul Harris squatted down beside Mick's chair, placing a hand on his free arm. 'Sir, perhaps you should let him go, he's going a funny colour.'

Mick snorted, releasing his grip. The man stumbled to his feet, rubbing at his throat and glaring at Hetty. 'You should keep him under lock and key – he's a bloody maniac!'

Standing up straight Paul Harris said to the man, 'Perhaps you should take yourself off to the hole you crawled out of while you still can.' To Mick he said gently, 'Are you all right, sir?'

Mick didn't look at Paul but stared after the man's retreating back. Curtly he said, 'There's nothing wrong with me. You can go now.'

Hetty laughed, embarrassed by his rudeness. Over Mick's head she smiled apologetically, only for Mick to turn on her. 'Don't you dare humour me! Take me home.'

'Yes, all right.' She sighed. 'I'll take you home.' As she pushed Mick's chair past Paul she mouthed, 'Thank you.'

He smiled and she noticed how frail he looked. She glanced back at him. He was lighting a cigarette, watching them.

Emma said, 'Well! That was horrible.'

Margot looked at Paul anxiously. 'Are you all right?'

'Yes,' Adam said. 'You shouldn't get involved with people like that.'

Angrily Paul said, 'Didn't you hear? He called him a freak! I couldn't just sit here.'

Emma laughed. 'He seemed to be handling it quite well on his own.'

Paul looked at her in disgust. To Adam he said, 'And what do you mean, people like that? He was a major during the war.'

Under his breath Adam said, 'But the war's over now.'

'I'm sorry?' Paul frowned at him. 'Maybe you should speak up.'

'I said the war's over now. We should all start behaving like civilised human beings.'

'Really? Well, if men who've lost both legs fighting for *civilised human beings* weren't called freaks perhaps we might.' He turned to Margot. 'I think we should go home.'

He was walking too quickly and Margot stopped trying to keep pace and said, 'Paul, slow down.'

He stopped. Still angry he said, 'Sorry. Are you all right?'

'Are you?' Concerned by his paleness she said, 'You look ill.'

'I always look ill.'

'Should we stop at your father's house? We could catch our

breath and have a cup of tea.'

'I'd rather go straight home.'

'I just thought –'

'Dad only worries. He'll guess something's happened and start worrying.'

They were walking along the path leading to the park's main gate. Ahead of them Margot saw the girl from the butcher's shop pushing the major's wheelchair. The girl stopped and seemed to re-arrange the blanket covering what was left of his legs. Margot shuddered involuntarily and Paul turned to her. 'I'd like to introduce you.'

'Oh, Paul.' She frowned. 'I don't know …'

'Come on.' Holding her hand firmly he led her towards them.

Paul said, 'Major, I'd like you to meet my wife, Margot.'

The man glanced up. Sullenly he said, 'Mrs Harris. How do you do?'

'I'm fine, thank you.'

The girl smiled too brightly. 'Well, the baby must be almost due, is it?'

'Hetty! For God's sake don't start embarrassing her again.'

Margot blushed. 'No, it's all right. Yes, due next week.'

'I hope it goes well for you.' He looked at her. 'I wish you luck.'

Hetty smiled awkwardly. To the major she said, 'Come on, then, you. Let's get you home before you cause any more trouble.'

Almost at the park gates Patrick had changed his mind about going to see the band. They had started to play *Tipperary* and he imagined the soft, sentimental faces of the crowd and their maudlin voices as they sang along. He would feel like punching them until they stopped.

The tune followed him down the lane of Victorian villas that backed on to the park. When he came to the last of these houses, the oldest and grandest, he stood looking up at its blank windows. Paul had been born in one of its rooms that overlooked the cemetery. He thought of him working in the garden and remembered the letters. He'd written about the garden often, with each new season remembering what was about to come into its own, the words so poignant that sometimes he found he couldn't read on. He would picture Paul then in tin hat and great coat, caked in mud or soaked with rain, shivering and blowing on his hands as he lined the men up for inspection.

There was a gate in the garden wall and Patrick pushed against it, expecting it to be bolted. It creaked open, the swollen wood catching on the ground. Pushing harder, Patrick saw that the gate led on to a kitchen garden, neglected and overgrown and screened from the rest of the garden by a copper hedge and tall trees. Glancing over his shoulder Patrick edged through the narrow opening.

He stood on the threshold and looked around. In a cleared space was the remains of a bonfire and he walked towards it, turning over the ashes with the side of his foot until a smell of autumn hung incongruously on the late spring air. A robin hopped closer; it seemed expectant. He smiled to himself. The bird probably missed the harvest of worms and insects Paul disturbed as he worked. He closed his eyes, breathing in the scents of his garden. He missed him with a sweet longing that was every bit as sentimental as *Tipperary*.

Watching Paul inspect the men's feet, Thompson had said softly, 'Ever fancy it?'

Patrick had made himself smile. Looking down at the stub of cigarette burning between his fingers he laughed. 'You're a dirty-minded bastard, Bill. If I didn't know better I'd say you were bloody obsessed with him.'

For once the weather had been warm and dry, the sun beat down on their heads, the stink of sweat only partly camouflaged by the smoke from their cigarettes. They leant against the sandbag wall, feeling the drying sand shift and give against their weight. A bird sang, a short, surprising burst of noise. Paul crouched to examine another foot. Thompson said, 'He's a good lad for all that he's a fucking shirt-lifter, a sight better than the other lazy bastards.'

Patrick said, 'He's too soft on the men.'

'Aye, well.' Thompson crumbled what little remained of his cigarette between his fingers and pushed himself away from the sandbags. 'Unlike you and me, Patrick lad, he feels sorry for the poor buggers.'

It was true he'd felt little for anyone except Paul. Men were killed and were replaced. He had stopped crossing himself whenever he saw a corpse. When the earth released a bloated body to bob in a flooded shell-hole, when he saw the remains of men and horses scattered along straight, poplar-lined lanes, he only thanked God that it wasn't him, that he was still alive to keep Paul safe.

There was a noise and the robin flew into the hedge. A few yards away a youthful-looking middle-aged man in shirtsleeves stared at him.

'You're trespassing.' The man's voice was exactly like Paul's. Stepping towards Patrick he said evenly, 'If you're looking for work I've nothing for you.'

'Are you Doctor Harris?'

Paul's father frowned. 'Yes.'

'I'm a friend of your son's.'

'Paul? He isn't here. He doesn't live here any more.' He came closer, obviously curious. Patrick was surprised by how young he was, forty-five at most, his hair still thick and dark like Paul's, his eyes the same startling green. He smiled Paul's smile. 'Were you in the army with my son?'

'Yes.' Patrick looked away, unsure of what to do next. The doctor was slight like Paul and he felt big and clumsy beside him, a man easily mistaken for a casual labourer. The robin hopped down from the hedge and he watched it, feeling the weight of the other man's gaze.

Gently, as though he was a child, Doctor Harris said, 'Won't you tell me your name?'

'Jenkins.' Patrick looked at him. 'Anthony Jenkins.'

He nodded, although he didn't seem to recognise the name. Suddenly he said, 'Look, come into the house and have a cup of tea. I was doing a spot of gardening but frankly I hate it, you'd be doing me a favour by dragging me away.' He turned towards the house. 'I have a fruit cake that's begging to be eaten.'

He was shown into the kitchen, a huge, cluttered room, neglected and dingy. Newspapers fanned out on the floor beside an armchair and a half-empty bottle of whisky and a sticky-looking tumbler stood on the hearth. On the mantelpiece was a framed photograph of Paul and his brother. Patrick picked it up, smiling at the artful, back-to-back pose.

He heard George laugh. 'That's Paul's brother in the picture with him – I suppose you guessed. Two peas in a pod, Rob and Paul, everyone said so.' Taking the picture from him he replaced it on the mantelpiece. Without emotion he said, 'My eldest son was killed in an accident.' Turning away he said briskly, 'Tea. Tea and cake. Please, sit down, make yourself at home.'

Patrick sat on the armchair, trying not to look around too obviously. He would have liked to explore the whole house and imagined walking from room to room, opening cupboards and drawers, searching for sides of Paul he suspected he kept hidden. Already he'd realised that the ordered, elegant home he'd imagined Paul growing up in was nowhere near the reality, and that his father was nothing like the old, fussing man he'd pieced together from the little Paul had told him. He smiled to himself, searching his pockets for his cigarettes. He hadn't expected George to be fanciable.

'You smoke, too? Why do all you young men smoke?' Doctor Harris sighed. 'No, don't answer that. I know.' Setting a tray of tea on a side table he said, 'Paul smokes like a chimney. I never see him without a cigarette these days.'

'How is he?'

'Oh, you know.' Sitting down in the chair opposite he said, 'I suppose you know he was wounded? That he lost an eye?'

Patrick nodded.

'He copes all right with that. His nerves are terribly bad, though.' He glanced at him. 'I suppose that's something else you'd know all about, Anthony?'

Patrick smiled. 'My nerves are pretty bad, too.'

'Sometimes I look at Paul and wonder if perhaps they should have kept him in hospital even longer.' He laughed lightly. 'I'm sorry, you didn't come here to listen to my worries.'

'I'm sure he appreciates your concern.'

'Oh, he doesn't! He thinks I fuss. Least said soonest mended, that's Paul. If you ask Paul everything's *fine*. Even when it obviously isn't.'

He poured the tea and handed him a cup and a plate of dark, moist cake. 'Did you know Paul was married at Christmas?'

'Married?'

'He obviously doesn't write to you?'

Patrick sipped his tea. Placing the cup in its chipped saucer he said, 'No, we lost touch after he was wounded.'

'Were you over there long?'

'Three years.' Patrick stood up. 'May I use your bathroom, Doctor Harris?'

Patrick stood in the bedroom he'd decided was Paul's. The bed had been stripped to its mattress; the wardrobe doors hung open revealing only a few coat hangers; dust had settled on the wooden floor and dulled the colours of the Persian rug. He sat down on the bed and stared towards the sash window. A horse chestnut tree grew close to the house, blocking the sunlight and tapping its heavy, candle-like blossoms against the glass. Beside him was a pillow and he picked it up and hugged it to his body. He closed his eyes, breathing deeply to catch Paul's scent, remembering.

They had waited in position for almost an hour before dawn, sinking into soft mud with the weight of equipment on their backs. The porridge in Patrick's belly had become an anchor, holding him fast to the earth. He imagined standing up, as he must in a few minutes, imagined that it would be a slow, unwieldy business, graceless and panicked. In truth he knew he'd be first to his feet when the signal came, that he'd run faster than anyone – a devil, Thompson called him, swept on the gales of hell. He closed his eyes, more scared than ever. He crossed himself.

Paul crawled on his belly towards him, slowly making his way down the line, whispering encouragement and stopping occasionally to check on individual men. He stopped for a little while with Cooper. Patrick was certain he was praying with the boy, and knew it would be a short, sensible Anglican prayer. Paul squeezed Cooper's shoulder as though murmuring a final benediction. He moved towards him and Patrick held his breath.

'Sergeant Morgan ...' For a moment they pressed themselves further into the mud as a machine gun opened fire. When it ended he felt Paul's hand on his shoulder. 'All right, Sergeant?'

'Sir.'

'The cooks are bringing hot tea down the line. Shouldn't be long now.'

'The tea or the off, sir?'

'Both.'

'Good luck, Lieutenant Harris.'

Paul smiled at him. 'I'll see you in the German trenches, Sergeant.'

He remembered that Cooper bled to death in his arms, his blood soaking his tunic so that later he would pick off the dry crust, noticing how it cracked into crazy-paving patterns beneath his busy fingers. Cooper's blood stayed beneath his fingernails for days, and sometimes he imagined it was pigs' blood, that he hadn't been clean since the slaughtering in the shop's yard. He remembered that in the German trench Paul had used his pistol to shoot the machine gunner and that he seemed not to notice the blood and brains that splashed his face. Worse than the noise and confusion, worse than Cooper's bloody, silent death, was his fear for Paul, the terror of having two lives to lose instead of one.

From the bedroom doorway Paul's father said, 'Have you seen enough?' Patrick looked at him blankly, he had forgotten where he was for a moment, and the doctor said coldly, 'You knew Paul well, didn't you? Is it still going on?'

'I'm sorry.' Patrick stood up, the pillow falling at his feet. 'I should go ...'

Doctor Harris stood aside, allowing him through the door. As Patrick brushed past him he said, 'Leave my son alone. He's married now. His wife's expecting their child. Leave them be.'

Without looking back Patrick ran down the stairs and out of the house.

*   *   *

Mick said, 'Where the fuck have you been?'

'Is it any of your fucking business?'

'Well, I know where you haven't been. I know you haven't been buggering that vile little queer. I know that much at least.'

Patrick sighed. 'Mick, just keep your disgusting mouth to yourself.'

'Do you want to know how I know?' Wheeling his chair close to him, Mick smiled slyly. 'You do. I can see it. Desperate to know. Well, I saw him. Him and that sweet little wife of his. She looks about ready to drop. Funny, he doesn't look capable of screwing a woman, let alone getting one up the stick.'

Patrick turned away from him. 'How was Hetty? What did she think of the new bed?' Lighting the gas beneath the kettle he glanced at him. 'I hope you're careful – it's surprising who's capable of getting a woman up the stick.'

'And it's surprising who isn't! Christ! Who would have thought that a brother of mine –'

Patrick laughed. Grasping the sides of the wheelchair he brought his face up close. 'Who'd have thought it, eh, Mick? A brother of yours! Jesus – the great Major Morgan has a fucking fairy for a brother! It's just not on, is it?'

'You make me sick.'

Patrick straightened up. 'I make myself sick.'

'Then stop! There are women who'd give their eye-teeth to be with you.'

'I know. I'm gorgeous. They make great big eyes at me in the shop.' Rolling his eyes in impersonation he smiled bitterly. 'And you know what? They make me sick, as well. In fact if I think too hard about them I actually vomit.'

He began to make tea. As it brewed he buttered slices of bread, then went to the pantry for ham and pork pies. 'Are you hungry? I thought we'd have a Sunday tea, a proper Sunday tea like Mam used to make. I've made a blancmange, there're tinned pears, too.'

'Did you know his wife's expecting a baby?'

Patrick placed the plate of bread on the table. 'Yes, I know.'

'And doesn't that concern you at all?'

'No.'

'For pity's sake, Pat! Have you seen that poor girl lately?'

Patrick turned to face him. 'What do you imagine is going to happen, Mick? That he'll leave her? That we'll set up home together and humiliate her by walking down the street holding hands? He sees me for a couple of hours a week, the rest of the time he's with her.'

'It's still adultery, Patrick. And what if you're caught together? You'll both go to prison.'

'They won't catch us together.'

'People talk …'

'Talk!' Scornfully he said, 'I don't give them anything to talk about, Mick. You do, though. They talk about you and Hetty. Perhaps you should care more about her reputation than mine.' He poured out the tea. 'Come and sit at the table, have a ham sandwich.'

Mick ate in silence and from time to time Patrick studied him. It must have been seeing Paul's wife that triggered this righteous anger. For a moment he felt sorry for the girl, a feeling immediately taken over by his jealousy of her.

Pushing his plate away Mick lit a cigarette. 'I made a fool of myself today. Someone called me a freak so I tried to throttle him.'

'How is that making a fool of yourself?'

'Oh for Christ's sake – look at me, Pat! Picking a fight when I'm stuck in this bloody thing? I just made a show of myself. A fucking freak show.' He bowed his head, turning a box of matches over and over on the table. Softly he said, 'Do you remember when Dad burnt all my notebooks? Everything I'd ever written thrown on the fire, page by page. He made me watch, remember? My nose all bloody from the beating he'd given me. I felt like a freak, then. A freak for writing and a freak for not standing up to him.'

'We were sixteen, Mick. Don't you remember how frightening he was?'

'I felt so angry. So angry and all I did was stand there because I was so bloody scared of him. I never wanted to feel so helpless again. But now, here I am. Worse than helpless.' He laughed bleakly, stubbing out the cigarette. 'Do you know what the worst of it was? Your little *friend* Harris had to step in to save me, made me realise what an arse I was making of myself.' He glanced at Patrick. 'Quite commanding in his way. I could almost understand what you see in him.'

'What? In a whey-faced little pansy?'

'Well, he does look like he needs a bloody good dinner inside him. Is he ill? He looks ill.'

'He's fine.'

'Just so long as you can bugger him, eh?'

Patrick stood up and began clearing the table. Catching his arm Mick said, 'You'll be careful, you and him, won't you? Promise me you'll be careful.'

'I promise.'

He nodded. Releasing his arm Mick said, 'Leave this now. Let's go out for a drink. I feel like getting pissed.'

Chapter Twenty-four

HETTY WATCHED HER MOTHER wrap the matinee jacket and bootees she'd crocheted. 'There,' Annie said. 'That's neat enough, isn't it? You'll take it round to her later, won't you? Doesn't harm to be neighbourly.'

Hetty sighed. Reluctantly she said, 'Yes, all right. But you should take it, it's your hard work.'

'She'd rather have someone her own age to talk to. I wouldn't know what to say to someone like her.'

'She's not royalty, Mam. Her dad's only a vicar.'

'All the same.' Annie looked at her. 'The major told me you're going to see him this evening?'

'Yes.'

'That's nice, he gets tired of being on his own.' She smoothed the brown paper she'd used to parcel the baby's clothes. 'He seems to like you – it was *Hetty this* and *Hetty that* when I was giving him his dinner.'

Cautiously Hetty said, 'You like Mick, don't you?'

'The major? He's a gentleman.' Annie picked up the parcel and put it on the dresser. 'Set the table for us, pet. Your dad will be home for his tea soon.'

In her bedroom Hetty lay down on the bed. She remembered the first and last piece of advice her mother had ever given her. It had coincided with her first period: '*Never lie down with a man until you're married.*' She'd learnt more from dirty jokes amongst the girls at the sugar factory. She thought of Milly Jackson, weeping in the factory yard because the lad she had gone with had been killed at Ypres. Over and over she'd stressed that she'd only done it with him once. Only once and

211

now he was dead and she was expecting. The small band of women gathered round her tut-tutted in commiseration, not so much for the death of her lover, more for the fact she'd been so unlucky. *Once!* Behind the weeping girl's back the women smirked at each other.

She had lain down with Mick three times. After the second time they made love she had forced herself to look properly at his legs. The stumps looked as though they had been patched over with ragged scraps of flesh, each placed haphazardly on top of the other, the healed skin forming a mass of protective scars. She had touched his left thigh gently, just above where his leg had been amputated, watching his face. He had only smiled his extraordinary smile.

She knew why her mother didn't guess what was going on between them. To Annie he was a neutered man, one whose potential for getting a girl into trouble had been taken away along with his legs. Besides, no normal girl would want to *lie down* with a cripple. But when they were together his wheelchair was forgotten, although she knew that if it hadn't been for the chair she wouldn't have climbed into his bed until they were married. She closed her eyes, appalled all over again at the wanton way she behaved when she was with him and the excuses she made to herself. Nothing was normal, the war had seen to that, so she slept with Mick because she wanted him, because the opportunity was there and no one suspected enough to call her a slut. And because she loved him, of course. She opened her eyes, listening to her mother's bangs and clatters from the kitchen. She loved him, and that wasn't an excuse, it was a reason.

Margot Harris smiled over the little jacket and held up each bootie in turn to admire it. She smiled as she folded the garments back into their paper and reminded Hetty once again to thank her mother for her kindness.

'Would you like a cup of tea?' Margot began to get up but her movements were awkward and Hetty stood up quickly.

'I'll make it.'

'Oh, don't bother. I hate tea these days, I don't think we

even have any milk, anyway.'

'Would you like a glass of water?'

'I'd like a cigarette but I've none left. I'm desperate for Paul to come home just so I can smoke his.'

'You smoke?'

'Awful, isn't it? I don't think Paul minds.' She glanced around the untidy kitchen. 'He doesn't mind anything, really.'

Hetty sat down again. After an awkward silence she said, 'It was good of Paul to help us on Sunday.'

'Your friend didn't think so.'

'Mick was upset, I'm sorry he was so rude.'

Margot laughed oddly. 'I didn't want him to step in like he did. I wanted someone else to do it. But it seems he *has* to take responsibility for everything.' She creased her face suddenly, pressing her hand to her side. 'Ouch. Little monkey's never still.'

'Are you all right?'

'I think so.' She smiled. 'Don't look so worried.'

'Do you want me to stay until your husband gets home?'

'There's no need. I've got days to go yet.' Shyly she added, 'But stay, if you like, I don't have many visitors. I'm sorry I can't offer you any tea.'

'That's all right.' Nodding at Margot's bulging waist she said, 'Do you think it's a boy or a girl?'

'A boy, he kicks so hard. Here.' Taking Hetty's hand she pressed it against her body. Hetty felt a balled fist punch at her and she laughed, meeting Margot's gaze.

'You must be excited now it's so near.'

'Yes, I suppose I am. Paul is.'

'He looked so proud of you on Sunday.'

'Did he?' She looked down, picking at a snagged thread in the tablecloth. 'Well, I'm proud of him.' Looking up she asked, 'Have you known your friend long?'

'Mick? Not long, really.'

'I remember him at that dance at New Year, he looked so striking in his dinner jacket.'

'Mick likes expensive clothes. I think he misses his uniform.'

'I think Paul does, too.' Margot opened the paper and drew the baby's jacket towards her. Her fingers worried the lacy stitches around the jacket's hem. 'What's Mick's brother like? Paul sees quite a lot of him.'

'Patrick?' Hetty paused, not sure how she might describe him. She realised that despite working for him for almost a year she barely knew Patrick Morgan. Besides, since getting to know Mick she took no notice of Patrick, he seemed like a poor imitation in comparison.

Margot looked up at her. 'Patrick, yes. Tell me what he's like.'

Hetty was surprised by the sharpness in her tone; it was as though she was desperate to know. Disconcerted, Hetty said, 'We don't speak very much. He's quiet. He keeps himself to himself.'

Margot nodded and seemed to accept this poor description. At last she said flatly, 'He seems nice, anyway. Kind. A nice, kind man.'

The back door opened and Hetty looked up as Paul Harris walked in. He smiled in surprise. 'Hello, there.'

'Paul, this is Hetty, we met on Sunday in the park.'

'Yes, of course. How are you, Hetty?' He kissed his wife's cheek. 'Hello, sweetheart.'

Margot gave him such a shameless look of love that Hetty glanced away, embarrassed. Making an excuse she left.

Paul said, 'I promised I'd go for a drink with Patrick tonight, but if you like I'll stay here with you.'

'If you promised you should go.' She was frying bacon. 'You shouldn't break promises.'

'Not a promise, exactly. And I worry about you … look, why don't I walk you to your mother's? You can spend the evening with her and I'll come and collect you on my way home.'

'I'd rather be on my own – I'd know if the baby was coming tonight. In that book I borrowed from your father it says a woman knows instinctively …' She blushed. After a moment she said, 'Go, you know you always enjoy it.'

Paul laughed strangely and she frowned at him. 'You do, don't you?' When he didn't answer she prompted, 'You do enjoy seeing him, don't you?'

'For God's sake, Margot!' He gazed at her angrily. 'If you don't want me to go, I won't, it doesn't matter.' He lit a cigarette, his movements quick and impatient. Exhaling smoke he said harshly, 'You should go to your mother's, stop me worrying.'

She set a plate of bacon and eggs in front of him. 'All right, I'll go to Mummy's. If you're going to make such a fuss I'll go.'

'It will be a change for you.'

'Will it? A change to listen to her telling me how disappointed she is in me?'

He rested his cigarette on the ashtray as he began to eat, ready to smoke between each mouthful. 'Your mother's not that bad.'

She sat down. After a moment he pushed his half-eaten meal away and lit a fresh cigarette from the butt of the last. Wearily he said, 'Stay here, if you want, I'll only be gone an hour, two at most.'

'Aren't you going to finish your supper?'

'I'm not hungry.' He got up. 'If you don't mind I'll go now.'

Chapter Twenty-five

PAUL GOT UP FROM Patrick's bed. He was thirsty, a raging thirst that often came after sex and was made worse by supper's cheap, salty bacon. Naked, he went into the tiny room on the other side of the hall with its sink and single cold tap. Waiting for the water to run icy cold, he held on to the edge of the sink. Drops splashed his body, cooling him, and he stuck his face under the tap, swallowing greedily.

Patrick watched him from the doorway. Wiping his mouth with the back of his hand, Paul brushed past him into the bedroom and lay down on the bed.

Carefully Patrick said, 'Paul? Come on, you know I hate it when you're like this.'

'Like what? Too thoroughly fucked to talk to you? Just give me a minute.'

On the bedside table his own face looked out at him from a silver picture frame and Paul turned away to avoid its gaze. The photographer who'd taken the picture owned a magpie, tame as a canary, which had watched him from a perch behind the camera and talked in the high-pitched, grating voice of an effeminate inquisitor. The bird was a prop, showing off its metallic tail feathers in dull pictures of mothers and babies, soldiers and sweethearts. In France, in a photographer's studio, there existed a picture of himself and this bird, man and magpie holding the other's gaze as though spellbound. He hadn't wanted that picture, he'd remembered that birds were unlucky, and had bought only the one of him alone to send home. Keen to keep the magpie photograph, the photographer said it would be displayed in his window and titled *English Officer with Pica*.

The mattress dipped as Patrick lay down and Paul tensed in

case he should touch him. Patrick liked to hold him after sex, manhandling him roughly until he was comfortable, his body giving off too much heat and scent. Moving away from him he said, 'I have to go soon.'

'You've only just got here! You can't go.'

'I daren't leave Margot for long. She could have the baby at any time.' He lit a cigarette. 'I'll smoke this and then I'll go.'

Patrick sat up. Taking the cigarette from Paul he crushed it out between his fingers and tossed it on the floor. 'We haven't finished yet.'

'Yes, Patrick, we have.' He reached for his cigarettes again but Patrick caught his wrist, pinning his hand above his head.

'No, *Lieutenant*, we haven't.' He kissed him, forcing his tongue deep into his mouth. Still holding his hand above his head, he reached down with his other hand and grasped Paul's cock. He pulled his face away. 'You know how quickly I can make you hard again.'

'Patrick, please. Let me go.'

Patrick smiled slowly. 'You could always fight me off. Try it.' He gazed into Paul's face. 'You're not putting up much of a fight, Lieutenant Harris. Now I think that's because you don't want to go anywhere.'

Paul grasped his hair, jerking his head back. 'I said let me go.'

Patrick smiled. 'Hair pulling, that's a girl's game, isn't it?'

Digging his fingernails into Patrick's scalp Paul pulled his head back even further. Patrick released him, only to move quickly to kneel astride his body. With a hand on each of Paul's shoulders he kissed his mouth lightly. 'All right, if you're going to be in this mood I give in. You win.'

He lay down and lit two cigarettes. Passing one to Paul he said, 'Thanks for helping Mick the other day.'

Paul laughed shortly. 'We both made total fools of ourselves.' He thought of the way Adam had sneered at him, remembering that he had given him the same look the first time he'd seen him in uniform, as though he couldn't quite believe he would do something so brainlessly patriotic as join the army. 'Christ,' he'd said. 'All you need is to grow a moustache and you'll look like every other idiot in the country.'

On the High Street below the window a tram rattled by. The bed creaked as Patrick rolled on to his side to look at him.

'You and Mick would get on, if you met properly, you have things in common.'

'Like what?'

'You were both good soldiers.'

'He might have been.'

'He was. And so were you.'

'And so were you.' Paul got up and began to dress. Buttoning his shirt, he said, 'The three of us, good, brave and true. We all had a topping time.'

Patrick laughed. 'Do you remember when we came across that demolished shrine? You should have seen Bill Thompson's face when you flung the Virgin's head into the sky. He was so shocked. I don't know what shocked him most – that it was sacrilegious or that you were so angry. We'd never seen you angry before – poor little Collier almost burst into tears.' Patrick gazed at him. 'It rained so heavily that day. I just wanted to get you away somewhere dry and quiet and calm you down. Somewhere away from that bloody smirking Jenkins.'

The mention of Jenkins's name made Paul's heart race. Trying not to think about him, he fixed on the memory of that day, how they had been marching all afternoon in the rain before they came across the shell-blasted shrine to the Virgin. He had been at the head of the platoon and had stopped to make sure no one was lagging too far behind. Rain dripped from his helmet and the waterproof cape he wore; he was blinded by rain, made invisible by it. On either side of the road the poplar trees were no more than a grey colour wash, the fields beyond a flood plain. Hunched against the downpour the men filed past him. He'd called out encouragement and sounded like a parody of himself; the little reserve of strength he had left had dwindled almost to nothing. Jenkins had been with the platoon a month. A month had been all the time he'd needed to demolish him.

Draping his tie around his up-turned collar he saw that his hands were trembling cigarette ash to the floor. He felt Patrick's eyes on him.

Patrick smiled. 'Come back to bed? It's early yet.'

'I have to get back.'

'Oh, for Christ's sake!' Patrick sprang from the bed and crossed the room. Holding him at arms' length he frowned. 'Have I done something wrong?'

'No.'

'Then what is it?'

'Nothing! All right?' Paul shrugged him off. 'Don't talk about the past, that's all. I don't want to talk about it.'

'I'm sorry. It's just that sometimes I think it's the only thing we have in common.'

'We're queer, isn't that enough to have in common?'

'No! That's like saying – I don't know – two men have lots in common because they're on a sinking ship together … I want more than that …'

Paul stepped past him but Patrick caught his hand. He led him back to the bed and made him sit down. Sitting beside him he took his other hand and held them on his lap. After a while he cleared his throat nervously. 'I have a confession to make. I went with someone. A man I picked up.'

Paul sighed, wanting only to get away. Patiently he said, 'Patrick, you don't have to tell me – and don't feel guilty. I understand.'

'Don't you want me to be faithful?'

'How can I ask that of you?'

'I want you to. And I want you to be faithful to me, I don't want there to be any other men.'

'There aren't.'

'Is that the truth?' Searching Paul's face he said, 'The man I picked up had a picture of you by his bed. He kept a box of your letters from France beside it.'

Paul drew his hands away from Patrick's. He tried to picture Patrick and Adam in bed in that squalid room and found himself wondering how the fastidious Patrick had brought himself to lie down on Adam's sheets. He imagined the disgust that Patrick would have struggled to conceal once the sex was over. Feeling weary suddenly he lay down on the bed and pressed his hands into his eyes.

After a while, aware of Patrick watching him, he laughed bleakly. 'So, you slept with Adam. Well, ours is a small world, I suppose. Was it any good? He can lack imagination in bed, I find.' He lowered his hands to look at him. 'Although usually I forgive him – he tries so hard to be *good*.'

'You still see him.' Patrick sounded incredulous.

'Do you?'

'No!' Patrick stood up. 'No, for Christ's sake! It was once, months ago, before you and I started meeting here. Are you still going to his house? How often? Do you love him?'

'It's none of your business, Patrick.'

'Yes it is! Of course it is! I love you!' Standing up he said, 'Do you love him more than you love me?'

Wearily Paul said, 'Look, I have to go – I promised Margot –'

'Promise me you won't see him again.'

'I promise.'

'I don't believe you.'

'Then what can I say, Patrick?' Exasperated suddenly he said, 'Anyway, what does it matter?'

'It matters to me! Does he know about us?'

'No.'

'Should I tell him?'

'Oh for God's sake, Patrick. Listen, Adam's just Adam, I've known him for years.' He almost added that there was nothing between them any more because since Sunday it seemed true.

Patrick slumped down on the bed. He held his head in his hands and looked so defeated that Paul knelt in front of him. He touched his knee. 'Patrick? Come on, you knew I wasn't a blushing virgin.'

'Were there many before me?'

'A few –'

'A few?'

'Yes. I told you.'

Patrick met his gaze. 'Davies?'

'What?'

'Second Lieutenant Davies, the poor little sod who could never take his eyes off you. Did you seduce him?'

'*Seduce* him?' Paul stared at him in astonishment. 'For Christ's sake, Patrick – you make it sound as though it was a fucking debutantes' ball! Were we buggering each other between bombardments? Did I *miss* something?'

Patrick bowed his head again. 'I'm sorry. It was just a stupid rumour. I never believed it, not really.'

'Not *really*? Do you honestly think so badly of me? You know what things were like over there – you know what the boy was like …' He felt sick suddenly. He remembered how Davies always seemed about to cry, how he'd wanted to offer his usual hollow encouragement only to be repelled by his snivelling. Eventually he found he was unable to even look at him, afraid that the boy's weakness might break his own puny resolve. He knew that Davies watched his every move. Ironically he'd believed he'd hated him. Agitated he got up and walked across the room, only to turn to face Patrick again. 'What was said?'

'That you and he … it was rubbish, everyone knew it was a lie – I shouldn't have said anything, it was only because I felt so jealous –'

'What was said!'

Patrick hesitated. Avoiding his gaze he said quickly, 'That you were found together, in your bunk. It was nonsense, of course it was. Jenkins was a liar – no one believed what Jenkins said.'

Jenkins. Afraid his legs would buckle he leaned against the wall. Patrick got up and stood a few feet from him. Cautiously he said, 'Paul? Are you all right?'

Paul wanted to say yes, that there was nothing to worry about, that he could push Jenkins from his mind if he really tried hard enough, but the words wouldn't come. Jenkins was suddenly alive and in their room. Wanting to run, instead he felt Patrick pull him into his arms as though he thought he was going to fall.

At first the pains made her smile. At last something was happening and Margot paced round and round the kitchen table, occasionally using a chair to support herself through a contraction. She looked at the clock. Soon Paul would be home and he could ask their next-door neighbour to fetch the midwife. Excited and afraid at once, she stopped pacing to double up against a stronger pain. Her waters broke.

Margot stared at the stain spreading over the floor, truly scared now. She remembered what she'd discovered in the book on pregnancy and knew that she needed help. Between pains, she slowly made her way next door.

'Mam!' The child who answered her knock stared at her as he shouted for his mother. Supporting herself against the doorframe, Margot tried to smile at him. From the kitchen came the smell of steak and kidney pie and a woman wiping her hands on an apron. The woman frowned. 'What's up?'

'I think my labour's started.'

The child giggled, covering his mouth with his hand, and the woman clipped him round the head. Taking her arm she said, 'Come on, love, let's get you home. You'll be all right, I'll look after you.' She turned to the boy. 'Run round to Miss Rowe's, tell her to come straight away. You hear? Straight away.'

Helping her up the stairs her neighbour said, 'Where's that lad of yours?'

Margot gasped for breath, lowering herself painfully on to the bed. Finally able to speak she said, 'He should be here soon.'

'Do you want me to send Alfie to look for him when he's fetched the midwife?'

Another pain came and she clenched her body against it. As it passed she said, 'He'll be here … I'm sorry, I've forgotten your name.'

'Moira.' She smiled. 'Do you think that daft husband of mine has had the sense to turn the gas off on that pie?'

'I'm so sorry to be a nuisance.'

Moira laughed. 'Don't you worry about it!' Closing her eyes tight Margot felt the other woman's arm around her, helping her up the bed. 'Don't hold your breath, love, try and breathe, it'll soon be all over.'

Patrick led Paul to the bed and made him lie down. Kneeling on the floor he said, 'I thought you were going to faint. Are you all right?' When Paul didn't answer he said helplessly, 'Maybe have a sleep, eh? You'll feel better.' Paul closed his eyes and Patrick sat back on his heels, ready to watch over him on his knees all night as a penance for his jealousy, and for being such a fool as to mention that little bastard's name.

He remembered how Jenkins had whispered, 'I can't do this, Harris. I can't.'

They had just started out on a raid. Patrick saw Paul signal for him to stop and motion that he and the other men should stay where they were. Halfway across no-man's-land, Patrick tried to ignore the whispering going on between Paul and Jenkins and concentrate on the sequence of events he and Paul had planned that would give them the best chance of surviving the night. Jenkins had sat with them and Paul had patiently tried to explain each stage to him. He wouldn't listen. It was as if he didn't believe he would actually be made to do any of it. Patrick could see Paul despairing; he knew as well as he did that if they didn't work together it was more likely that one of them would be killed.

Even before they set out Patrick knew the venture was doomed. The men could see Jenkins working himself up into a state before they'd even left the trench and it made them jittery to imagine that an officer might bugger their chances. Sensing their disquiet, Paul had talked to the men individually, knowing each one well enough to personalise the reassurance. To him he had said only, 'Is there anything you feel we need to discuss again before we go, Sergeant?' He had shaken his head. He had known Paul wouldn't reassure him: they were in this together as equals.

Paul climbed the ladder over the top of the trench, followed by the men and then Patrick himself. Jenkins's fear radiated from him like a bad smell; when his turn came he froze on the first rung. After a moment Paul scrambled back down into the trench.

Patrick heard Jenkins's frantic whispering and crawled back. He peered down to see what was going on. In the darkness Paul's face was white but his hand held his pistol to Jenkins's temple steadily. Snivelling, Jenkins climbed the ladder.

In no-man's-land between the trenches, Collier turned to look at him and Patrick tried to reassure him with just a movement of his eyes. Pressing his body into the ground with an idea of muffling the terrible noise his heart was making, he saw that the rest of the men were still and silent as the ground itself. He thought of the bodies left after a battle and felt his flesh crawl as though the worms had made an early start on him. He began to pray, picturing the crucifix that was safe beneath his uniform.

Paul and Jenkins began moving towards him and Paul signalled that they should move on again. Again Patrick began to visualise the plan. He saw himself cutting the German wire and moving closer and closer towards their trench. He pictured the layout of the land they were crawling through and knew that in a few yards it would begin to slope. To their left was a shell hole marked by rusted wire and the ragged scraps of cloth that clung to the barbs. On windy days the cloth would flap like birds desperate to escape a trap and the eye was deceived into believing that there really was something alive in the waste the shells had made. Now, though, the air was still and the only movement he could see was that of the dark outline of the man ahead of him.

After a few feet he sensed something was wrong and looked back. Jenkins had stopped crawling. Once again Paul signalled that he and the others should stop, and once again he heard the same, frantic whispering. Patrick decided he would rather know what was going on than wait helplessly. He shuffled back until he found himself next to Paul.

With his mouth close to Patrick's ear Paul whispered, 'I can't get him to move!'

'What do you want to do?'

Before Paul could answer Jenkins was on his feet. In a half crouch he ran back towards their line.

The sniper's shot was too low. It hit Jenkins in the shoulder, knocking him off his feet and into the shell hole. Paul stared after him. After a moment he dropped his head to the ground, banging his forehead against the frozen mud and Patrick was scared he was about to lose his nerve, too. But at last he looked up. 'They'll know we're out here now. You and the men go back. I'll get Jenkins.'

'I'll help you, sir.'

Paul held his gaze and Patrick began to worry that he would insist on the order. At last, to his relief, he nodded. 'All right. Send the others back first.'

Kneeling beside Paul, Patrick kissed his head lightly. He remembered how Jenkins used to hum *The Boy I Love* under his breath whenever Paul was in earshot and how Paul would pretend not to hear although Patrick could see his body tense as well as Jenkins could. Often he thought about killing him, how, with a carefully planned accident, he could spare Paul his torment. His thoughts became elaborate fantasies in which Jenkins's death was replayed over and over. He told himself that one more death in the scheme of things wouldn't matter and, despite his creeping doubts, that fantasies didn't matter at all.

When he'd given the order for the others to return to their trench, Patrick had crawled back to the shell hole. He'd wondered at his heart's capacity to go on beating at such a pace and couldn't imagine it ever recovering to a normal beat. When the single shot sounded he thought for a moment that he was hit and he'd rolled into the shell hole, afraid of the pain to come. He'd found himself next to Jenkins's body. He remembered crossing himself cursorily, a habit he had thought he'd forgotten. He felt he should have said a prayer but he knew there was no point. Already the mud had begun to claim Jenkins; he might have been dead for centuries.

Paul placed his pistol back in its holster and looked at him as though challenging him to speak. He kept silent. After a moment, Paul leaned across the body and closed Jenkins's eyes.

Hetty slowed her usual fast walk as she neared home. She turned, hearing footsteps hurry behind her and saw the midwife and Alfie Simms. The little boy grinned at her. 'We're helping Mrs Harris have her baby.'

The midwife laughed. 'That's enough, Alfie. Mrs Harris

won't want the whole world to know.'

Surprised, Hetty said, 'I was only with her a couple of hours ago.'

They had reached Margot's open door. The midwife said, 'Come in, if you're her friend, then this young man's Mammy can get back to her family.'

Reluctantly Hetty said, 'I don't want to get in the way.'

The woman laughed, already climbing the stairs. 'Don't worry pet, I'll let you know if you do.'

Margot had stopped asking for Paul and had begun to cry for her mother. Feeling useless, Hetty said, 'It's all right. She'll be here soon.'

Heaving herself up the bed, her chin pressing hard on to her chest, Margot clutched Hetty's hand. She grunted, a deep, animal-like noise, her face red and sweaty with effort. The midwife smiled, looking up from between her splayed knees. 'Oh, you're a good brave girl! You'll have your baby in your arms in no time.'

'Oh God!' Margot cried. 'Oh God help me …'

All at once the bloodied baby was laid across Margot's belly, arms and legs flaying, screaming outrage at being forced out into the cold. Hetty laughed in astonishment and the midwife caught her eye and grinned with relief.

Paul got up. Beside the bed, Patrick scrambled to his feet but Paul ignored him and went into the kitchen. He splashed cold water on his face. His eyes were sore and he took out his false eye and held it under the running tap. Replacing it, he remembered how he had woken in a field hospital with bandages around his face and how he had panicked because, for a moment, he'd believed he was back in school and this blindness was some new trick of Jenkins's. Then he'd remembered that a shell had exploded as he and Sergeant Morgan were returning from the aborted raid and that suddenly he was covering his eyes with his hands and wouldn't allow anyone to prise them away. He'd remembered too that Jenkins was dead and that the relief he'd felt when his tormentor's body slumped against his had immediately become something else he had to keep at bay along with fear and cowardice and grief. It would be best to keep silent, he decided; there would be less chance of a breach in his defences.

Patrick said carefully, 'Paul? Are you going to be all right?'

Paul could see how frightened Patrick was; Patrick knew as well as he did that Jenkins had wrecked everything. Because there were no words to help he simply kissed him. 'I should go,' he said. 'Margot will be worried.'

The midwife hesitated at the front door. 'You'll stay with her until that husband of hers shows his face?'

'Yes.'

The woman sighed. 'The buggers like to keep out of the way until it's all over. They don't like to hear their wives suffering. It makes them feel guilty.'

Closing the door behind her Hetty looked up the stairs. She had left Margot dozing, the baby swaddled and asleep in the great ugly cot. The midwife had said to make her a cup of tea and so she went into the kitchen to put the kettle on, wondering if Paul Harris had thought to buy milk before he disappeared. She glanced at the clock on the dresser. It was only eleven o'clock. She'd been sure it was later.

She heard the front door open and went out into the hallway. Paul Harris frowned at her. 'Where's my wife?' There was panic in his voice and he looked past her into the kitchen. 'What's happened?'

'She had the baby –'

He was running up the stairs at once.

His eyes were swollen and he looked like he had been crying. Half asleep, Margot reached out and touched his face as he knelt beside the bed. He really was the most beautiful man, even when he cried. She wondered why he'd cried but it seemed not to matter now that he was here. She felt euphoric with relief and laughed, but it was a weak little noise and she felt it should have been louder. Paul smiled at her, fresh tears in his eyes that she wiped away. 'It's a boy.' Her voice was hoarse and too quiet so she repeated, 'A boy. I think we should call him Robert.'

Chapter Twenty-six

HETTY WATCHED FROM BEHIND the French windows as Patrick thrust the spade into the heavy clay of the flower bed, burying it deeply and with such force she wondered at the effortless way he lifted it out again. His sleeves were rolled up past his elbows, his muscles bulging with the effort of the work. The rose bush he was digging out trembled, scattering white petals at his feet. She thought of confetti and smiled to herself. Patrick stopped to wipe his brow with the back of his hand and caught her eye. He gazed at her coldly.

Mick said, 'Quite a specimen, isn't he?'

Startled, she turned round. Taking off his glasses Mick folded them in their case and looked out of the window at his brother. 'Pat's always turned heads. I've seen him walk down the High Street and half a dozen women have stopped to look at him go by.' After a while he turned to her. 'You know I'm afraid to tell him, don't you.'

'You'll have to tell him soon.'

They watched Patrick take off his shirt, unbuttoning it slowly as though he was aware of their eyes on him. The shirt was dropped to the lawn where it lay crumpled in the long grass. He stretched, arching his neck so that the curve of his throat was exposed to the sun. There were sweat patches on his vest; a crucifix nestled in his chest hair, too delicate a thing for such a broad, powerful man. Hetty turned away too quickly. Beside her Mick bowed his head, closing his eyes as though the sunlight hurt.

'I think I should go,' Hetty said. He nodded and she crouched beside his chair, covering his hand with hers. 'You'll tell him today, won't you, before we go to Mam's?'

'Yes.'

She kissed his cheek, imagining that Patrick had become the watcher.

Patrick washed his hands at the kitchen sink, lathering the soap and scrubbing the mud from beneath his fingernails. Soil always made him feel unclean; he hated the creatures that crawled through it, the worms recoiling from the cold of the spade, the fat slugs contracting to hide their underbellies. He had come across a dead blackbird, maggots gleaming beneath its body. His nostrils flared in disgust as he remembered. Behind him Mick said, 'You've caught the sun on your shoulders, you should rub on calamine lotion, stop it getting sore.'

'I'm all right.' He scooped up handfuls of water to wash the sweat from his face. Groping for the towel he asked, 'Has Hetty gone?'

'Yes.'

He threw the towel down. 'What do you want to eat?'

'I'm not hungry. Sit down, I'll make us a cup of tea.'

'I'll do it. It takes you three times as long.'

'You've left your shirt in the garden.'

'It was hot out there.'

Mick lit a cigarette. Looking down at it he said, 'I've asked Hetty to marry me. She said yes.'

'Really? Well, well, brave little woman! Good for her.' He pulled out a chair and sat down, turning Mick's box of matches over and over on the table in front of him. Sensing Mick's anxiety he glanced at his brother. 'It's all right, Mick. I won't hang around getting in the way. You can have the house, you and Hetty.'

'It's your house, too, we thought we could divide it, you could have the upstairs –'

'I don't think so, Mick.'

'You could live above the shop.'

Thinking how cold and lifeless those rooms were without Paul in them Patrick laughed bleakly.

Mick said, 'I love her, Patrick. If it wasn't for her, well … I can't believe she's taken me on.'

'Oh, you're a handsome bastard, Mick, I'm sure that has something to do with it.'

He looked down at the box of matches, thinking of Paul and the first time he'd taken him to the rooms above the shop. He remembered the effort he had to make to stop himself calling him sir and how gauche he had felt, huge and clumsy beside this slight, gorgeous man who talked and carried himself like an officer. Yesterday afternoon, as Paul stood in the shop for what Patrick knew would be the last time, he had almost looked like any young father who lived along the terraced streets, a beautiful, frail impersonation of one of those exhausted men. Only his voice had kept its officer's authority.

Patrick said, 'Paul's wife had the baby. A boy.' He laughed emptily. 'He was with her, I didn't keep him from his duty.' After a moment he said, 'He's going away. To university. He came to see me after I closed the shop yesterday. He told me then.'

Paul had refused to go upstairs to their room. Standing in the shop he had said, 'It's not for a few months, the new term doesn't start until October, but I've decided to give up teaching and move back with Dad. Margot will be more comfortable there.' On a rush of breath he went on, 'It's best I go away, Patrick, best I'm on my own. I'm no good to anyone. You understand, don't you? It's for the best.'

He had wanted to kneel at his feet and beg him not to go. He pictured himself doing just that and knew that Paul would be dismayed, and that they would end up in their room making love because retreating into the mindlessness of sex would be so much easier than such an embarrassing scene. But he knew they would lie together afterwards and the familiar emptiness would creep back and Paul would still leave, as he always did: too quickly and silently as if he felt words might encourage him.

Mick said gently, 'Patrick?' He wheeled his chair closer to him and touched his arm. 'Will you be my best man?'

Patrick said, 'I would have taken care of you, you know that, don't you? No matter what.'

Hetty's mother had set the table in the parlour. Sardine sandwiches, scones and a pink blancmange for afters were all laid out on the best lace cloth she had spent the morning starching. A vase of Sweet William stood next to Albert's photograph on the mantelpiece, their scent spiking the parlour's fusty, unused air. Beside the flowers the candle's flame was a pale ghost in the sunlight.

Wheeling himself into the little room, Mick said, 'You shouldn't have gone to so much trouble, Annie.'

'No trouble, Major. It's just a bit of tea.'

'You must call me Mick.'

Her father laughed awkwardly. 'Aye, mother, you're not on parade now.'

Giving him a withering look Annie said, 'Hetty, you can help me in the kitchen.'

As Hetty edged past Mick's chair he squeezed her hand. She smiled at him nervously, wishing her mother had served the tea in the kitchen, as she would've for any other young man she brought home. Tea had been days in the planning, furniture had been moved to accommodate the wheelchair, her father ordered to be on his best behaviour, scrubbed, shaved and sober. Catching her father's eye she realised he was as nervous as she was, and she smiled at him.

In the kitchen Annie was brisk. 'Set the tray with the best cups, see that you don't use the chipped one, mind, the major won't drink from a chipped cup.'

Hetty sighed. 'He wouldn't mind, Mam. You don't have to put on a show for him.'

'Don't I? Why not? You know – he might have been Albert's commanding officer. What would we do if *he* came to tea, eh? You'd want everything right then.'

'He wasn't Albert's commanding officer.'

'No, but if he *had* been.' She sat down suddenly, her face flushed. 'I'm just saying if he *had* been.'

Hetty squatted at her side. 'It's all right, Mam, don't get upset …'

'I got a letter from his captain, you know? Saying what a

good lad Albert was. I used to imagine him coming here in person, handing over Albert's few bits and bobs. Daft, really. He probably hardly knew who Albert was.'

Hetty found her eyes straying to the photo of Albert her mother kept on the dresser. He had been her mother's favourite, but she hadn't minded – she had her father, after all. The plain, no-nonsense boy in the photograph gazed back at her and she looked away quickly, not wanting to believe any more than her mother did that he was dead.

Straightening up she said, 'Shall I make the tea?'

'I'll do it. You can put a few of those biscuits out. We'll show the major a nice spread.'

Mick ate three sandwiches and two scones, her mother constantly pressing him to eat more. As she filled his teacup for the third time he cleared his throat, smiling at her. 'Mr Roberts, Mrs Roberts.' Reaching across the table he took Hetty's hand. 'I've asked Hetty to marry me and she said yes.'

As though relieved it was finally out in the open Joe said quickly, 'Well! Married, eh? I'm very happy for you both. We both are, aren't we love?'

Hetty looked at her mother. She swallowed hard, tasting the vinegary sardines again. 'Mam?'

Annie turned to Mick. 'Do you love her?'

'Yes.'

'She won't be your skivvy, you know. You'll have to treat her well.'

'I know, I will.'

Annie turned to her husband. 'Get that bottle of sherry out, Joe. We'll have a bit of a toast.'

In his room Patrick spread Paul's letters over the eiderdown and arranged them into date order. Starting with the earliest he read each one again. He knew them all by heart, the familiar descriptions of men and landscapes, endearments and questions and jokes he didn't get. Paul had drawn in the margins, recognisable caricatures of Thompson and Cooper and Hawkins, but there was nothing of him, he didn't even mention his name. They hardly knew each other then, of course.

Patrick tossed the last letter down. It described a ruined church and each time he read it he stood again on its stone flagged-floor and looked up at the wooden sculpture of Christ still nailed to his cross. Paul wrote how the nail through his feet had fallen away, the agony preserved in the perfect round of the nail-hole. He had inserted his finger into the hole, felt the splintered wood, the soft pad of sawdust. The wood had smelt so bitter he could taste it.

Patrick's fingers went to his own crucifix and traced its raised outline through his shirt. He remembered how Paul had once rubbed its figure of Christ between his fingers, his expression as curious as a heathen's; after a moment he'd smiled, eyebrows raised as though Patrick had told him he believed that fairies lived in the bottom of the garden.

He tied the letters together, resisting the urge to keep one back to hide between the last pages of his mother's bible. Those last, all at once colourful, pages depicted the map of the World of the Patriarchs, the Travels of the Apostles and Paul's Missionary Journeys. As a child he would trace the red lines promising himself that one day he would follow the maps from Ur through Damascus to Beer-sheba, from Jerusalem to Antioch. Even as a child he knew he would welcome the heat of the sun on his face and the feel of dry sand beneath his feet and that he wouldn't miss the mud and rain and cold of Europe a bit. After Mick's wedding he would go to Palestine; he would find a dark-eyed, olive-skinned boy who loved him and wouldn't feel ashamed.

Taking the letters, Patrick left the house and walked towards the rows of terraces that ran from the High Street. In an alley he stopped, scanning the line of wooden gates that led into the backyards of the little houses. He guessed which gate he wanted from its peeling paint and pushed it open cautiously. At once he knew he'd guessed correctly. The yard he found himself in was obviously neglected: there was no woman in this house to scrub the back step or whitewash the walls. Beneath his feet the cobbles were slimy with moss and he remembered almost losing his footing on that night months earlier when he had followed *A* into this house.

For a moment he waited just inside the gate, as ready to turn back as he had been since leaving home, but then the back door of the house opened. *A* stood in his shirtsleeves frowning at him fearfully. He was holding on to the door as though ready to close it quickly and slip the inside bolt, barricading himself against past indiscretions. Patrick noticed that the hairs on *A*'s forearms had raised as if he had seen a ghost. He stepped forward cautiously, aware that sometimes he could appear frightening.

'Hello.' Patrick smiled awkwardly. 'Hello again.'

'You shouldn't be here.' The man's voice broke and he cleared his throat, glancing nervously over his shoulder into the dark interior of the kitchen. Turning to him he said, 'Not here.'

Patrick took another step forward, conscious of the slipperiness of the ground. 'Do you have someone with you?'

'No. It's just –'

'I won't keep you.' He thought how odd the expression was, as though he could hold him against his will. He remembered the skinniness of *A*'s body beneath his own, how he'd felt he would crush the life out of him, how he was frail compared to Paul, who only appeared breakable. *A*'s fright was genuine and so he said carefully, 'I won't stay. I just wanted to return these.' He held out the letters and saw them now only as a poor excuse. He thought of Paul writing them and his heart felt like a stone suspended in mud.

Adam took a step back and opened the door wider. 'Come in. Quickly.'

He made a pot of tea. He said, 'I'm sorry I don't have any sugar.'

The kitchen smelt of dirty dishcloths; a pair of longjohns and a vest hung grey as corpses from a clothes-horse in front of a banked-down fire. School exercise books were stacked in piles on the floor, one of them open and straddling the arm of the only easy chair. Patrick sat at the kitchen table. He cleared a toast-crumbed plate to one side and set the letters down. He pushed them away a little, hoping they could be ignored. Adam glanced at them only to turn away to rummage in a cupboard. 'I have biscuits,' he said. 'If you'd care for one.' Sitting down opposite Patrick he placed a plate of shortbread between them and smiled too brightly. 'I'm afraid they may be a bit soft. It's the damp. The house is damp. The doctor says it doesn't help my asthma.' He hesitated. Glancing at the letters again he said, 'Asthma kept me out of the war.' He smiled bitterly as though remembering some humiliation. 'Unfit for active service – almost any activity at all, in fact.' For the first time he met Patrick's gaze directly. Behind the thin lenses of his spectacles his eyes were hard and brightly defensive. Patrick held his gaze, knowing exactly what a recruiting sergeant would have made of this man; he thought of the scathing remarks he may or may not have spared him.

Adam poured the tea and Patrick saw that his hands shook a little as he handed him his cup and laughed nervously. 'You know, I don't know your name.'

'Patrick.'

'Adam.' After a moment he said, 'That what's the *A* stands for. Adam. He – the person who wrote those letters – he couldn't write my name, obviously. Well – it's *obviously* if you've read them, I suppose. Have you read them?'

'I'm sorry.'

'Oh, don't be. Really, don't be! I don't even know why I kept them. He would have been amazed that I didn't simply burn the lot.'

'Why didn't you?'

'I forgot about them, to be honest.'

As if he knew how blatant his lie was he took off his glasses and polished the lenses on a corner of his shirt. He wasn't wearing a collar and his sleeves were rolled up past his elbows as though he was about to do heavy work. His fingers were ink-stained, the nails bitten to the quick. Patrick thought of Paul taking one of those childish-looking hands and pressing its palm to his mouth. He would have just arrived here, still stinking of the long journey home, the rattle of the train still in his head, fear as dogged as a shadow at his heels. He would toss his kit bag down and pull Adam into his arms and they would cling together wordlessly. Or at least Paul would be silent; there were so few words in him he could barely imagine his greeting.

Adam might dare to speak. Adam would have a mouthful of words for Paul to suppress.

Patrick picked up a biscuit and took a careful bite, expecting staleness. But the shortcake was sweet and buttery; he finished it in a couple of mouthfuls and washed it down with hot, strong tea. He felt comforted, as though he hadn't realised how hungry he'd been.

Sharply Adam said, 'Why did you bring the letters back?'

'They're yours.'

'But you wanted them.'

'They were on my conscience.'

Adam laughed shortly. Disconcerted, Patrick looked down at his teacup. He thought of the boy who wrote the letters, a sweeter, more optimistic Paul than the man he knew. He looked up at Adam, wanting to guess from his expression how much he still loved Paul, his need to know as irresistible as the urge to worry a rotten tooth.

Adam suffered his gaze only for a moment. He stood up abruptly. 'We'll go upstairs. That's what you came for. All I can say is I'm glad you had the excuse.'

Patrick followed him up the stairs. He felt outsized, his feet too big for the narrow treads, the threadbare carpet disintegrating with each heavy step; the house seemed to shrink so that he felt he would have to bow his head as he walked through the bedroom door. He remembered how Adam's bed had seemed small as a child's and imagined it buckling beneath his weight. On the landing he stopped, his hand still grasping the stair rail; the walls were closing in on him. He saw Paul in the shell hole calmly closing Jenkins's eyes; there was blood on his fingers where they had brushed against the wound in the side of the man's head. He had wiped the blood on his tunic, casually, as though it were dust from a bookshelf. There was a fine spray of blood on his face. This had seemed ordinary, too.

Patrick sat down on the top stair. He held his head in his hands and part of him was aware of how melodramatic he must look to the frail, wary man waiting in the bedroom doorway. He told himself that in a moment he would clamber to his feet and behave in a way that was as close to what was expected of him

237

as he could manage. He would make love to *A* and it would be Paul's body he was breaking into, fucking him with all his heart and strength that he might weaken him enough to be comforted. It was terrible how brave Paul was; by rights such brittle self-containment should have been easy to break.

Paul had said, 'I love you, Patrick.' He said the words instead of goodbye, standing in the shop doorway before leaving to walk in the direction of Parkwood and his wife and child.

Adam sat down beside him, keeping still and silent so that eventually Patrick felt himself leaning against him, felt the other man's arm rest lightly around his shoulders. He smelt of coal fires. He remembered how sweet he tasted when he'd kissed him. Patrick closed his eyes; his breathing became steadier. After a while Adam took his hand and led him to the bedroom.

Free first chapter of

All the Beauty of the Sun

Soho, May 1925

WATCHING ANN BRUSH HER hair, Edmund had the idea that he should ask her how he compared to the other men she slept with. Did she like him more? Was he in some way better or worse? Clumsier perhaps? Or more tender, energetic, desirable? He wondered if he really, truly wanted to know, because of course, no one asked such questions, no one with any pride, or any sense at all of conviction. Lawrence Hawker, for example, would never be so crass. Hawker was older, a careless, sophisticated man, someone who, in Edmund's heart of hearts, he thought of as one of the grown-ups.

Edmund knew he should, conventionally, be jealous of his rival; but jealousy would make him unconventional within their tight little circle. Besides, Hawker and he weren't rivals: Ann slept with them both, and he suspected that Hawker cared even less about this than he did. All the same, Edmund would like to know if she cared more or less about him. He supposed he wanted to know that at least. At least he would like to know that he made some impression, some *something*.

Lying on his back in her bed, his hands clasped beneath his head, the sheet crumpled beneath his body, he laughed because there was something absurd in all this that he hadn't realised until now; he had been taking promiscuity seriously when perhaps he should have thought of it as a parlour game: *bed-hopping – the winner the first to finish with his pride still intact.*

Ann turned from the mirror above the fireplace to frown at him, hairbrush poised mid-stroke. Blonde hairs curled from the bristles, bright in the lamplight. She was naked and her skin was pale and quite perfect, wondrously so. No wonder Joseph Day wanted to paint her so often; they all did, but it was only Day who was skilled enough, whose finished results Ann decided were worth the uncomfortable, boring hours of modelling.

Turning back to the mirror she asked, 'What are you laughing at?'

He wondered how she might react to his question, *Who do you prefer, Lawrence Hawker or me? Which of us thrills you most?* He might ask if she had slept with his friend Andrew, too – although he suspected Andrew was queer. He thought of Andrew, decided it would be best not to think about him, not now, but when he was alone, perhaps. For now he imagined asking her, *Am I different in any way?* She would laugh; he imagined she would say, 'Silly boy!' But all the same, the thought of differences could not be unthought; he knew that he would return to these differences, worry them over and over; he knew that this worrying could overwhelm him.

The bedcovers were in deep folds at his groin and he pulled them up to his chin, cold suddenly. Her scent lingered on the sheet, warm and touching like cheap violet sweets; earlier he had noticed a blood stain on the side where she slept and had been reassured, even as a part of him wanted her to be pregnant, that part that was irrational and boorish and as desperate to be confirmed as virile as any man who had ever lived. But that part of him seemed particularly unconvincing, an under-rehearsed act he was performing for a knowing, critical audience. Besides, paternity couldn't be assured, of course; also there was the used johnnie flaccid on the floor beside the bed; he was always very careful, very afraid of disease. 'VD kills in a particularly nasty way,' his father had told him, and he should know, the great doctor having witnessed such deaths. Edmund remembered the rest of this lecture from his father as particularly oblique, even by his father's standard, how he had talked about how he must be sure of himself and not go rushing at windmills. He had been sixteen at the time, his virginity still shaming. Perhaps his father had sensed this shame, although he didn't like to think so.

Ann picked her knickers up from the floor and began to dress. Her room was on the second floor above a pawn shop and was just big enough for the bed and a chest of drawers and a chair strewn with her clothes. A midnight-blue party dress hung from the picture rail beside a pale lemon blouse with a pussy-cat bow and jagged sweat marks under the arms. Face powder dusted the chest of drawers, where an unscrewed lipstick lay beside the crumbling square of mascara he had seen her spit into to moisten the blackness for the spiky brush. A crumbed plate and tea-stained cup, an empty milk bottle and an ashtray were lined up on the windowsill. Her shoes were everywhere: separated, upside down, small hazards of pointed heels and trailing laces. A stocking dangled limply from the bedstead, still holding the shape of her leg and foot, the toe stiffening a little; as she sat on the bed to roll up its pair she said, 'Get dressed or we'll be late. I don't want to be late for Lawrence.'

'No, of course you don't.'

She glanced at him, perhaps suspecting his jealousy, if indeed he *was* jealous. She looked away again, paying attention to her suspenders. 'I promised Lawrence I wouldn't be late – this is an important night for the gallery.'

'Whatever time we turn up, we'll be first. I'll be surprised if the others even bother.'

'Andrew's going – he's told everyone they should see this artist's pictures.'

He snorted: how like Andrew to be so impressionable; he had his fancies, his enthusiasms that he would quickly forget. Next week there would be someone else to rave about. The thought of Andrew's excited gushing made him close his eyes in despair.

Ann patted his leg beneath the sheet. 'Come on. Don't look so glum. You laugh for no reason and then you look glum like this,' – she pulled a face.

She stood up and returned to the mirror to pin up her hair, humming tunelessly under her breath. Occasionally she sang snatches from a repertoire of music hall songs – songs that even he, sheltered middle-class boy that he was, recognized as full of double entendre. *Dirty girl,* he thought, as he often did. The kind of girl he couldn't take home to his mother, the kind of girl a man practised on – as if anyone needed to practise. Perhaps he did. Perhaps the more he practised the more he would straighten himself out. He was using her – the thought had occurred to him before, of course. But didn't everyone use everyone? Agitated, he tossed aside the bed covers and gathered his clothes. Ann went to the window and drew the curtains. The clock on her mantelpiece chimed the hour; the coals on her fire shifted and caved in. Outside a drunk warbled a song he was sure Ann would know. Edmund pulled on his trousers and tucked in his shirt; he buttoned his flies and fastened his collar and noticed a stain on his frayed cuff. He found his tie draped in a pleasingly louche manner on the end of the bed and put it on. Ann straightened the knot, standing back to regard him quizzically.

'Don't be sad,' she said.

'I'm not.'

She put on her coat, handed him his, held out his scarf, all the while watching him as though she was nursery nurse to his wayward child. Ready, she unlocked the door and stepped out into the dank, dark little passageway, preceding him down the steep flight of stairs.

He was sad, despite his protestation. Yet he knew thaere was no reason for his sadness. Until the idea he'd had about questioning Ann over how he compared with Lawrence Hawker, he'd been fine, but a feeling of melancholy had crept over him, a feeling he knew had been lying in wait for him for a little time now, only foiled by drink and sex. In the King's Head last night he, Andrew, and Day had drunk until Susie would no longer serve them, and then they had staggered to Andrew's rooms and seen off a bottle of port. Port, for Christ's sake, inducing the most savage hangover he'd had for a while. That morning, as he and Barnes had opened the bookshop where he worked, Barnes had wrinkled his nose. 'You smell like my old Aunt Florrie on Christmas night.' Stepping closer he made a show of sniffing him. 'You should wash more, nice boy like you, frequent a decent barber.'

He had instinctively rubbed his chin; it wouldn't have been the first time he'd forgotten to shave. Barnes pulled up the blinds on the front windows and Edmund had stepped back from the sunlight, wincing. 'Bitten by the vampire, were we?'

Barnes had said; then in his ordinarily weary voice added, 'Go and make the tea. There are some aspirin behind the caddy.'

Walking along Percy Street, Ann's arm through his, Edmund thought that perhaps sad was not the word for his mood; rather he was disappointed; rather he had walked into a brick wall behind which lay all his hopes and ambitions, everything he had once fondly hoped he would be. If he stepped back and jumped as high as he could, he could just about see over this wall, catch tantalizing glimpses of a life he might lead if only he wasn't so damnably lazy, if only he gave up his job at the bookshop and got down to some serious work.

Serious work. This was his father's expression, the two words always shackled together like prisoners on a chain gang. Serious work was cutting open bodies, delving about in their insides, stitching them back up restored, more often than not. Serious work was not painting, not unless he was deathly intense about it, prepared to work and work and work and still get nowhere, never catching up with the little talent he supposed he had. Seriously, he should paint and do nothing else, caught up in a maniacal mindfulness, not eating, not sleeping, fractured from the ordinary, a transcendental life.

Such seriousness seemed preposterous to him. Slowly Edmund had come to realise that he was possessed of a clerk's self-conscious heart. There were times when he could even bring himself to feel content working in the bookshop, the slow hours ticking by in steady, companionable quiet. He liked the smell of the books, particularly the old, next-to-worthless ones, those they left out in boxes on the pavement in front of the window, their spines fading without the protection of lost dust jackets. He liked the pathos of those books and their forgotten authors, those many who had tried and not quite failed; he knew he couldn't work in an art gallery, where that same, soft feeling would be unbearable.

Like it or not, however, he couldn't entirely escape into the bookshop and pretend he had never had an ambition. He knew those who did work and work and didn't give up in a fit of horrible self-awareness and pique: Andrew, who had actually sold some of his seascapes; he knew, in a way, Day, who would probably be famous some day, if he didn't kill himself first. And of course, he knew Ann, their muse. He was surprised when she decided she would like to go to bed with him, but her enthusiasm for his body did help to relieve the depleting ennui that lately he couldn't shake off, even if afterwards he was pestered by questions and doubts.

He was aware of Ann's arm through his, her warm, vital closeness. She walked quickly, easily matching his pace, although she was so much shorter. She'd once laughed, 'Don't I look like the scullery maid out with the young master?' He was six foot three inches and broad-shouldered. As blond as her, he looked younger than his years, and as she was older than he was, he knew that she didn't take him seriously. There, that word again. Andrew, Day and all his other friends were serious. He was not.

They turned into a street where once-grand houses had been converted into flats: the cold, damp basements for the poorest; the larger, drafty rooms with their cracked window panes and bare, creaking floorboards for those who were a little less desperate. When he had first left home, he had lived on this street, in a room he thought must have been the maid's in better times: cramped beneath its sloping ceiling it was certainly like the maids' rooms in his parents' house. His window had looked out over rooftops; if he craned his neck, he could see the dome of St Paul's. Through the gaps in the floorboards he could eavesdrop on his downstairs neighbours – Russian Jews, whose exoticness made him feel as though he had arrived at a place even further away from home than they were.

As they passed his old flat, and he looked up at the attic window to see if there was a light, Ann squeezed his arm. 'This artist – Lawrence said his work is all about the war.'

There was no light; he imagined that the attic room – where he had once, with such hope and enthusiasm, painted the rain-darkened view of roofs – was unoccupied, settling even further into disrepair. There would be dead flies on the sills, the undisturbed dust no longer agitating in the deep shaft of light that fell at noon across the sagging bed. There would be a stronger smell of damp, more evidence of mice and a colder draft beneath the door. Perhaps he could go back there, start again as if the last year had never even begun; as if he was still that enthusiastic boy, the money his father had given him for this *experiment* miraculously unspent, his naivety still happily in place.

As if he could be that time traveller, he promised himself he would work; he would put his weight behind breaking the stubbornly unyielding shell of his talent. But he remembered that the money was spent; he remembered the bookshop, its easy cosiness; he thought about his new room, its tidiness because he had realised he couldn't pretend to be a man who didn't care about a certain level of comfort and order; he recalled how cold and lonely, how *untypical* of him, that first little flat had been.

Cautiously Ann persisted, 'This artist. His name is Paul Harris – he fought during the war, Lawrence told me. That's what he paints – the war. Battle scenes. Dead soldiers.'

He glanced down at her, her head at the level of his heart, her face turned up to his, her cheeks pink from the cold. In a certain light she could look very young, younger than he was. He would paint her like this; recreate these exact circumstances – close to her, looking down at her as she looked up at him – to capture her vulnerability, her occasional, surprising shyness of him. The portrait would catch only a moment of truthfulness, such a fleeting moment it would hardly be true at all. He put his arms around her, pulling her close so that he wouldn't have to see how anxious she looked.

'I heard the paintings were controversial.'

She pushed away from him. '*Controversial*? What if we can't look?'

He sighed, feeling large and foolish and shallow – the worst of these feelings because he knew he would be able to look, to be critical or envious or dismissive – any of his usual responses – but he would *look*. He couldn't be afraid all the time, or made to feel grief whenever it was expected. He cleared his throat and felt larger and more foolish still. 'Shall we not go?'

'I have to go.'

'Then we'll go together,' he said, remembering that of

course she had to be there – Lawrence Hawker was expecting her. He pulled her arm through his again, patting her hand, ashamed of his cowardly resignation. 'Best foot forward?'

She laughed as though he wasn't quite right in the head. 'Left right, left right?'

'Indeed.' He had patted her hand, and now this gesture seemed to him to have struck the wrong note: it was too comradely, too affectionate, he supposed, and it came to him that perhaps affection was all he felt. He had the urge to say that he didn't care to be one among others, just to hear her reaction, but such grandstanding would only be part of that act he seemed intent on performing, and in truth her reaction meant little to him – he had an idea that she was acting a part, too, and there was comfort in this idea: he couldn't hurt her, just as she couldn't hurt him.

All the Beauty of the Sun

Soho 1925. Two young men meet – for one of them this is love at first sight, for the other only lust and guilt.

In 1925 Paul Harris returns to England from self-imposed exile in Tangiers for an exhibition of his paintings. He leaves behind Patrick, the man he has loved since they met in the trenches in 1918, wanting to explore the kind of life he might have lived had it not been for the war. In Bohemian Soho, he meets Edmund whose passionate love changes Paul's idea of himself. Paul begins to believe that he may have another life to live, free of the guilt and regrets of the past. But the past is not easy to escape, and when Patrick follows Paul to London a decision must be made that will affect all their lives.

ISBN 9781908262011   £7.99

Paper Moon

The passionate love affair between Spitfire pilot Bobby Harris and photographer's model Nina Tate lasts through the turmoil of World War Two, only to be tested when Bobby is disfigured after being shot down. Wanting to hide from the world, Bobby retreats from Bohemian Soho to the empty house his grandfather has left him, a house haunted by the secrets of Bobby's childhood. Here the mysteries of his past are gradually unravelled.

Following on from *The Boy I Love*, Marion Husband's highly acclaimed debut novel, and *All the Beauty of the Sun*, *Paper Moon* explores the complexities of love and loyalty against a backdrop of a world transformed by war.

ISBN 9781908262745   £7.99

Á

Accent Press Ltd

Please visit our website
www.accentpress.co.uk
for our latest title information,
to write reviews and
leave feedback.

We'd love to hear from you!